OHIO
DOMINICAN
UNIVERSITY™
SINCE 1911

my lost and found life

my lost and found life

• • •

MELODIE BOWSHER

Published by Bloomsbury Publishing, New York, London, and Berlin
Distributed to the trade by Holtzbrinck Publishers

Library of Congress Cataloging-in-Publication Data
Bowsher, Melodie.
My lost and found life / by Melodie Bowsher.—1st U.S. ed.
p. cm.
Summary: When her mother is accused of embezzling a million dollars and vanishes, spoiled, selfish Ashley must fend for herself by finding a job and a place to live.
ISBN-10: 1-58234-736-0 • ISBN-13: 978-1-58234-736-3
[1. Abandoned children—Fiction. 2. Homeless persons–Fiction. 3. Mothers and daughters—Fiction. 4. Coming of age—Fiction.] I. Title.
PZ7.B6795My 2006 [Fic]—dc22 2006006432

First U.S. Edition 2006
Typeset by Westchester Book Composition
Printed in the U.S.A. by Quebecor World Fairfield
2 4 6 8 10 9 7 5 3 1

Bloomsbury Publishing, Children's Books, U.S.A.
175 Fifth Avenue, New York, NY 10010

For Mia and Luca
And especially for my mother

• • •

chapter one

Five days before I graduated from high school, my mother embezzled a million dollars and disappeared.

Thinking back, I can't recall anything unusual about that day. No "funny feelings" tickled the back of my neck; no suspicions nagged my subconscious. Some time later, when I looked up my horoscope for that day, I found the stars provided no hint that I would never again feel safe or confident about the future. I would have laughed in scorn if anyone had predicted that I, the homecoming queen, the most popular girl in my high school, would soon be homeless and alone, bedding down in an unheated camper with a knife under my pillow.

Even now, five years later, I still wonder—if I had known, could I have somehow changed the outcome?

That morning began in the usual way. I ignored both my alarm and the sunlight streaming through my bedroom window and stayed burrowed in my warm bed. I was often late and sometimes skipped first and second periods entirely. I was an expert at imitating my mother's handwriting and always wrote a plausible excuse for myself: *Please excuse Ashley's tardiness, as she wasn't feeling well, blah, blah, blah.* I wasn't fooling the school's attendance secretary, but she was obviously sick of dealing with me. The administration was pretty lax with the graduating seniors spring semester, no doubt in happy anticipation of our imminent departure.

That particular morning I managed to throw off my comforter at the last minute and rushed around, showering, applying makeup, wriggling into my jeans and favorite red tank top, pulling on my wedge sandals, and stuffing my gear into my backpack. A generous squirt of Obsession on my neck and I was ready.

As I dashed for the front door, my hair still damp, I saw that my mother was on the telephone. That, too, was ordinary—she was always on the telephone, speaking in a low, intense tone to someone. I assumed she was talking to her best friend, Gloria, or her loser boyfriend, Phil. I assumed that nothing my mother was talking about would be of interest to me. I was wrong about a lot of things back then.

Even if she hadn't been on the telephone, I didn't want to talk to my mother that morning. We'd had a screaming match the night before. To tell the truth, I didn't want to remember what I'd said or how my mother had looked, standing on the lawn with the rain pouring down, her nightgown soggy and clinging to her torso, her face twisted, tears running down her cheeks and melting into the rain. I was determined not to think about that. Pretending was a skill we both had perfected over the years.

School ended at noon all that week, and when the final bell

rang, I lingered to gossip about graduation and the senior trip to Hawaii, only five days away. That made shopping for the trip a priority. Mara was showing off her new bag, which she bragged was a Gucci, like mine. I gave her a scornful smile and whispered in my best friend Nicole's ear, "Oh, puh-leez. Who is she kidding? I can spot a knockoff a mile away."

My boyfriend, Scott, tried to persuade me to go surfing with him and his buddies at Granada Beach. But I didn't feel like watching and cheering while he played jock all afternoon, especially since the coast is usually foggy in May. Instead, I told Nicole I'd go shopping with her at four, then steered my little red Jetta toward home.

Now that last night's storm clouds had cleared, it was one of those picture-perfect spring days. I put the sunroof down and felt a warm glow on my neck and shoulders. Every garden I passed seemed to be bursting with flowers. I could almost smell the blossoms.

As I drove, I sang along with Sheryl Crow on the radio.

Twenty minutes later I was stretched out on our redwood lounge chair, clad in my size 2 bikini and tropical suntan oil, with a diet soda by my right hand and cell phone at my left. My cat, Stella, was lying beneath my chair, lazily licking her orange fur while remaining alert for any stray butterflies or bumblebees that might need chasing. Thumbing through the latest issue of *Lucky* magazine, I began planning all the clothes I would buy to wear in Hawaii. I wanted to find a really hot red dress. I considered red my signature color, and not just because it looks fabulous with my shoulder-length dark hair. Red is center stage and that's always where I like to be.

I had the volume on my boom box cranked up. I guess that's why I didn't hear the doorbell. What got my attention was a head appearing over the back gate—a male head, a cop's head.

The cop barked, "If you turned down that damn music, you'd know I was ringing your bell."

I glared at him and reached over to turn down the volume. I recognized him immediately and my defenses went up. He was the jerk who had given me a long lecture and a speeding ticket two weeks earlier. Anyway, there aren't that many cops in Burlingame, one of the many suburban communities strung along the bay between San Francisco and San Jose. Burlingame's finest regularly patrolled the neighborhood around the high school, so they were recognizable to all of us.

"My mother isn't home," I said, hoping to deflect him.

Ignoring my comment, he opened the gate and strode into the backyard. Behind him the gate swung shut with a loud clang. He stomped over to my chair and stood there, giving me the usual badass cop stare as if I had just robbed a liquor store or something. He was thirty or so and sort of cute, but he had that burly body and accusatory attitude they all have.

"Now, how could you know I want your mother?" he asked.

"Why would you want me?" I said, putting on my impassive face, the one I'd learned to use when dealing with my father or jerks like him. "You're blocking my sun."

He didn't move, just continued to stare at me. Why is it that cops always make you feel guilty even if you haven't done anything wrong? I sighed and reached for a shirt to pull over my bikini top. His chilly gaze made me uncomfortable. It definitely wasn't the admiring stare I was used to getting from guys. Stella came out from under the chair and rubbed up against his ankles, and he knelt down to stroke the soft fur under her chin. Cats have no loyalty.

"Well, it just so happens you're right," he said. "If your mother is Diane Mitchell. Remind me what your name is again."

"Ashley," I said. "Ashley Marie Mitchell. Why are you looking for my mother?"

He ignored my question, the way cops do.

"I'm Officer Strobel, Ashley, and I need to talk to your mother right away. Where is she?"

"At her office, I suppose. Look, I've turned down the music. That should satisfy the old busybody next door."

I picked up Stella and tried to stroke her, but she struggled to get free, so I let her go. She stalked away and arranged herself on a sunny patch of grass just out of reach, her whiskers twitching as she actively ignored us both.

"I'm not here about a noise complaint. I need to see your mother. Is she here?"

"She's at her office," I repeated slowly as if speaking to a half-wit. "That's where she always is. The Simmons Company in Redwood City."

"She's not there, and they're looking for her. Any other ideas?"

"Has something happened to her? Are you trying to say she's been in an accident?" He was making me uneasy, though I didn't want to show it.

"There have been no accidents reported."

I waited for him to say something more, but he didn't. *What was he after?*

"Maybe she had a doctor's appointment or something. It's not a big deal. Call her cell phone. She always has it on."

"We did. She didn't answer." His tone was flat, yet challenging. "It *is* a big deal because we need to find her now."

With an elaborate sigh I reached for my cell phone and dialed her number. After six rings, I heard, "This is Diane. I'm not available at the moment. Leave a message at the tone and I'll call you back just as soon as I'm able."

"This is Ashley. Call me the minute you get this message," I said, and hung up. "Okay, now are you satisfied? When she calls me back, I'll tell her to call you, *officer.*"

"When did you see her last?"

"This morning, before I went to school. Why?"

"When you saw her, did she tell you her plans for the day?"

"No."

He kept looking at me, so I added, "I was late for school and left in a hurry."

"Well, how about last night? What did she say last night about her plans for today?"

I was starting to get uneasy in the face of his persistence. "Nothing."

"Your mother didn't say one word to you last night about her plans for today. What did the two of you talk about?"

I wanted to say, *None of your business,* but his stony look intimidated me.

"Nothing much. Just the usual stuff about school." I was determined not to tell this bully about the ugly fight we had. "Look, why are you trying to find Diane?"

"You call your mother 'Diane'?"

"That's her name," I snapped.

"Most of us call our mothers 'Mom' or 'Mother,' " he snapped right back. "Why don't you stop giving me attitude and tell me exactly what your mother did and said last night?"

"We didn't talk," I lied. "I was at a friend's house and came home late. If you want to know what my mother did, try asking her best friend, Gloria, or Phil, her boyfriend."

"I will. You can give me their numbers in a minute. When does your mother usually get home and start cooking dinner?"

I snickered. "Diane doesn't exactly rush home to fry a chicken or bake a cake. We both have frozen dinners or maybe pizza and not always at the same time."

"Home, sweet home," he said.

"She's busy," I defended her. "She works long hours."

"Maybe too long."

"What does *that* mean?" I said, scowling at him.

"You'll find out soon enough. How old are you?"

"Eighteen. Why?"

"Old enough."

"Old enough? For what?" I said, not even trying to keep the sarcasm out of my voice. "Are you coming on to me?"

He snorted. "Don't flatter yourself. Old enough means, legally, you're an adult. How about acting like an adult and letting me look around inside?"

I was flabbergasted. "Are you crazy? Do you think she's hiding under the bed or tied up in the closet? She's. Not. *Here.*" My voice rose on the word *here* and turned it into a shriek.

"Look, either you let me look around or I'll be back with a search warrant."

"What! You *are* crazy! What could you possibly want with my mother that would involve a search warrant? If you think she's some kind of drug dealer, you're delusional."

"Why would you mention drugs?" He gave me a menacing look. "Are you afraid I might find some inside?"

"No, I'm not," I said. Suddenly I was tired of answering his weird questions while he avoided answering any of mine. "Okay, fine. Go ahead and look all you want. You won't arrest me for not making my bed, will you?"

Without replying, he crossed the deck and walked in the back door. I took a swig from my Diet Coke can and followed.

Officer Strobel gave the kitchen a cursory look.

"Oh, look, there's her favorite coffee cup," I said, pointing to a mug on the gleaming granite countertop. "Maybe you should have the contents analyzed."

Mr. Cool Cop ignored me and walked through the dining room and into the living room. We had redecorated just a few months ago, and I was proud of our elegant new furniture, silk drapes, and Oriental rugs.

"Very nice," he said. "You live well."

"Naturally," I said, with the nonchalant air of a duchess speaking to a dog.

He was impervious to my scorn. Glancing around, he pointed to the side door. "Where does that lead?"

"We hide our washer and dryer out there."

He continued down the hall, glancing into the guest bathroom and then the family room, where we kept our computer and new flat-screen television. At the doorway of my bedroom, he stopped and stared at the chaos of clothes, papers, and books strewn across the bed and floor.

"Looks like someone already tossed this room." He smirked.

I pushed past him and closed the door in his face.

"She's not in my room."

When he reached my mother's room, he surprised me by walking across it, opening the door to her walk-in closet, and stepping inside. I perched on the edge of the bed, pretending to study the red polish on my toes, and called after him, "You forgot to check under her bed."

"Where does she keep her suitcases?" he asked.

"On the floor on the left side of the closet."

"There aren't any here," he said.

"Of course, there are," I said impatiently, and pushed past him to stare at the place where her matched set of dark green luggage should have been. The suitcases were gone! I stood there, my mouth gaping. My mother wouldn't go on a trip without telling me, would she? No, she wouldn't, I told myself, trying to erase the memory of last night's hysteria from my head. Suddenly, I didn't feel like being a smart-ass anymore.

"She must have put them in the garage," I muttered, more to myself than to him.

"Is there anything else missing—any clothes or shoes or toiletries?" he asked.

"How would I know?" I responded, gesturing toward the bulging clothes racks.

He studied my face for a moment, then asked, "Can I use your phone?"

Without waiting for an answer, he picked up the receiver next to my mother's bed and dialed. "Hey, Donahoe. I'm at the Mitchell house. No, she's not around. Uh-huh, just the daughter. She says she doesn't know her mother's whereabouts. Looks like she might have skipped."

"Skipped!" I repeated, staring at him in shock.

Glancing at my horrified face, he turned his back to me and added, "Uh-huh. I'm going to talk to the boyfriend and then I'll come back to the station. It's early yet."

The minute he put down the receiver, I screeched, "Why did you say 'skipped'? What the hell is going on?"

"There's some money missing from your mother's office, a lot of money, and we want to find out what she knows about it."

"You mean you think she stole it," I hissed. "Well, you're out of your mind. My mother wouldn't do something like that."

"Maybe so." Strobel nodded without conviction. "In the meantime, I need those phone numbers you mentioned. By the way, what does your mother drive?"

"A Mercedes. Blue."

"Do you know the tag number?"

I looked at him, confused at the question.

"The number on her car's license plate," he added.

"No, I don't know it."

"That's okay, I can get it from DMV," he said, snapping open his notebook.

I gave him both Gloria's and Phil's phone numbers and protested once again that he was crazy for even suspecting my mother of wrongdoing.

Strobel closed the notebook. “That’s all for now. If your mother comes back, tell her to call the police department right away. She should ask for me. Tell her it will be a lot better for her if she calls us.”

He gave me another badass cop stare and left, pausing only to give the driveway a searching look as if he expected to see armed thugs hiding behind the rhododendrons.

“Asshole!” I mumbled as I watched him walk away.

The minute I shut the door, I bolted for the telephone and called Gloria myself.

chapter two

Nope, no idea where she is," Gloria wheezed into the phone, sounding as if she had just run a marathon. "Actually, I haven't spoken to her in a few days."

I didn't bother to ask why she was panting. Nor did I tell her about the police.

"I thought you two talked every single day," I tweaked her.

"You must be thinking of you and your girlfriends. Your mom and I have lives," she retorted with a right-back-at-ya attitude.

"This is really important," I insisted. "I *have* to find her right away. Help me out here, Gloria."

"I would if I could. Look, I'm kind of busy right now."

Gloria was always in a crisis—for heaven's sake, it can't be that hard to handle a couple of preschoolers. My mother and Gloria had been friends since high school, even though they weren't much alike. Diane had hatched me at a young age, while Gloria was one of those career women, a bank vice president to be exact. Six years ago, though, she had finally married another banker and started popping out kids. Now she had two little boys when, at her age, she should have been having grandchildren practically.

Even though she and my mother were tight, I wasn't so crazy about Gloria. I overheard her once telling my mother she shouldn't give in to me so much and that I was turning into a spoiled brat.

"My mom didn't say anything about going out of town, did she?"

"Not a word. Why? Where would she go?" Gloria said in a distracted tone. "Uh-oh, there's someone at the door. Gotta go. Tell Diane to call me later."

She hung up. Officer Asshole must have arrived. I smiled inwardly, just a little. A few minutes with him and Gloria would be the one badgering me with questions. In the meantime, I dialed the number for Phil's gas station.

To my complete embarrassment, my mom had been going out with a mechanic for the past three years. I had to admit Phil was handsome in a rugged, outdoorsy way. He even had plenty of hair. Still, he wore cowboy boots and drove a truck. I wished my mother would date a doctor or lawyer or at least someone who wore a suit, carried a briefcase, and drove a Beamer.

Phil owned a Shell station down on El Camino Real, the main drag through our little burb. Reynaldo, the Mexican guy who worked for him, answered the phone. He said Phil wasn't at the station. "I think he's at home," he added when I pressed him.

When I called Phil's home number, a woman answered.

Her voice sounded familiar, but she was definitely not my mother. She called, "It's for you," and Phil picked up the phone. I was curious who the woman was, but I let it go for the moment. I had enough to worry about.

I asked him if he'd seen or talked to Diane today. Without a trace of embarrassment, Phil claimed he hadn't seen her "in a while."

There was an awkward pause as I tried to take in his meaning. And then he hung up on me! I stood there, staring at the receiver, angry and more bewildered than ever.

Before long, Gloria showed up at the front door. She dragged her two hyperactive horrors into the living room and began interrogating me. What did my mother tell me? Where could she be? And on and on. But I didn't have any answers. She kept repeating over and over, "I can't believe this. This is crazy," until I wanted to slap her silly. Naturally, I restrained myself. Besides, knowing Gloria, she probably would have slapped me back.

"I wanna go home," whined her five-year-old, and the younger one stopped chasing Stella long enough to chime in.

Finally, Gloria stopped barking questions at me and herded them outside. I should have been relieved, but I didn't know what to do with myself after she backed her big SUV out of our driveway. I was alone again in the empty house, confused and impatient, with my mother's whereabouts a complete mystery and the police lurking, if not in the driveway, then at least in my imagination. My stomach was in knots. I didn't feel like sunbathing or watching the tube or eating. Even shopping didn't sound like fun anymore. I called Nicole and backed out of our shopping excursion without telling her the real reason.

All I could do was wait and worry. But sitting and waiting was too passive for me. I wanted to take action—any action. So I cleaned my bedroom. In a storm of activity, I hung up clothes, made my bed, and tried to organize the chaos, all in an effort to keep my anxiety under control. In the back of my mind, I also thought it would please my mother when she came back. I was certain she would come home and set the police straight.

I found myself wishing I had a father or uncle I could call—someone who would fix this or make it all go away. But my father was dead. To tell the truth, a live Jimmy wouldn't have been any comfort anyway. My darling daddy had spent his whole life obsessed with himself.

Jimmy had been movie-star handsome, and women had fawned over him—my mother included, at least when I was little. Before he died, she seemed less infatuated than exasperated by him, as if he were a cat that couldn't be taught to use the litter box instead of the bathroom rug. By the time I was ten, it was clear even to me he was a loser, a pathetically unsuccessful actor who spent his time drinking in bars and bitching because the world failed to recognize his genius.

Diane always told a romantic tale of being alone in the world and then meeting my father at a wedding where he was tending bar. He claimed to have studied at the Actors Studio in New York, but somehow ended up in San Francisco instead of Hollywood. Anyway, they married, Diane had me, and we all lived unhappily ever after until he fell and cracked his skull outside his favorite tavern. I was fourteen when he died, and I didn't miss him a bit. Why should I? It wasn't as if I had ever been "Daddy's little girl."

Jimmy always said he was an orphan, but I didn't buy it. His relatives had probably disowned him long ago. Even if he'd had parents, siblings, or other relatives somewhere, I'd never know now that dear old Dad had gone to the happy hour in the sky.

As for my mother's family, they too were firmly planted in Holy Cross Memorial Park. There was no one left among the living. Only my mother and me.

As the minutes and hours dragged by, I paced, channel-surfed with the TV's remote control glued to my hand, and paced some more. I tried to watch a movie on the tube, but it was hopeless. I couldn't sit still or concentrate. The knot in my stomach had moved up and was now firmly lodged in my chest. My emotions teetered between fear and anger. What was wrong with Diane to worry me like this? If she thought scaring me was going to change my mind and make me sorry for what I said, she was wrong, wrong, wrong. I was not going to be manipulated, and I was surprised my mother even imagined this kind of trick might work.

Several times I picked up the telephone receiver and listened for a few seconds to the dial tone, just to make sure the damn thing was working. My cell phone was fully charged. I plugged it into the wall anyway just to make absolutely certain. My mother didn't call.

Around nine the phone rang, and I leaped for it. But it was only Gloria.

"She's not back," I told her with an edge in my voice. "Listen, I want to keep this line open in case she calls." I didn't wait for her answer before hanging up.

The only other person who called that night was Nicole. While I was tempted to unload the whole story on her, I didn't. I reasoned that my mother would reappear any moment, and in the meantime, I didn't want Nicole's mother, Cindy, to find out. Although Gloria was bossy, she wasn't mean. But Cindy was a total witch, and she didn't like me. If she found out, in no time the whole town would know about the missing money and the police wanting to question my mother. Besides, I was certain that the whole thing was a mistake—it had to be.

Every time I heard a car enter our street, I rushed to the window and peered out. A couple of times I saw a police car cruise by and slow down as it passed our house. Officer Strobel and his cohorts were keeping an eye out for my mother, the dangerous fugitive.

Around midnight I turned out the lights, crawled into bed, and hugged my pillow to my chest. Sleep seemed impossible. I couldn't stop worrying. My eyes stayed open, staring into the darkness. Even though I've never been a crier, I found myself fighting back tears. Where was my mother, and what was this all about? I was never afraid to be home alone at night, yet suddenly, our house exuded an eerie atmosphere. The whole place seemed empty and vaguely sinister, as if the walls, the furniture, and even the very air around me were thick with tension. It felt as if the house, too, were watching and waiting for my mother.

Sometime after two I gave up trying to sleep, wrapped my

comforter around me, and moved cautiously through the dark house to the living room. Without turning on any lights, I opened the drapes and propped myself up on the sofa cushions so I could watch the front yard and the street beyond. Through the open window I could smell the scent of the jasmine blooming along the front porch. The house was so still I could hear every noise outside as if I were eavesdropping on the sleeping neighborhood. Mrs. Musick's back gate was banging in the cool breeze. Across the street the Goldmans' Irish setter was barking, probably at Stella, who liked to prowl the neighborhood at night. Or maybe raccoons were visiting again—I could hear a rattling noise from the direction of the garbage cans. Our house creaked and groaned as if it couldn't settle down either. A scrap of paper danced down the empty street. I listened and watched and at some point I finally fell asleep.

chapter three

i woke up to the sun shining in my eyes through the open drapes and Stella yowling up at me from the living room floor. Reluctantly, I sat up. A quick glance at the driveway confirmed my mother's car still wasn't there. I staggered into the kitchen. The clock said 6:47. I groaned and groped in the cupboard for the cat food, knowing Stella wouldn't let up until I fed her. That, at least, was normal.

After scraping some pukey brown muck into the cat dish, I stumbled down the hall and flopped on my bed. But even though I was exhausted, I couldn't get back to sleep. Last night's anger had dissipated, leaving only anxiety in its place.

Finally, I pulled myself up again and stared at my reflection in the mirror. Same old Ashley—in fact, I looked good. How weird, when I felt as if I should have worry lines on my face or some other blemish to mark the misery of the last seventeen hours.

Since no real alternative presented itself, I got ready for school. Staying home waiting for my mother all day would drive me completely off my rocker. Besides, I knew she'd show up—of course she would. In the meantime, I would do what I do best: look good and pretend I didn't have a care in the world. This whole mess would be cleared up before the day was out. It had to be.

Just to give me a happy reminder, a cop car cruised slowly by as I went out the front door. I ignored it.

I tried to sashay through the morning, pretending that nothing had changed. It wasn't hard to fool Scott. He was, as usual, oblivious to anyone else's feelings. As he droned on, describing yesterday's surfing, I stared up at his tanned face and sun-bleached hair. No doubt about it, he was a great boyfriend—good-looking, tall, a star athlete, a good dancer, and the owner of a brand-new Jeep Cherokee. Plenty of girls (including Mara) had tried to get their hooks into him over the past two years, but I knew how to reel him in when he got restless. Like most jocks, Scott enjoyed a challenge, so I never let him get too sure of himself. He also liked the prestige of having the homecoming queen as his girlfriend.

Believe me, there were plenty of guys who wanted me, even though I didn't put out. But why should that matter, when a hand job or blow job would do just as well? Sex was too risky, too messy, too much like surrender as far as I was concerned. I liked to be in control and keep Scott happy while teasing him with the promise of total capitulation in the future.

Today, though, Scott's lack of awareness annoyed me. In fact, no one at school noticed anything unusual about me although I was fighting hard to control my panic. Why didn't my mother call? Where was she? I wanted to go home to see if she was there, and I was afraid to go home in case she wasn't.

There was no real reason to be at school—lessons and tests were over. All of us, students and teachers alike, were just serving out our sentences. In first period we watched a boring movie, and during second period we erased pencil marks from our textbooks. In third period, American Government, we slouched in our chairs while Mr. Grant, a pint-sized bully, blathered on.

Then my cell phone rang.

Everyone in the class turned around to stare as my phone beeped out a rendition of "What a Wonderful World." Mr. G. paused in midcliché and raised his eyebrows in exaggerated astonishment.

Ignoring all of them, I snapped my phone open and whispered, "Hello."

No response.

Mr. G. barked out, "Ashley!"

I ignored him and looked down to read who was calling. The screen said "Blocked ID."

"Hello," I said again, much louder this time. *"Hello."* Still, no one spoke. Frustrated, I pounded the buttons. But it was no use—the phone was dead.

By this time Mr. G. had moved to my desk and stood there like a prison guard ready to clobber an unruly inmate.

"My, my," he said with undisguised glee. "Taking calls during class, are we? It must be of earth-shattering importance. Was it from the White House perhaps? Or maybe the governor wants your opinion on the state budget crisis?"

"I'm expecting an important call," I answered defensively. "From my mother."

"Your mother? Come, come, Ashley, I'm sure you can do better than that. What do you think, class? Does anyone here believe for one minute that our fair Ashley would disobey school rules to take a call from her mother?"

Several students tittered in response.

Smirking, Mr. G. continued. "Whatever your *important* call concerns, I fail to see why you should take up class time with it. If you're overdue for a bikini-wax appointment, it has nothing to do with American government, does it?"

A few of the geeky boys guffawed at this.

Just in time the dismissal bell screeched, and everyone surged toward the door. I quickly moved with them, and Mr. G. called after me.

"Don't bring that phone in here tomorrow, Ashley, or I'll own it."

Nicole was right on my heels and grabbed my arm in the hall. "What was that all about? What's going on?"

"What do you mean?" I feigned ignorance.

"Why would your mother call you during school? And why were you acting so weird last night on the phone? Something must be wrong." Her blue eyes blinked up at me in concern.

I stared at her silently for a moment, weighing exactly what or how much I should tell her. It wasn't that I didn't trust her. Talking about it meant that I couldn't pretend anymore that it wasn't really happening.

Nicole and I had been friends since fourth grade. I could count on her. I found that out when we were only ten. One

Friday afternoon the two of us were dropped off at my house after a gymnastics class. My mother wasn't home from work yet. We came dashing in, giggling and happy because Nicole was sleeping over that night.

I should have been warned by the smell.

"P-U, what's that stinky smell?" I said as we crossed the living room. That's when we saw him. Outside the hallway bathroom, my father was lying facedown on the carpet, his gray pants and jockey shorts pulled down around his ankles. Jimmy's body was twisted so we could see his naked butt, hairy legs, and soft, fleshy penis drooped to one side.

We stood there for a moment, mouths open, staring at him in shock. I couldn't help staring at his penis, which looked like one of those pale, slimy Italian sausages my mother sometimes cooked.

"Is he . . . all right?" Nicole asked.

I gave his closest body part, his upper arm, a sharp tap with the toe of my shoe. He snorted and stirred slightly without getting up. His eyes stayed closed, and I could see drool pooling in the corner of his mouth. The odor of alcohol emanating from him made my stomach lurch.

"No," I said. "He's drunk. He's a dirty, disgusting drunk. Let's get out of here."

We went outside and sat on the porch. I was so humiliated that I wanted to run away and never come back. But I put on a big act and pretended nothing had happened, even though I wasn't able to meet Nicole's eyes. We were still sitting on the porch when my mother's car pulled up a few minutes later. I lied and told my mother we hadn't gone inside yet. Diane went in the house and came out again ten minutes later, giving me a searching look.

"Let's go out for pizza" was all she said. "Your father isn't feeling well."

When we came home, Jimmy was in bed. The hallway still reeked of urine. We pretended not to notice. After Nicole left on Saturday, I worried that she would tell her mother or someone at school on Monday. I kept expecting Cindy to call and say my father was a pervert and Nicole couldn't come to my house ever again. Her mother didn't call, though, and no one said anything at school because Nicole didn't tell. She never told anyone. I loved her for that.

From then on, Nicole was my best friend. I protected her whenever anyone tried to bully her—even her mother. So it was time I filled Nicole in on my situation. But I only managed to get out the words "I need to tell you something" before Mara came prancing up to us.

"Wait till you see my new blue bikini," she boasted. "You'll die when you see it. It's very, very hot. Where did you buy yours, Ashley?"

Even on a normal day I found Mara annoying. Although she was part of my crowd, I didn't trust her, and with good reason. The girl was a complete wannabe and imitated everything I did. If I bought a pair of high-heeled suede boots, within days Mara would be clip-clopping down the hall in an identical pair. She even went to Sheila, my hairdresser, and asked her for the same hair cut. Being around her was like having an evil twin or clone or something.

"Don't you ever think about anything except clothes?" I

snarled. "I swear, if you were going to have your head cut off on the guillotine, you'd be wondering what you should wear on the scaffold."

"God, what is your problem?" Mara squealed indignantly.

"Guess what!" I said. "Some of us have real stuff to worry about."

I stomped away, and Nicole scurried after me to find out what was up. She followed me to the school parking lot and we sat in my car, talking. It was a relief to finally tell her about my mother.

Her jaw dropped at my news. "No way! *Your* mother? It can't be true. I don't believe it."

"Believe it. I'm totally freaked. No one can find her, and the cops keep driving by my house." I looked in the rearview mirror as if they might be pulling up behind me in the student lot. "I don't know what to do."

"God, I hope nothing's happened to her. What if she's been kidnapped or something?"

"You're not cheering me up, Nic."

"I'm sorry, I'm sorry," she apologized. "I mean, this is awful. I don't know what to say. This kind of thing just doesn't happen. To your mother, of all people."

"That's what I thought, but it is happening. It's a nightmare." I blinked back tears. "We're supposed to be leaving for Hawaii on Sunday, and I have no idea where my mother is. And what am I supposed to do for money? I just don't know what to do. Maybe Diane has been kidnapped. Or what if she's being framed for a crime she didn't commit—you know, like in a movie? You know my mother. She doesn't have the gumption to be a crook."

"Yeah," agreed Nicole. "She's definitely not the type. What does Gloria say?"

"Oh, she's hopeless. She doesn't know anything, she's so wrapped up in those brats of hers. And when I called Phil, there was some woman there. Her voice sounded familiar but . . ." I shook my head. "Well, anyway, I think he's dumped my mother. He sure didn't seem worried about her whereabouts."

"Men can be such jerks," she said. Maybe she was thinking about her own father, who had ditched Cindy two years earlier for a woman from his office. Nicole had idolized her father and couldn't forgive him for his desertion.

I squeezed Nicole's hand and we sat there, brooding about men and our mothers and the enigma of adult relationships.

"I guess I should go talk to Phil in person," I decided, rolling down my window to let in some air. We were having another day of dazzling sunshine. "Maybe if I corner him, he'll have to tell me what's going on."

"That's a good idea. What about calling your mom's office and talking to someone there?"

"No way! I'm not Nancy Drew, Girl Detective. Anyway, listening to someone accuse my mother of being a thief would *not* be fun. That's the last thing I need."

"Sorry. You're right. Do you want me to come with you to see Phil?"

That last part was said very bravely, but I wasn't fooled. Nicole hated confrontations. I smiled and shook my head. "No, I'll do it by myself. But come over later. I don't want to be alone. Waiting for my mother is driving me stark raving mad."

"I have to do some errands for my mother, but I'll come over around three," she said, opening the car door.

I sighed and pulled my hair up off my neck. "Nicole, be careful you don't let something slip about this. Especially not to your mother. Please!"

"I won't," she promised.

As I watched Nicole walk away, I thought maybe I should have told her the other part of the story. Maybe I should have told her about the vicious quarrel my mother and I had the night before she went missing. But my side of that argument wasn't very pretty, and I was ashamed to repeat it.

. . .

Even though Phil's gas station is always super clean, I could still smell the acrid odor of gasoline as I walked inside the garage. Overhead, a black Lexus was suspended on the hydraulic lift. Phil was in the back, leaning against his workbench, with a cell phone pressed to one ear. He raised his eyebrows when he saw me, said something into the phone, and hung up. He was dressed in his usual faded jeans, denim shirt, and shitkicker boots as if he were just off the range from wrestling a few broncos. I always considered his look totally phony—this is California, after all, not Montana.

Reynaldo was nowhere in sight.

"Well, well, what an honor—a visit from the Duchess," Phil quipped, leaning back against the workbench with his arms crossed in front of him. "Careful you don't get those dainty sandals dirty."

He always thought it was funny to refer to me as "the Duchess." I gave him a *Ha, ha, how amusing, you hopeless dork* look.

"Have the cops been to see you?" I said.

He nodded warily. "Yes, but I couldn't help them. I haven't seen Diane much lately."

"What does that mean? The two of you have been a couple for years. Now suddenly you hardly know her?"

Phil shrugged. "Things kind of tapered off between us."

"This is the first I've heard of it," I sneered. "What happened—you dumped her?"

"Duchess, you're too wrapped up in yourself to notice anyone else," he shot back. "No, I didn't dump her." He gazed down at his hands as if he were studying them. They were big hands, callused and stained.

"Yeah, so, if you didn't dump her, what happened?" I persisted.

Finally, he looked up and straight into my eyes. "I don't really know what happened. She never seemed to have time for me. She's been awfully busy, or at least that's what she said. I thought maybe she was seeing someone else. Someone at her office."

"At her office? Why would you think that? Are you sure you're not just making excuses because you're cheating on her?"

He shot me a hostile look. "Sure, I'm seeing someone else now. But I'm not cheating on anyone. Diane and I are still friends. If anyone did any dumping, it was her. Anyway, our relationship just never went anywhere. You were always more important than me."

I ignored that old, tired complaint. Phil had always been jealous, because we both knew I came first with my mother.

"Why do you think she was seeing someone from her office?"

"She spent so much time there, late nights and weekends, and she was always talking to someone at work by phone. I saw less and less of her, and when I asked what was going on, she never really answered. I asked her a hundred times to go away with me, just the two of us in my camper. I wanted to go to Oregon or Yosemite or even just to Reno. She always claimed she couldn't leave you or she was too busy at work. She always made excuses, although . . ." His voice trailed off.

"Although what?" I hissed.

He didn't answer me.

"What?" I demanded.

He stared at his hands again. "Although if she were embezzling money, that would explain it. She would have been spending more time at the office, wouldn't she? Trying to cover her tracks?"

"Embezzling! My mother—an embezzler? Jesus, Phil, Diane is not some criminal mastermind. You can't honestly think she's guilty!"

"I don't know, Ashley," he said slowly. "I would never have thought so, but I always did wonder where she got all the money she spent on you and redoing the house and that Mercedes. The two of you spend a lot of money."

"We don't spend any more money than anyone else," I protested.

"Maybe so, but on a single mother's salary? She's a bookkeeper, not a bank president. Most people around here spend that much because they're pulling down big bucks in high-powered jobs, with two parents working."

I didn't know what to say. I had never really thought about it. I had no idea what my mother's salary was. All I knew was that when I wanted money, my mother would come up with it. Would my mother steal money to keep me in designer jeans? I wanted to say no, but I was terrified the answer might be yes. I couldn't help but remember my mother sobbing in the rain two nights ago, "It's never enough for you. No matter what I do, it's never enough."

chapter four

I opened the front door and grimaced at the sight of the two uniformed men standing there. "You again! Have you found her?"

Strobel gave a negative headshake, but I knew the answer from the expression on his partner's face. Officer Donahoe looked as if he had poured sour milk on his breakfast cereal.

"Why don't you just tell us where she is?" Donahoe snarled. "You don't seem to realize you're in a bad spot. If you're not careful, you could be charged as an accessory. I don't think you'll like doing mother-daughter time in San Quentin."

His voice sliced through the air with the whine of a weed whacker. Donahoe's obnoxious tone matched his equally obnoxious manner. Three days had elapsed since my mother went missing, and this was the fourth time the cops had stopped by the house. Apparently, Officer Donahoe never tired of trying to browbeat me into telling him my mother's whereabouts.

"I confess, copper. Go ahead, put on the cuffs and throw me in the slammer," I retorted, holding out my wrists. "The loot is stashed in the cookie jar, and my mother's at the Four Seasons."

"This isn't a joke, little lady. You'll start taking this seriously when you find yourself in jail." Donahoe glared at me and I glared right back.

"Oh, yeah, some joke. My mother is missing; she's probably been kidnapped, but the cops won't lift a finger to find her and you keep hassling me. That's my idea of a really big joke."

Donahoe snorted, waved what he called a warrant in my face, and pushed past me into the house. Strobel raised his eyebrows and followed his partner inside. The pair of them had arrived to search for evidence or maybe to find out if some of the missing cash was stashed in my mother's underwear drawer, under her bikini panties.

Instead of following them inside, I slumped onto the settee on the porch. I could hear a woodpecker *rat-tatt*ing away from the telephone pole across the street. I felt like going over with a hammer and lending a hand.

I was enduring another gorgeous spring day. It felt as if the weather were mocking me in my misery. The day should have been cold and bitter, with black skies and ominous clouds ready to pour torrential rain down on everyone and everything. I needed pounding hail and savage winds and ear-shattering thunder. I wanted to see wildly destructive tornadoes tearing up the landscape. As it was, all of the storms were raging inside me.

Yesterday, I had even swallowed my pride and asked Gloria if she would lend me the money for Hawaii, just until my mother came back. She exploded into the telephone.

"You can't be serious. Your mother is missing and you want to run off to Hawaii and get a suntan! Why does this not surprise me? Just when I think you couldn't possibly be as narcissistic as I imagine, you demonstrate you really are that shallow."

I hung up on her. What *was* her problem? She had no idea what hell I was going through. What did Gloria expect me to do? There was nothing to do except wait, and that was the hardest thing I'd ever done.

That night a reporter from the *San Francisco Examiner* had called, asked for Diane Mitchell, then tried to question me when I said she wasn't home. I slammed the receiver down without answering.

Today, page six of the *Examiner* contained a four-paragraph article, with the headline:

Burlingame Woman Sought in Fraud Investigation

Burlingame, CA—Police have filed fraud and grand theft charges against Diane Mitchell, 42, of Burlingame. Mitchell allegedly embezzled $1.2 million from her employer, Warren Simmons & Co., in Redwood City. Mitchell, a bookkeeper for Warren Simmons for the past nine years, is missing, and authorities fear she may have fled the country.

"She was a trusted employee for years, and we totally relied on her," said Arthur Warren, chief executive officer of this well-known architectural and engineering firm. "We're all still in shock."

> Burlingame Police say the fraud was uncovered by independent auditors brought into the company in preparation for a merger. They did not disclose what led them to suspect Mitchell of the theft. Two months ago Warren Simmons announced its proposed acquisition by Martinez Engineering, the largest firm of its type in the Bay Area.
>
> Ashley Mitchell, 18, the suspect's daughter, has been questioned, but no charges have been filed. Mitchell had no comment when reached at their Burlingame home.

Those four paragraphs were wreaking havoc in my life. At school, there were two equally distasteful reactions: some people were so-o-o kind and treated me as if they were oh-so-sorry for me, while others just whispered and turned away as if I had a communicable disease.

The school administration fell into the pseudo-sympathetic category. Mr. Rachesky, the iron-jawed principal, took me aside to ask if they could "do anything" for me. I told him I was fine.

Predictably, Mara was one of those that put on a bogus "you poor thing" act. I was lucky enough to avoid running into her all morning. Then, right before dismissal, I heard her singsong voice behind me.

"What are *you* wearing to graduation?" I heard her say to someone. I kept my back toward her and my face averted, but it was no use. She spotted me and danced over.

"Oh, Ashley, how *are* you?" she said in her most sugary-sweet tone. "You must be going through *hell.* You poor thing, I guess this means you won't be going to *Hawaii.* We should all do something, like, take up a collection for bail."

With my teeth clenched, I said, "Oh, Mara, that's so-o-o sweet. You don't need to worry about me, but I'm really touched because I didn't know you ever thought about anything except what clothes to put on your back."

I walked away without waiting to see what she would say next.

Scott's attitude was the most hurtful of all. He ignored me—*me,* his girlfriend. When I finally thrust myself into the middle of his little group of poseurs, they all scattered as if there were a fire drill in progress.

"Oh, hi, Ash," he said casually, looking down at his shoes instead of meeting my eyes.

"Oh, hi, Scott," I mocked him in a loud voice. I was angry and ready to rock and roll. "Maybe you'd like to explain why you walked right by me after French class as if you didn't even know me."

"Hey, don't go postal on me," he protested, finally looking up. "I didn't see you."

"Like hell you didn't. I know you saw that article in the newspaper. I know everyone has read it, and anyone who didn't read it has heard about it by now."

"Yeah, that was weird. I can't believe your mom would . . ." He let it trail off.

"I don't believe it. And I can't believe all my friends, even my own boyfriend, would start acting as if I'm a criminal."

"Come on, Ash, I don't think you're a criminal," he said, rocking back and forth uncomfortably. "It's just that, well, you know my old man. He's being a real prick. He gave me his 'I'm a big-shot partner with a distinguished law firm' speech and said he can't afford to have anyone in his family mixed up with an embezzler and the police and all that. He raised holy hell last night and told me to stay away from you, or else he'll take my Jeep away."

"Your Jeep. Great, I rank right up there, don't I? Right below that piece of metal. Thanks for nothing."

"This is just for a few days. Your mom will show up and fix everything. We just have to cool it in public until we get to Hawaii."

"I don't want a boyfriend who pretends he doesn't know me in public. And it looks like I'm not going to Hawaii. Right now, I don't have any money to pay the balance due. Anyway, the cops are all over me. Yesterday, they told me not to leave town, just in case I was thinking of taking off for Argentina with a suitcase full of cash."

"Not go to Hawaii?" Scott was truly shocked. "We've been looking forward to this all year. The cops can't do that. You need a lawyer. We can't let them do this."

"And where would I get the money for a lawyer?" I scowled. "Earth to Scott! I already told you I don't have the money for Hawaii. Lawyers aren't free either."

"I'd loan you some cash for Hawaii, but I'm busted. I need to tap my old man before liftoff or the whole trip will be a real drag."

I stared at him in disgust. I had just told him I was being

harassed by the cops, but all Scott could think about was Hawaii and how to get spending money from his tight-ass father. I was lost—completely adrift, with no money and no one to help me. I wanted someone's arms around me, someone who would hold me tight and murmur, "It'll be all right, baby." Truthfully, I wanted my mother, but a little TLC from Scott would have helped.

"My hero," I answered, my voice dripping with sarcasm. "I wasn't asking for money, but I expected more than this from you. I hope you and your Jeep are very happy together."

I stalked off, minus one boyfriend.

. . .

Graduation day was a complete fiasco. The only reason I showed up for the ceremony at all was to prevent my former friends and their respectable, law-abiding parents from whispering that I was too ashamed to appear. Let them dare to judge or pity me. I would hold my head high and spit in their eyes. That was the only thing my mother had ever insisted on—that I hold my head up, no matter what.

So I faced down all of them on graduation day. The hardest part was enduring the chilly reception when my name was called and I walked to the podium. Unlike Scott and others in the popular crowd, my march across the stage was not heralded by any outburst of enthusiastic applause, cheers, or congratulatory war whoops from friends and relatives. For me there was only silence, followed by embarrassed, tepid applause. My heart was pounding and my face was hot with humiliation, but I maintained my icy control and survived the ceremony.

After all the diplomas had been handed out and all the speeches given, everyone congregated on the lawn in front of the school. Each new graduate, wearing a white cap and gown and a bright smile, posed for pictures surrounded by a joyous crowd of relatives and friends. They all had mothers and fathers and brothers and sisters and aunts and uncles and cousins and grandparents. Only I was alone. No one came over to hug me and say "I'm so proud of you." I wanted my mother so badly I ached. How could she do this to me?

Ironically, I'd never minded being an only child. Now, standing on that lawn, I'd have given anything to have a sister or brother to cheer me on.

I was making my way through the crowd when Nicole came up behind me and grabbed my arm. "Ashley. Come with us. We're going to lunch at the Portabella Bistro to celebrate."

I hesitated. "We?"

"Oh, you know—my mother, my brothers, and my grandmother," she said, making a face. "Then tonight I have to go to dinner with my dad and *that woman.*"

Now that her parents were divorced, poor Nic had to play the do-everything-twice game.

I stood there, jiggling my car keys in my hand. Seeing my hesitation, she pleaded, "Please, it'll be fun."

Looking over Nicole's head, I could see her mother standing beside her Beamer, watching us from across the lot. Clad in a floaty yellow dress with her platinum hair curling around her sly face, Cindy looked like a lemon meringue pie—one with the sugar left out. In her eyes I recognized a trace of triumph at my comeuppance. I gave her a defiant look, hugged Nicole, and answered, "Sure."

But as I climbed behind the wheel, a police car cruised by on the adjacent street, reminding me of just how different I was from all the other graduates. My whole body suddenly felt heavy, weighed down with worry and misery. There was no way I could face two hours of fending off Cindy's cutting remarks and pretending that everything was wonderful. Instead, I turned my car in the opposite direction of the restaurant and drove home to brood about how my life sucked.

chapter five

Graduation night always means lots of parties, but I felt too wounded to call around and find out what was happening. I stayed home, having a one-woman pity party, moping and listening to a CD of my-boyfriend's-left-me-and-I-think-I'll-kill-myself songs. Around ten I heard a car horn honk. I looked outside and saw a long white limousine pulled up to the curb. Out popped the platinum-and-purple head of Tatiana, better known as Tattie, the wildest girl in the entire school.

"Hey, let's get crazy. It's party time!" Tattie shouted as I opened the front door. I could hear the raucous rap of OutKast blasting from inside the limo. The music was so loud the car was vibrating.

Why not? I thought. Waiting and moping wasn't doing me any good. Why not get crazy?

"Give me two minutes," I yelled back, and dashed into my bedroom to don my shortest, hottest skirt, a red halter top, and a pair of sexy high-heeled sandals.

I was surprised at this unexpected invitation. Tattie and

I had never been close. She was a little too over the top for my taste. While my ears and belly button are pierced, Tattie wore six earrings in each ear and one in her eyebrow plus a stud in the side of her lip. She also had a tattoo of a tiger on her backside, which everyone could see when she bent over. Most of her outfits were tight and garish and looked as if she bought them at Kmart. Still, she had a great body, and she had been voted "Best Figure" in the entire school. The guys liked to say she had quite a rack.

As I walked up to the limo, I saw that tonight Tattie's notorious breasts were corralled inside a low-cut leather and lace camisole.

"Get in, get in," she urged me, pulling on my arm. I was barely inside before the limo took off amid a loud chorus of shrieks. The back was crowded to the max with the laughing, gyrating bodies of ten excited new graduates, male and female, sipping beer or wine coolers. The smell of marijuana was thick in the air. Someone must have slipped the driver a big wad of cash to make him ignore what was going on. This group was definitely ready to party.

I wondered what had prompted Tattie to invite me along, but I didn't ask. I was just glad she did. Last winter both Tattie and I had lead roles in the school's musical production of *Chicago.* (Ironically, Nicole could outsing us both, but she cringed at the very thought of singing a solo onstage.) At rehearsals we discovered a mutual affinity for playing practical jokes and generally acting up.

At the final cast party, we outdid ourselves by doing a provocative little dance that ended when we flipped our skirts up and mooned everyone by wagging our thong-clad butts. That dance was the upper limit of my wildness, though it was probably the tamest story circulating about Tattie.

After the play was over, Tattie and I didn't become best buds or go to the mall together. Still, we remained friendly.

As I settled into a seat near the door, Tattie passed me a plastic cup full of brew. "Welcome to the club, girlfriend," she said.

I wondered what club she was referring to—the losers club? The misfits club? The let's-get-high club? I didn't say anything, though, because tonight I was just thankful to be a member of whatever club would have me. At the same time, I hoped I wouldn't run into Mara, Scott, or any of my old crowd—they would probably think it was pretty funny to see the bunch of oddballs and freaks I was hanging out with. Or maybe they would feel sorry for me. I wasn't sure which reaction would be worse.

The limo's first stop was a rave party in Redwood City where everyone jumped out to dance in the street with several hundred other gyrating tweakers. A boy with a Mohawk offered me some Ecstasy, but I passed. A few puffs on a joint together with the beer I'd been drinking made me feel sufficiently mellow. After a couple of hours we went on to some random party at an estate in ritzy Hillsborough. Eventually the cops showed up and everyone took off.

Around two we ended up back at my house since no parents or disapproving adults would interfere. I danced up a storm and hooked up with a semicute guy from another school named Ryan. He was a good kisser, and I felt more relaxed than I had in days. Of course, Ryan had to push it and whisper

"Let's go in the bedroom" in my ear. I ignored him after that and eventually he split.

Around four I stumbled down the hall to my room and collapsed on my bed without undressing. At some point the sound of frantic catlike scratching on the other side of my closed door pierced my slumber. I didn't move—Stella would have to wait for her breakfast.

It was midafternoon before I finally emerged and tottered toward the kitchen. As I passed through the living room, I paused in what had become an involuntary action—checking the driveway for my mother's car. It wasn't there.

Once I had fed the cat and downed some aspirin, I paused to survey the damage. Glasses, empty wine bottles, beer cans, and the remains of what appeared to be a pepperoni pizza were strewn here and there. The hall phone was off the hook, CDs were tossed on the floor, and the place smelled like a brewery. Fortunately, I didn't see anything that looked like permanent damage. I did notice, though, that someone's skirt and sandals had been abandoned near the sofa.

A quick look around the house revealed that Tattie was the owner of these garments. I found her sprawled across my mother's bed, dressed only in a thong, with her spiked hair sticking up like a rooster's feathers from the pillow. Stella ran in ahead of me, jumped on the bed, and sniffed the pillow as if she was identifying the species of this mysterious stranger.

"Go away, cat," Tattie said in a husky voice as she sat up and wrapped the top sheet around her shoulders. She lit a cigarette and inhaled deeply. I should have told her not to smoke in my mother's room, but I didn't.

"Do you need to call your mother?" I asked.

Tattie gave me a sleepy smile. "Don't worry. *She* won't even have noticed I'm not there."

It was no secret to me or half the town that Tattie's mother was a big drinker. She tended bar in a bowling alley and was prone to oversampling what she served.

"God, I feel like I smoked four thousand cigarettes last night," Tattie said, coughing and rubbing her eyes. "Maybe I did."

I pulled the drapes open to let the sun in, looked out the window, and sighed.

"What are you so down about? High school is finally over—we're free at last."

"Yeah, sure, everything's great. The sun is shining, the birds are singing, and my mother is missing."

"Gawd, I'd be thrilled if my mother disappeared," she said.

"Yeah, well, I'm almost out of money, and I don't know when my mother is going to show up."

"You need some money? No sweat, just have a garage sale and sell some of this stuff." She waved her hands, gesturing at all the stuff in the room.

I was taken aback. "What do you mean? Sell our furniture and clothes? I can't do that. What would my mother think when she came home and found I had sold all her things?"

"Hey, that's what she deserves for leaving you busted. Anyway, if she comes back, she's going to understand you had to sell the stuff. If she doesn't come back, it won't matter."

"My mother will be back," I barked at her.

"Okay, relax, don't freak out. She'll be back," Tattie said, backing off. "Then take some clothes down to one of those secondhand clothing stores. I hear Couture Closet will give you cash on the spot if you have really good stuff."

I looked inside my mother's bulging closet and thought that maybe Tattie was on to something. Maybe I could even sell a few outfits I didn't wear anymore.

After taking a shower, I drove Tattie home. I came back determined to choose some stuff to sell. But once I stepped inside my mother's closet, I was immediately overwhelmed by the familiar scent of her White Shoulders perfume. Standing there, she seemed so close that I expected to turn around and find her behind me. I stroked the soft cashmere of her favorite navy blazer, the one she wore to work on so many mornings. Her silky blouses with those ridiculous bows at the neck were hanging there too. If she would just come back, I would never make fun of them again. If she'd just come back, I'd be a perfect daughter. I would. I really would.

I grabbed her satiny blue bathrobe and slipped it on over my clothes. It was as close to having her arms around me as I could get. Tears, the same tears I had been fighting to hold back for days, began to trickle down my cheeks and then turned into a flood. My heart hurt so much I didn't think I could bear it. I sank down on the carpet and bawled like a baby—a baby who wanted her mother and couldn't find her.

Finally, I pulled myself together and escaped to the bathroom. I had barely managed to wash away the evidence of my tears when the doorbell rang. It was Nicole.

"Where have you been?" she said in an exasperated tone, plopping down on the sofa. "I must have called you a dozen times."

"Oops, sorry. I was going to come say good-bye. I thought you'd be busy packing. The plane leaves in just a few hours."

"I'm not going," she replied.

"What?" I was stunned. "Have you lost your mind?"

"I don't want you to be alone when everything is so weird right now."

"That's insane. Why should you skip a great trip to Hawaii just so we can both be miserable? I'll be fine. There's nothing you can do, believe me. There's nothing anyone can do right now."

"Hawaii won't be any fun without you. Anyway, you wouldn't go without me," she insisted.

"Yes, I would," I said, and it was true. I wouldn't want to go without her but I would. "Listen to your big sister. There's absolutely no point in you staying here."

While I always called myself her big sister, in reality I was only four months older than Nicole. Sometimes, though, it seemed like four years.

"I can't believe this is happening. It isn't fair," she said.

Inside my head, I could hear my mother's voice telling me over and over that life isn't fair. I hadn't ever believed her until now.

Seeing that Nic was on the verge of tears, I tried to make a joke. "Hey, I know without me you won't be able to enjoy the sun and sand and waves, not to mention all those hot-looking surfers. But I need you to ruin Scott's trip and make sure he doesn't have any fun."

She didn't even crack a smile.

"Anyway, your mother will never let you drop out now,

not after she's already paid big bucks for the nonrefundable deposit."

"I'll make her understand," she muttered.

"Don't waste your breath. You know and I know that whether you sing or say it, your mother isn't going to listen, not even if you get down on your knees."

"About my mother . . . ," Nicole began, and then stopped.

"What?"

"I asked her if you could come and stay with us until your mother comes back but . . ."

I hooted with sarcastic laughter. "Wow, I can imagine what she said to that. I'll bet your mother is really enjoying the mess I'm in."

Nicole flushed. She didn't say anything, just reached up and began twisting a lock of her hair around her finger. We both knew that Cindy had never been my biggest fan, even in grade school. She told Nicole that I was "insolent." Nicole's dad liked me, though; he said I was spunky. But when he took off with the other woman, Cindy's mild dislike of me intensified. Junior year, when Nicole dropped out of the school's production of *My Fair Lady* and I took over the lead role, Cindy was furious. She also blamed me when Nicole wouldn't try out for cheerleader, and she was livid when I was named homecoming queen, even though I made sure Nicole was a princess in my court. Cindy just wouldn't accept that her daughter hated the spotlight and nothing was going to change that. For years I tried to coach Nicole and teach her how to put on the whole self-confident act I'm so good at, but she just couldn't do it.

Really, it was sweet of Nic to try to persuade her mother to take me in, though I could have told her it would never happen.

"Thanks anyway," I said. "But honestly, I need to stay at my house in case my mother calls."

She was still mechanically twisting her hair, so I reached up and grabbed her hand. "And stop yanking on your hair!" I scolded her. "You've already got a tiny bald spot there."

She dropped her hand. "Sorry. I'm trying to stop, really I am. I'm just so worried about what's going to happen. I don't just mean Hawaii, but about college and everything. What if your mother doesn't . . . ?" Her voice trailed off.

For years Nicole and I had been planning to room together at an East Coast college. After applying to at least a dozen, we both had received acceptance letters in April from Boston University.

"You worry too much," I said, without admitting I was having the same fears. "My mother will probably show up tomorrow. When she does, I have a plan."

"What?"

"I'll make her pop for a ticket so I can join you in Hawaii."

"That's a great idea," Nicole said eagerly. "She should buy you a first-class ticket. It would only be fair, after all she's put you through."

I nodded agreement without telling her how unlikely I thought that was. I was beginning to doubt there would be any quick and easy solution to this mess. My mother would come back, of that I was sure. But when she reappeared, she would almost certainly be hauled off to jail and wouldn't be in any position to pass out money for first-class tickets to Hawaii.

The last couple of nights I'd been troubled by dreams in which my mother was captured and dragged off in handcuffs while TV cameras filmed her humiliation (and mine). It seemed too horrible to even hope for such an ugly conclusion. Yet at least I would know where she was and if she was all right.

Nicole eventually went home to finish packing for Hawaii. When I hugged her good-bye, I held on tight for a few extra seconds, comforted by the reassuring arms of someone who cared about me. Then I let go.

chapter six

That night, while Nicole and all my former friends were in the sky en route to Hawaii, I was in my car on my way to Tattie's place.

Tattie lived in a white stucco bungalow along the access road facing the freeway. While there is no such thing as a "bad" neighborhood in Burlingame, her street came closest, with its small houses and even smaller yards. Her house was the least impressive on the block since it needed repainting and the front yard had more weeds than grass.

I parked at the curb behind Tattie's dented Honda and walked up to ring the doorbell. Before I could even press it, the door swung open and I was staring straight at two breasts threatening to burst out of a low-cut green top.

Tattie's mother gave me the once-over and yelled behind her, "Don't you even think of going somewhere before you get this place cleaned up! Get your little friend here to help you."

With that, she barreled past me and headed for the driveway.

I stood watching as her sizable bottom convulsed inside too-tight black pants.

Her mother pulled herself into the driver's seat of a yellow Mazda with a deep crease in the passenger-side door. She paused to check her face in the rearview mirror. Her hair was dyed an aggressive shade of red, and she was wearing more makeup than you'd see at an Estée Lauder counter. She and Tattie obviously shared a love of excess.

"Are you lost, Miz Ashley?" Tattie said from behind me in the doorway.

"Bored," I answered, and walked inside. "I came over to see what you were doing."

"You've come to the right place," Tattie said. "The excitement never stops around here."

She walked through the living room, and I followed her, trying not to wince or hold my nose. Her house was a complete mess, with newspapers and clothes and dirty dishes everywhere. And the place smelled—the rancid odor of cooking grease and soiled laundry fought with the heavy floral scents of air freshener and hair spray.

She walked into a tiny bathroom and paused in front of the mirror to apply blush to her already red cheeks. I stood leaning in the doorway since there wasn't anywhere I wanted to sit down.

"What flavor of excitement are you serving tonight?" I asked.

"That all depends," she said. "Just wait and see. You like this shadow?"

She was applying glittering gold cream to her eyelids.

"Wow," I said for lack of a better comment.

"Makeup is kind of my mask," she admitted, letting her mouth hang open slightly as she applied more mascara to her eyelashes. "I even sleep with it on so I don't scare myself in the morning. I'm kind of a hag that way."

"You look more biker babe than hag in that outfit," I said. She was wearing all black, from her low-cut top to her leather miniskirt and matching boots.

She laughed and said, "We make quite a contrast. You look like Little Miss Gap or something."

I smiled, although my designer jeans and form-fitting pinstripe jacket cost a lot more than anything from the Gap. She clearly didn't recognize classic style when she saw it.

"Time to boogie," she said. "Let's haul ass. I'll drive."

We climbed into Tattie's Honda and took off for San Francisco, or "the City," as it is referred to by everyone who lives in the burbs. The minute I slid into the front seat, I made a mental note to never ride in her car again. Part of the floorboard beneath the passenger side was missing. I had to balance my feet carefully so that my foot didn't slip through the hole and hit the pavement below.

She drove fast, and twenty minutes later we pulled off the freeway onto Cesar Chavez Boulevard. As we sped down debris-lined streets past grimy buildings with peeling paint, I began to get uneasy. I was not familiar with this part of San Francisco and didn't want to be either.

"Where are we going?" I asked, realizing I should have asked this question before.

"The Cactus Club. I need to see my friend Tony," Tattie said.

"What if they card us?" I asked.

"Aren't you twenty-one yet, little girl?" She laughed. "No problem, they know me."

When she stopped in a bus zone outside a dingy-looking bar, I said, "Hey! I'm not sure—"

But Tattie jumped out, yelling, "Come on!" as she headed inside.

I stayed where I was, weighing my lack of options, until a big diesel bus pulled up next to the car and stopped. The huge doors opened with a loud hiss and I saw the dark face of the bus driver scowling down at me. A couple of men emerged from the bus and zigzagged around the car to reach the sidewalk. "Stupid bitch," I heard one of them mutter. "Don't know any better than to park in a bus zone."

"It's not my car," I called after him. He didn't turn around. Sighing, I got out of the car and skittered into the bar. It was like stepping into a dark, smelly cave. Tattie was seated on one of the bar stools, laughing flirtatiously at a mustached bartender. I sat down on the stool next to her.

"Tony, this is Ashley."

I nodded.

"She's the one I was telling you about," Tattie continued. "Can you fix her up?"

"Oh, yeah." Tony leered at me. "I'll be happy to take care of her, don't you worry."

I shifted uneasily, leaning my arm on the bar and then moving it when my flesh stuck to the tacky surface. Actually, the whole place was tacky, with an unpleasantly boozy odor—it smelled just like my father used to, and that wasn't a good thing.

Tattie got up, announced she had to pee, and sauntered toward the back. A few seconds later, Tony followed her. I sat there staring at my reflection in the bar mirror until some weirdo wearing an Oakland Raiders cap sat down on the stool next to me.

"Hey, gorgeous, can I buy you a drink?"

"No, thanks," I said. Was he kidding? He was way old and had long sideburns. "I'm fine. I better go see where my friend went."

"Oh, don't worry about her," he said, leaning toward me with his mouth open wide. I could see his teeth needed a good flossing. "I'm betting she's real busy right now. I'll entertain you till she comes back."

Without answering, I walked toward the back. I didn't see Tattie, so I tried the door to the toilet. It was locked. I could hear giggling inside and some other unidentifiable sounds. I stood outside the door, reluctant to return to the bar alone.

After a few minutes, Tony walked out of the toilet with some money in his hand. He gave me a smirk as he brushed by and said, "You come back, sweetheart. Anytime."

Then Tattie reappeared. "I've got what I need," she said. "Let's blast."

Out in the car, Tattie tucked a plastic bag into the glove compartment and flipped me a card. "Your new ID," she said.

It was a driver's license for an Elizabeth Castillo, age twenty-two, and the only thing she and I had in common was dark hair. "Thanks," I said, not really meaning it. I was feeling more depressed by the minute. Instead of sunning myself on a Hawaiian beach, I was hanging out in raunchy taverns and meeting sleazy drug dealers.

"What next?" I muttered, more to myself than to Tattie.

But she answered me. "Why don't we go back to your house?"

I could have kissed her, I was so relieved. As we drove the sixteen miles back to Burlingame, Tattie used her cell phone to invite a few of her friends to my place.

Maybe I should have told her to forget it. But I didn't have anyone else to hang with. I reasoned that at least Tattie didn't look down on me or talk shit about my mother, the notorious embezzler.

We had barely turned into my driveway when they began arriving. None of them were part of the popular clique at school, but I knew them.

First to arrive was Mike, a pint-sized wisecracker with a shaved head and baggy jeans. He strolled in with a skateboard on his shoulder and his girlfriend, Shirlee, at his heels.

"Gee whiz, Ashley, first last night and then today. We're getting to be, like, best friends," said Mike in a falsetto. "I feel cooler already, I mean, like, I am the coolest dude around. I mean, like, oh, my gawd."

Shirlee giggled as if he were the funniest human on the planet. She was known for giggling at anything anyone said, including herself.

Next came Brian—also known as Brain because he was a total computer geek who made straight As. Rumor had it he could hack into any network no matter how tight the security.

"I brought refreshments," shouted Brain, pointing to a cooler he was carrying. "Cold Jell-O shots and beer."

Brain was half-Vietnamese, or maybe all—he could have been one of those adopted babies. In school it was hard to keep your own story straight, much less anyone else's. So many of the kids were of mixed ancestry that it was no big deal. Money, not race, was always what counted.

Webb was the last one to arrive, swaggering in the door to a welcoming chorus of "Hey, dude!" and "What's happening, dude?" His first name was Robert, but everyone always called him by his last name. Webb was the male version of Tattie. Scott always said he was a loser. True, he cut school a lot and his grades weren't good. But he was a daredevil on snowboards and dirt bikes. I heard he had even tried skydiving. If he had been a dog, he would have been a rottweiler, while Scott was a classic golden retriever.

"Hey, Webb," said Mike. "That was quite a show you put on yesterday."

"Show? What show?" I asked.

"You mean you haven't heard?" Tattie hooted. "Our friend here got banned from commencement because of a little prank he pulled."

Brain leaned forward to fill me in. "You know that little shed over on the edge of the football field?" he said. "Well, Webb tried to send it into orbit with a few well-placed pyrotechnics."

"I made a slight miscalculation," Webb allowed.

"It was a beautiful sight," Brain continued. "Rockets, Roman candles, the whole works. Two fire trucks were on the scene and a platoon of firemen, but the shed burned down to the ground. I hear the school board was on the warpath and a couple of the big hot dogs wanted him busted."

Mike guffawed. "It's a good thing you're leaving town, dude. Otherwise, they'd have your dick in a wringer for sure."

Webb leaned back in the chair with a smirk on his face. "They haven't made a wringer big enough for my dick."

"So I've heard," I interjected.

Shirlee giggled, and Webb honored me with a smile. He was known for his devastating smile and his ability to charm the pants off almost anyone. In fact, he had charmed the pants off quite a few girls in our class.

"Believe it," said Tattie, sticking out her tongue and wiggling it in a provocative manner.

"Are you speaking from experience?" Brain asked playfully, pretending to hold a microphone up to her mouth. "Enquiring minds want to know."

She grabbed his hand and cooed into his make-believe microphone. "I always speak from experience. But that's ancient history."

"Ancient, ancient history. The crustacean period. When dinosaurs roamed the earth," Webb added.

"You mean Cretaceous period," I said.

"Whatever," he grunted, and gave me a challenging look.

"Whatever," I agreed.

"Okay, we're all here. Let's get started," announced Tattie, climbing to a perch atop the back of the sofa. "Welcome, Ashley, to the other side of the tracks, home of the outcasts and troublemakers. Zoned for those who can't or won't fit in, who don't give a fuck, who don't buy into the bullshit. Let the games begin."

"Do you have a special game in mind?" I asked while the others whooped and whistled.

"I have enough Vitamin E for everyone here," she said. "You, girlfriend, are in for a really big treat."

"I'll pass," I said, and everyone began booing and catcalling.

"Oh, no, you don't. This is special for you. We're all old hands at this. You have been through a lot of bad shit and need some serious cheering up. This will definitely do the trick."

"What if it's been cut with something? Dying would not cheer me up."

Someone made a clucking noise. I ignored it.

"Relax, I guarantee you this is grade-A stuff, nothing mixed in," Tattie assured me. "Tony would not give me bad shit."

I didn't say anything, but I was still reluctant.

"It's perfectly safe," Shirlee added earnestly. "I don't do drugs, not even aspirin. Only E. It really is pure ecstasy, pure bliss."

"There's nothing better than the first time you try E," said Brain. "It's totally dope. You feel like you're floating above the whole world, and at the same time everything seems so crystal clear."

Everyone nodded in agreement.

"What are you, the Ecstasy fairies?" Webb intervened. He was sprawled in our cranberry red wing chair, a beer in one hand. "Leave her alone. Maybe she can't handle it. If she's not up to it, she's not up to it."

Tattie shrugged and began handing out the little white pills.

I watched Webb grab one. He gave me an I-dare-you look,

swallowed it, chased it down with a swig of beer, and grinned. No doubt about it, the guy did have a great smile going for him, along with that whole dark-and-dangerous-bad-boy look.

I reached over, took a pill, and swallowed it. "Let the games begin," I said.

chapter seven

At first I didn't feel any different. We listened to music and talked about everything and nothing. Silly Shirlee began to babble about color and how everyone's aura was a different shade. I tuned her out. Gradually, I became aware that an amazingly good feeling had come over me, something between the warm, cozy feeling of curling up on the sofa with a good book, and the euphoric giddiness of the day I had been named homecoming queen.

I felt like my mind was completely in tune and yet goofily happy. All my defenses and my distrustful attitude fell away as if I were shedding a worn-out skin I didn't need anymore. Suddenly, I felt very warm. I pulled off my blouse to reveal the camisole underneath.

"Someone's feeling it," Webb said, and gave me a glass of water to drink. His thoughtfulness rocked me.

Everyone began to open up. Brain told us that his mother had left yesterday for a rehab clinic.

"It won't work," he said. "She's gone twice before and

nothing ever changes. She's pathetic. I don't have any respect for her. Or my father. No matter what happens, he pretends that everything's okay. Even after she ODed on wine and sleeping pills and had to have her stomach pumped, he pretended it was just a little accident."

"The typical all-American parents—all fucked up," snorted Webb.

"Parents are so totally whacked," Mike agreed. "It's always all about them—how hard they work, how much they've done for us, how grateful we ought to be—"

"How they deserve some happiness, too," interjected Webb. "That's my mother's favorite line. Who's she kidding? My mother has never denied herself anything. She's had four husbands, for Christ's sake."

"None of them remember what it's like to be young," said Shirlee.

"Oh, I don't know," said Tattie. "I'm not convinced the Mad Russian has ever grown up."

Everyone laughed. Tattie always referred to her father as the Mad Russian because he was born and raised in Moscow. Once he had been a businessman, but now he was a cab driver in Vegas.

"He always has some con or other going," Tattie added. "He stole money from his job, just like your mom. Only reason he's not in the slammer is the company didn't want any publicity."

"My mother isn't a thief!" I screeched, and then was transfixed by a new and profound thought.

"You know, I don't really know what my mother is." I looked

at their faces and words began to fly out of my mouth. "I don't think that I have ever really thought about who she is. She was my mother. Her job was to make me happy. My dad was a drunken bastard, and it made me furious to see her treat him like a prince. She was always trying to please him, but she tried to please me, too. It's sad to think how hard she tried to please us both—and I kept pushing her and pushing her. In a way, I despised her for being so weak, for always giving in. I was mean to her; it was all about me, me, *me.* I was the fucked-up one, and now she's gone."

I started to cry, and they all took turns hugging me. I felt so connected to them. I loved these people, my new, compassionate friends, and I told them so.

"Ashley, you are getting way too deep," Tattie said.

"That's why the first time is always the best," Brain said. "It's like taking a truth serum, and all the crap in your life disappears. Your entire view of existence is altered."

"Not for me," said Tattie. "Hey, I'm not seeking spiritual enlightenment. I want some fun, capital *F-U-N.* It's time for some action. Let's go to the Last Call."

Tattie literally propelled us out the door and into my car. I was just going with the flow, full of energy and up for dancing or some way to express the elation I felt.

The Last Call is known for being the spot where everyone in the City goes after the clubs close. The place doesn't even open until midnight, and the music keeps pumping into the morning. Maybe it never stops. In the old days I would have considered the people there dorky or strange. That night, though, I was full of Ecstasy-inspired fellowship and high spirits. Everyone was cool; everyone was my friend. We danced for hours, swept up in a collective rapture under the flashing lights and moving to the endless techno music.

Before long I was soaked in sweat and thirsty as hell. Webb continued to look after me, making sure I drank enough water to keep hydrated.

When we finally arrived back at my house, everyone collapsed in the living room. Webb started giving me a back rub, and it felt so-o-o good. Sitting there with Webb's strong hands kneading my shoulders, I made my decision. To hell with Scott and all this virginity crap. It was time to go for it. Ignoring everyone else, I grabbed Webb's hand and pulled him down the hall to my bedroom. It seemed like the perfect night to take the plunge and get the whole thing over with.

Webb gave me a really long, soft kiss, and then stopped.

"Hey, look, I've always thought you were very hot. But I'm not looking for a girlfriend, you know. Nothing permanent. I'm leaving here soon."

"Who says I'm looking for a boyfriend?" I said, pulling him down on the bed. "Good grief, what does it take to get laid around here?"

He pulled a condom out of his wallet and waved it.

I smiled and kissed him again, a kiss that went on and on. All my nerve endings were tingling. For a guy with a hard body, his skin felt surprisingly smooth. I was glad he wasn't too hairy, as that might have put me off the whole thing, and I didn't want to lose my nerve. I sniffed his neck and inhaled his scent. If everything I'd heard about Webb was true, he would know what to do and what to put where.

He did know. The whole thing was fine, honestly—much better than I expected. For one thing, I discovered that when you're the one wanting it and pushing for it, you don't feel as if you're losing control or relinquishing your power. I loved having him stroke my skin and suck my breasts, and the quick, sharp pain when he entered me wasn't too bad. When he pulled me on top, I really got into it, and unrecognizable sounds started to come out of me. Then I felt a tiny, warm explosion inside. It wasn't a big shuddering lollapalooza like you see in the movies or one of those multiorgasmic things you hear about. Still, it felt good. Maybe it was a mini-orgasm, but it was my first involving a partner, and I felt very proud. The whole thing wasn't nearly the ordeal I had expected.

. . .

I woke up the next morning with the inside of my mouth as dry as sawdust, and a sore head. Webb had stuck around, hogging my twin bed, and I gave him a small kick and told him I felt awful.

"That's the price of tripping on E—you have a sore jaw in the morning."

"Why didn't anyone tell me there was a price?" I groaned.

"Come on, it's no worse than a hangover, and the trip was a whole lot better than drinking booze, admit it. At least on E, you don't stumble around, get mean, or throw up."

He got up and went into the bathroom. When he came back, he handed me a glass of tap water. I watched him pull on his jeans and black T-shirt. He had a great body, no doubt about it.

"I wish I could hang around, but I have to split."

I nodded. I didn't feel like conversation anyway.

"Listen, don't be like Tattie. Don't start mixing E with acid or doing drugs every day. It takes a couple of days before it's totally out of your system," he cautioned me. "You need to wait and see what happens."

"What does that mean?" I said sharply, sitting up with the comforter pulled around me.

"It's just that some people get really down afterward. Not everyone. But someone I know did. If you start to feel depressed, that's what's going on. It'll pass."

"Great," I mumbled. "As if I'm not depressed already."

"It probably won't happen. I've never felt down afterward. Lately, I haven't felt much of anything. The first time is always the best, and I've never had the high that I got the first time. I had more fun watching you last night than tripping on it myself."

I smiled weakly and flopped back on the bed.

Webb took off after saying he'd call me, and it was all I could do to keep from saying "Don't bother." I was just relieved to have done the deed at last. And I was miserable enough these days without getting involved with bad-boy Webb.

. . .

I hung out with Stella for what was left of the day, waiting to feel better. The tightness in my jaw started to go away, but my depression didn't. I stayed on the sofa, mindlessly channel surfing and unable to get interested in anything.

As the sky darkened, so did my mood. I couldn't stop

thinking about my mother and my situation, and everything seemed hopeless. Last night's revelations had stuck with me, and I couldn't forgive myself for the contemptuous way I had treated her. All the thoughts I had been struggling to keep at bay were on the top of my mind now, and I felt a dull, aching pain as if I had a splinter in my heart.

It started to rain, one of those quick spring showers that douses everything and then is over. Sprawled on the sofa, I stared out at the rain and remembered what I had been avoiding for days—the memory of my mother on that lawn, sobbing and drenched, the night before she disappeared.

. . .

The argument had started when I came home from a night out with Scott and the gang. I was in a bad mood because Scott was pushing me on the whole virginity thing, and I just didn't feel like doing it. I saw immediately that my mother had been waiting for me. For the last few weeks, she had been acting weird.

Her first words were "I need to talk to you. I can't wait any longer."

With an exaggerated sigh, I perched on the arm of the sofa. "All right, make this quick," I said. "I'm tired."

She sat down on the sofa and reached over to take my hands in hers, but I pulled away, bored and ready to resist whatever she had to say.

"Yeah? What?"

"Sweetheart," she began, and then faltered. "Oh, God, this is too hard. I don't even know how to begin. I must have been crazy not to see this day would come. Now I don't know what I'm going to do or how to tell you."

"What's wrong with you? Have you been drinking? Just say what you're gonna say and let me go to bed."

"You know how much I love you, don't you? More than anything in the world."

"Yeah, I know," I said impatiently. "Get to the point. I'm not in the mood for this."

She stood up and began to pace around the room, talking feverishly without meeting my eyes. "The thing is, I've made some big mistakes and I've managed to put myself in a deep, dark hole. I don't know how to get out of the mess I've created. I feel like my feet are stuck in quicksand and I'm being sucked down. God, I've been so stupid." She drew a ragged breath and then went on when I didn't say anything. "Money, of course, it's always money. I don't know what's going to happen, but it's going to mean big changes for both of us. I'm sorry, I really am, baby. We just can't go on the way we have. I've put off telling you because I knew how disappointed in me you'd be. That's the worst thing about this, knowing that I've let you down. We're going to have to change our lifestyle, and it's going to be very hard for both of us, but—"

I interrupted this long flow of words. "What do you mean, 'change our lifestyle'?"

"Well, we can't live this way." She waved her hands around the room. "You know, spending money like there's no tomorrow. If I can hang on to my job, I should be able to pay your tuition and school bills, but there won't be anything left over for luxuries. To start with, I think you should get a job this summer."

At that I exploded. "A job? But I'm going to college soon—I want to enjoy my last summer of freedom. I'm supposed to relax and have a good time until I go to Boston."

"I'm sorry, Ashley, I can't help it. I know this is a big disappointment for you. I know I've let you down. But it will be all right in the end; we'll make it all right. And at least you have this trip to Hawaii. At least this year at school has been fairly easy for you."

"Easy? I just went through finals, for your information," I sneered. "Besides, any pennies I could earn wouldn't begin to pay for my clothes. Do you expect me to wear trash or shop at Old Navy? I need some fabulous new things to take to college with me this fall. No sorority will ask me to pledge if I look like a loser."

"I'm s-sorry, but I'm in trouble," she stammered. "I wish this weren't happening, but I don't know what to do. Everything's falling apart on me. I don't know what's going to happen. If worse comes to worst, I can put the house up for sale."

"What? What's wrong with you? How can I come home at Christmas if you sell the house? Have you lost your mind?"

She buried her face in her hands, so I could hardly hear her words. "I'm so sorry. You don't know how sorry I am. But I've made some big mistakes and now I have to pay."

"What are you talking about, *you* have to pay? It sounds like *I* have to pay. You always said my happiness was the most important thing in your life. How can you do this to me?"

She came over and stood directly in front of me, her eyes boring into mine in desperate appeal. "You have to understand, honey, I can't help it. I wish I could."

But I was too angry to answer that appeal. "You are pathetic!" I screamed. "I hate you! You are a complete failure as a mother."

That's when she slapped me. My mouse of a mother slapped me. I stared at her, both shocked and furious, then spat out the words, "Fuck you!"

Then, before I could say another word, she burst into tears. She was shaking uncontrollably.

But I was too wound up to stop now. With my eyes blazing, I spat out the words I knew would hurt her the most. "Don't expect me to feel sorry for you. You're a loser just like that drunk you called my father. The minute I can, I'm moving away and never coming back. You'll never see me again."

My mother staggered as if I had stabbed her. Her greatest fear always was being alone again, the way she had been when my grandparents died.

"I can't stand it here. I'm leaving," I said, and ran out the front door into the pelting rain.

She followed me like a crazy woman, oblivious to the fact that she was wearing only a thin nightgown. Behind me I heard her say, "It's never enough for you. No matter what I do, it's never enough."

As I backed my car out of the driveway, I saw her standing on the lawn, soaked to the skin and sobbing.

I drove around for an hour or so, until I calmed down. Then I came home. By this time I felt guilty about what I said, yet I was too stubborn to apologize. When I walked down the hall toward my bedroom, I saw the door to her room was closed. So I walked straight past it and crawled into bed.

. . .

The rain stopped and my sore jaw went away, but my bleak mood continued. Tattie called and wanted me to go out with her. I told her I was sick. Truthfully, I was sick, sick at heart. I couldn't stop thinking about the argument with my mother and hating myself for driving her away. She had deserted me because I was a horrible, evil person. I knew that now—maybe I had known it all along. I couldn't pretend or lie to myself anymore. My head and heart hurt so much that I couldn't move off my bed.

As the daylight vanished and night began, I lay awake remembering and reliving all the times I had treated my mother badly. When I finally closed my eyes, sleep didn't bring me any relief. I dreamed my mother was chasing me in her nightgown in the rain, only in my dream we were both running down a highway. Out of the darkness a big truck with blazing headlights bore down on her and struck her with a loud thump. I yelled, "Momma!" and ran back toward her. But after the truck roared past me, I saw only a dark and empty roadway. She was gone.

chapter eight

The ringing kept bouncing around in my brain until I finally realized it wasn't a dream. Someone was ringing the doorbell. I pulled myself out of bed, stumbled through the house, and opened the front door.

Facing me was a young Asian guy wearing sweats and a Giants baseball cap on backward.

"Ashley Mitchell?"

"Yeah," I yawned.

"You've been served." He thrust a folded piece of paper into my hand and departed, leaving me staring after him in confusion.

I opened the envelope and discovered it was a legal document that didn't make any sense to me. But one thing was clear: this wasn't a good omen.

. . .

Weeks had passed since my mother went missing. I had done absolutely nothing except wait, since, to be honest, I didn't know what else to do. I did stay away from Ecstasy. No way did I want to relive the quarrel with my mother again. Instead, I occupied myself by sleeping late, followed by surfing the Net or watching TV. In between, I would read, paint my nails, and talk on the phone. At night I went out dancing with Tattie to some club or other.

When the senior-trip gang had returned from their seven fun-filled days in Hawaii, I told Nicole all about losing my virginity with Webb. She was shocked. Nic wasn't very experienced with guys—her romantic nature always got in the way. She'd get a crush on someone for a while, but then go off him pretty fast when he got into a farting contest or got drunk and urinated on the lawn or some other stupid guy trick. I don't think they can help themselves; guys are just naturally gross. Poor Nicole, she actually believed her soulmate was out there somewhere and she'd find him someday. Till then, she refused to bend her standards or do the deed. For her sake, I hoped she'd find Mr. Perfect. I had no such illusions about the opposite sex.

Nicole found it hard to believe I'd done "it" just like that.

"It sounds so cold-blooded," she protested. "You don't even love him. Do you?"

"Don't be silly. I just wanted to get it out of the way, and you must admit he's hot. Anyway, it seemed like a good idea at the time."

"What if he tells someone and it gets around?" Nicole was so sweet, the way she worried about me.

"So what?" I gave her a sly smile. "I hope it does get around. I hope it gets all the way around to Scott. He missed out and I chose Webb. I hope that annoys the hell out of him."

. . .

Whether Scott ever found out or not, I had no way of knowing. I didn't see Webb again either. Eventually Tattie let it drop that Webb had a job working construction in the East Bay, and he was going to boot camp in September.

I had no idea what I would be doing in the fall or even tomorrow. Without my mother, there wasn't going to be any freshman year at Boston University or anywhere else. Unfortunately, my mother had not reappeared, except in my fitful dreams.

While I should have looked for a job, I didn't know how to go about it. If someone had offered me one, I would have taken it. But I just couldn't walk up to some counter and ask to be hired—what if they turned me down and everyone laughed? I'd die of humiliation.

Selling clothes to Couture Closet was the main source of my funds, and the pittance I received disappeared fast. It's a good thing I'm not a big eater and fast food is cheap. Still, I had to buy shampoo, tampons, cat food, and so on. I canceled the cleaning lady and the garden service but just tossed the rest of the bills on the dining room table.

Then the phone calls started—first, little reminders that our Visa bill or water bill was overdue, and then more strident requests for payment. I let the answering machine get them.

Police cars still drove past our house, but Strobel and his cohort didn't bother me anymore. They, too, seemed to be waiting for my mother to return. I couldn't imagine that she wouldn't, no matter how angry she was with me or what she had done. I tried to picture her as a fugitive—sunning herself on some

Mexican beach, sipping margaritas and forgetting all about her bitchy, selfish daughter. But I couldn't imagine it—that wasn't my mother. She loved me and she would come back.

Bad things are supposed to come in threes. My cell phone was number one. Service was shut off for nonpayment. Before I had recovered from that blow, my gas card wouldn't work at the pump.

"Look, there must be something wrong with your machine," I insisted to Reynaldo.

"Okay," Reynaldo shrugged. "I'll go call." He walked into the office and I could see him talking into the receiver while I waited by the pumps. He hung up and walked over to Phil's camper, which is always parked behind the station, except when Phil is off on one of his nature trips. He called inside and Phil emerged, carrying what looked like a fishing rod. They talked for a moment and then Reynaldo returned.

"They won't accept your card, Ash-lee," he said. "Phil told me to fill your tank anyway. It's on him."

I nodded stiffly and got back into my car. I knew I should thank Phil, but I was too embarrassed.

. . .

Being served, whatever that meant, was the third bad thing. I sat on the sofa a long time, stroking Stella's soft orange fur and talking to her about the situation. Unfortunately, "meow" was the only comment Stella made, and I didn't find it all that helpful. I was worried and needed to talk to someone, fast—someone who could help me figure this out.

As much as I didn't want to call her, Gloria seemed like the logical choice. She was smart, she was my mother's best friend, and she understood all the financial mysteries I didn't. My pride pinched me, but I didn't have any choice. I steeled myself and dialed her number.

Her voice was cool but she didn't hang up on me.

"Oh, Ashley. Any news? I left a message on your machine last week."

I knew she had. I had erased it without calling her back.

"The thing is," Gloria continued, "both Daniel and Matthew have been down with chicken pox, and it's just been one thing after another."

I politely murmured, "Oh, poor kids."

I doubt I fooled her with my feeble show of concern.

"They're feeling better," Gloria replied just as politely. "What are the police saying these days? Do they know anything more?"

"They're not exactly confiding in me, but I don't think they have any idea where my mother is. They haven't been back since they carried off some stuff."

"What did they take?" she asked.

"Papers, boxes of them. They seemed disappointed not to find a horde of cash stashed under the rug."

"Hmmm," she said, and then she abruptly switched gears. "Now, what can I do to help you?"

I was pathetically grateful for her sympathetic tone. Maybe this wouldn't be too bad.

"Well, I hate to ask but I do have a big problem. Someone

came here this morning and gave me some sort of legal paper. Served me, he said. I don't know what it's all about or what I'm supposed to do," I said, my voice trailing off.

"Served you?" she said sharply. "That doesn't sound good. I guess I better come over and have a look."

"I would be so grateful if you could do that," I said in my most earnest, good-girl voice.

"I'll be over tonight around eight-thirty, after I've put the kids to bed," she answered.

It was almost nine-thirty before Gloria showed up, but I was in no position to complain. Nor did I make any comment about the purple pantsuit she was wearing. Gloria had a passion for the color purple that was way over the top. I myself wore mostly neutrals—black, white, or beige plus my favorite, red, to shake things up.

"Thanks for coming," I said with my new mature attitude. "Would you like coffee?"

"No, thanks," she answered. "The house looks good. You surprise me, Ashley."

She walked over to the dining room table and pointed to the now gargantuan pile of mail. "What's all this?"

"The mail. I'm saving it for my mother," I said.

She picked up an ominous-looking envelope with a bold FINAL NOTICE printed on it. "Good God, Ashley, how can you just ignore these? Look at all of them. Visa, the gas company, the phone company—you should be paying these."

"With what?" I screeched, and then added more calmly, "Where would I get the money to pay them?"

"What about the money in your mother's checking account?"

"There isn't any left," I said. "I tried to use my ATM card last week, but it said 'insufficient funds.' "

"Well, ignoring these isn't going to make them go away. I'm surprised they haven't cut off your power yet or sent bill collectors to knock on your door."

"They stopped my cell phone service," I admitted.

"I guess somebody better take a look at these before you end up sitting here in the dark," she said. "Get me a bag."

She stuffed all the bills into a plastic grocery bag and then sat down. "All right, now let's see those papers that were served on you."

I handed her the envelope. Gloria put on her reading glasses and unfolded the papers. I watched anxiously as she read.

Finally, she looked up. "This is not good. It looks as if your mother's employer has put a lien on this house."

"What does that mean?" I said.

"I'm not sure. Nothing good." She thought for a minute and then stood up. "I'm going to have to find out more about this. Can I take this with me?"

I nodded.

"I'll let you know what I find out," she said, walking over to the door. "But you better prepare yourself. You'll probably have to find a new place to live."

"*What!* Where would I go? How will I live?" I was aghast.

"You get a job, like everyone else on the planet," Gloria said with visible satisfaction. "Your mother didn't do you any favors, treating you like a protected little princess, and I told her so, many times. You need to find a job and an apartment and learn to take care of yourself."

"A job! What do I know how to do? Drive a bus? Work at the drive-up window at McDonald's? I was going to go to college and have a career. This isn't fair. None of my friends have to serve tacos at Taco Bell. No, please don't say it. I guess I'm supposed to remember the starving children in Africa and how lucky I am in comparison."

"No, I'm not going to tell you anything because you're going to find out all by yourself."

chapter nine

Gloria called two days later and asked me to come over after her kids were in bed.

"You better sit down, Ashley," Gloria said. Her face looked ready to announce bad news.

"Is it that bad? Should I take a Valium first?" I wisecracked. I made my way through the obstacle course of Legos and other toys scattered on the carpet and flopped down on her recliner.

"It's not good," she said. She seated herself on the sofa, an arsenal of papers arranged on the coffee table in front of her. Carefully placing her pen on the table next to the papers, she gazed up at me with the look of a teacher about to begin her lesson plan.

"I did a lot of research on embezzlement on the Web," Gloria began. "I've acquired quite an education on the subject. This sort of white-collar crime is amazingly common, and often only a portion of the money is ever recovered. Most embezzlers go to prison, but others get off with just probation. Sometimes companies don't even press charges because they don't want the word to get out about how stupid and gullible they were."

"Obviously, that's not the case here," I said, sinking back into the cocoon of the recliner. "So I'd like the Cliff's Notes version. What's going on?"

"Richard talked to an attorney friend of his about this situation. According to him, putting a lien on the house was an aggressive strategy on the company's part. Your mother's employer is undoubtedly angry and looking for a way to recoup their losses. So they're staking a claim on some part of the proceeds when the bank forecloses and the house is sold."

I couldn't believe my ears. "What do you mean 'when the bank forecloses'?" I sputtered. "How can they sell our house?"

"Unless your mother gets back right away, it's going to happen very soon. The bank will take the house back and boot you out . . . evict you . . . because no payments have been made for nearly ninety days. It takes one hundred and eleven days by law in California for a mortgage lender to foreclose. Once they do, the sheriff will come in, nail up an eviction notice, and toss you out. That would be a humiliating experience, believe me."

"What!" I screeched, sitting upright as if a bolt of electricity had just been applied to my backside. "How can they do that? That's our house. It was my grandmother's house. They can't steal our house like that."

"Look, they're not stealing it. Even though Diane inherited the house from your grandparents, she's remodeled it extensively and taken money out of it over the years. The bank holds both a first and second mortgage on the place. They want their money. There's nothing complicated about it. Unfortunately, there's nothing left in your mother's checking account, and she doesn't seem to have a savings account, not even a college fund for you. I have to admit that surprised me. Do you know of any accounts that I don't know about or some investments perhaps?"

I shook my head wordlessly.

"How about a safety-deposit box?"

"No."

"I just don't understand it." She shook her head, then began gnawing on her lower lip. "How on earth could she have mismanaged her finances so badly?"

She paused for a moment, as if waiting for an answer, but I didn't provide one.

Gloria let out a long, exasperated sigh. "Well, here's the bottom line. You need about eight thousand dollars just to catch up on the mortgage payments. Even if you had the eight thousand, you'd still need enough money each month to keep up the mortgage payment plus another five hundred a month in taxes, insurance, and utilities. I just don't see any way you're going to be able to come up with that plus your own personal expenses for food, gas, and so forth. And there's no way that I can pay your mortgage in addition to ours every month."

I sagged back into the chair as Gloria kept talking and ruining my life.

"If I thought you could sell the house and make some money off the deal, I would go ahead and lend you the eight thousand contingent on the sale. But this lien means that you'd probably never see a dime of any sale proceeds. The Simmons Company wants to recover some or all of the missing money, and they'll fight you for every penny. Who knows how long that will take, even if they lose. Plus, we don't know where your mother is, and the house is in her name, so how can you sell it? It's a mess. I think you should move out and take everything you can while you still can."

I felt as if someone had just punched me. But her voice droned on.

"Hopefully, your car is in your name?"

I didn't respond, and she repeated impatiently, "The car is in your name, Ashley?"

I nodded assent.

"Good. Move out of there as soon as possible, and take everything that isn't nailed down. Probably they can't seize anything, but better safe than sorry. It could take years for the dust to settle. They're obviously very angry and willing to take an outrageous position to punish you and your mother."

I just sat there, motionless. My whole body felt numb as her words spilled over me like wet concrete, cementing me to the chair.

"This is so unfair," I whimpered.

"This isn't about fair, Ashley. Anyway, it could be construed as fair *if* your mother took that money. That really hasn't been established yet, not in a court of law. The presumption is that she's guilty because she's fled. She's not around here to argue any differently, and you're not in a position to do it for her."

She began rearranging the papers on the coffee table. "Who knows? Maybe they won't be that hard-nosed. They may be just trying to frighten you, reasoning that Diane will come back to rescue you. What they don't understand is that you really don't know where she is, and frightening you isn't going to help."

"How can I leave? Where will I go? What about our furniture?"

"Can you stay with some friends for a while? How about Nicole?"

"Cindy would never allow that."

"Then you need to start looking for a place to live. Check the newspaper and those apartment rental agencies. Or look on the Internet for someone who needs a roommate. As for the furniture, I talked to Richard, and he's agreed to store as much as will fit in our garage. But I can't get it all in, so you're going to have to select what you want to keep, and get rid of the rest."

"How can you do this, Gloria? She's your best friend, and you're going to let her house and her daughter go to hell just like that . . . as if it's nothing."

She shot me a hostile look. "I'm not doing this, dammit. This whole situation is out of control, and I can't do anything to stop it. I don't even know what I *should* do. She's my best friend and I'd do anything for her, but I don't know what she would want me to do. She's left us both in the dark. If only she would call or *something,* anything. I just don't understand it. . . ." Her voice trailed off, and she looked as bewildered as I felt.

She shook her head and started again. "The only thing that's clear to me is that you've got to start acting like a grown-up. And I'll help you keep as much of her stuff as I can. The house is a lost cause at this point. We can't fight that battle until Diane comes back. I wish I could do more, but with the kids and our own financial issues . . ."

I buried my face in my hands. "How could she do this, Gloria? Why? I know I was a brat sometimes, but I didn't ask her to steal money to make me happy. She was the mother. She was supposed to tell me no, wasn't she?"

Gloria paused, and then said, "I know, Ashley. It was her job, but as long as I've known her, Diane was a pushover for everyone else's needs and wants. We both know that your mother was always too nice and took the easy way when anyone pushed her. God, even I was guilty of it. When I wanted one thing and she wanted another, she always gave in and I got my way. Maybe that's why we were such good friends—I always was kind of the bossy one."

I was smart enough to refrain from agreeing with that assessment. "Why? Why was she like that? I'm not like that."

"No, you're not." She gave a hollow laugh. "I think it was because your grandparents were so strict and controlling. Me, I would have rebelled. But she bent over backward trying to be their good little girl. Once, in high school, she told them she was going to my house to study, but we met up with some boys instead. Her father called to check on her, and my mother told him we had gone out. When Diane went home, he told her that they were ashamed to have her as a daughter. She went crazy, begging him to forgive her. Even so, he wouldn't even talk to her for a month! She was completely cowed and would never go to parties with me again."

"Poor Mom!" I interjected.

"You'd think it would have been a relief when they died, but Diane was only twenty and she was so needy. She was lost without someone to love her and tell her what to do. Then she met Jimmy, and in no time he had her eating out of his hand. I don't suppose she had enough guile to get pregnant just to get him to marry her, so it must have been an accident."

I rose up out of the chair and stared at her in shock. "My mother *had* to get married? She was pregnant with me *before* they got married?"

"Yes." She raised her eyebrows and gave a little snort. "It shouldn't surprise you that Jimmy would seduce a naïve girl with a strong need to please. I imagine it was easy for him, though I don't think he meant to knock Diane up. He wasn't exactly the fatherly type. And then there was his gambling. Now that I think back, that could have been what led your mother to begin dipping into company funds. Sometime back, I remember your mother being beside herself because he was in debt to some pretty rough characters. He probably encouraged her to 'borrow' money from the company to bail him out."

"Yeah." I thought about that for a moment. "I can see that. But if she was ripping off the company to pay Jimmy's debts, why didn't she stop after he died?"

"Maybe she couldn't or she didn't know how to untangle the mess she was in." Gloria stood up and walked over to look out the window. "Look, this is all speculation. We don't know anything for sure."

"But they're accusing her of waltzing off with a million dollars. I can't see my mother slinging a mil in her handbag and flying off to Rio."

"I know." Gloria turned around and spread her hands in a helpless gesture. "I can't either."

"Well, my family seems to have a history of nastiness and criminal behavior. I'm amazed I'm not in Juvenile Hall already."

"You have plenty of good qualities too. You're an intelligent girl and can be very charming, just like your father. I know this is hard, but I'm betting you can handle it if you just learn how to use those assets. Your mother could have used some of your spunk. You can even demonstrate your mother's sweetness, though not very often."

I was astonished to hear Gloria praise me. I should have ducked outside to see if the moon was blue or something.

"You just need to learn from your parents' mistakes." She let out another long sigh. "You know, I thought Diane had finally gotten on track and found Mr. Right. Phil is a really nice guy, the exact opposite of your father."

I snorted. "Oh, yeah? That really nice guy is seeing someone else."

"What!"

I noticed with satisfaction that I had shocked her for a change.

"You didn't know? Phil told me that he and Diane hadn't been seeing each other for a while, whatever that means."

"That can't be true. She would have told me if she wasn't seeing him anymore. Just a couple of weeks before she disappeared, I remember her telling me how much in love she was."

"Did she say it was Phil? Because he claimed she was seeing someone from her office."

I had actually succeeded in silencing Gloria, which was quite an accomplishment. She stared at me, then whirled around and stared out the window again. Finally, she muttered, "I don't believe it. She would have told me. That can't be true."

"Believe it," I said.

chapter ten

I was awake half the night worrying about what Gloria had said. And things didn't look any clearer to me the next morning. I was desperate for someone to talk to, but Nicole was spending a few days with her grandmother in Pasadena, so I called Tattie. There wasn't any answer. I kept trying all day, and finally around six that evening, her mother picked up.

"Who is this? Ashley? Oh yeah, the embezzler's kid," she said, and I winced inwardly. "Well, you can't talk to her. She's done it now. The stupid little pill-popper has gotten busted, and that car of hers has been impounded. She's in jail and probably won't get out until Monday, if then."

"What!" I gasped. "Oh, my god! What can we do? Surely there's something we can do?"

"Not unless you have five grand for bail," she snorted. "I'm trying to reach that crazy Russian and get some dough out of him. His daughter will have to sit on her ass in jail unless he comes across with some, 'cause I sure as hell don't have any. Say, why don't you give me some of that money your mother stole?"

I hung up on the bitch.

A phone call to Brain, who always seemed to be in the know, confirmed what Tattie's mother had told me.

"Yeah, I heard about it," he told me. "She got pulled over for speeding and reckless driving. They found some pot and some pills. So they hauled her off to jail and impounded her car. Tattie is totally screwed."

I hung up the phone, horrified about Tattie's situation and sorry that I couldn't help her. At the same time, I found myself incredibly relieved that I hadn't been with her. You see, Ashley, I told myself, you thought things couldn't be worse. Obviously they could be worse.

Tattie's situation convinced me that I had to do something. But I didn't know how to get started. How could I find another place to live when I had no money to put down for rent or pay for moving expenses?

I did have one idea, though, an idea that had been buzzing around in my brain since Tattie had first mentioned that I should sell my mother's stuff at a garage sale. It certainly seemed like the easiest way to acquire a wad of cash.

When Nicole came back on Sunday night, I told her about my idea, and she was a big help. Turns out Cindy had been a garage-sale devotee for years. It figures—she was the type to take advantage of other people's misery. I had never been interested in someone else's used stuff, even though I had read that movie stars found antiques and fabulous vintage outfits that way.

Nicole said she'd make some signs for me and help me place an ad on Craigslist. That got the ball rolling on my cash-shortage problem, but I had two other problems: a place to live and a job.

"You should go to work at the Gap or, no, I've got it," Nicole suggested. "That store on Burlingame Avenue with the really trendy, cool stuff, you know, Star Baby. With your sense of style, you'd be perfect for them."

"True," I agreed. I have never believed in false modesty. "But what if I had to wait on one of the girls from school? It would be so awful to have Mara or someone like her order me around. Besides, do you really think that some store is going to hire an embezzler's daughter to run their register and count their cash?"

Nic was taken aback at that thought. "But how would they know?"

"Oh, come on, around here? If the store manager didn't know, one of the girls who worked there would, and she'd blab the whole thing. I've got to get a job in San Francisco."

"In the City!" Nicole said, shocked.

"It's not deepest, darkest Africa," I said impatiently. "It's only fifteen miles away. A city is the only place you can be anonymous."

"Why do you want to be anonymous?" she asked.

"Because if my whole life has to change, I don't want all my former friends looking down their noses and feeling sorry for me." I grimaced. "I can hear Mara now. 'Oh, poor Ashley, she can't go to college and has to shop at Target now. It's so sad—do you want some of my old clothes, Ashley, the ones I'm giving to the Salvation Army?' "

Nicole giggled. "She wouldn't do that."

"The hell she wouldn't," I snapped back. "Anyway, I'm not

going to give her or anyone else the chance. I need to create a whole new Ashley. I'm going to make a new life and new friends."

"What about me?" she said sadly.

"Oh, Nic, you'll always be my best friend," I said, and hugged her. "I don't want to do all this, I have no choice. I'm thinking a waitress job in the city would be good—you make all those tips and get free food. That has to be better than trying to squeeze some pathetic fat woman into a dress two sizes too small."

"Right," said Nicole, her voice trailing off in obvious doubt.

I longed to move far, far away to some new place where no one knew me, but I couldn't. How would I know when my mother turned up, unless I stuck around?

. . .

First, I thumbed through the newspaper want ads looking for a place to live. The listings were slim in number and expensive. So, I booted up the computer for the first time in weeks and started searching the Web for San Francisco rentals. I was shocked at the prices, which ranged from high to unbelievable.

I didn't even bother to write down the info on anything above $700 a month—and even that was stretching it. It was amazing to me that a room in a three-bedroom flat in North Beach could cost $1,100 a month. At first I thought it was a mistake and that was the cost of the whole apartment, but no, it was $1,100 *for each roommate.*

Most of the affordable rentals were out of the city in Oakland, the East Bay, or San Jose. Finally, I found three I might qualify for, so I called and made appointments to see the apartments. The next evening I dressed very carefully—trying to look good but not too good in black jeans, a crisp white shirt, and a tan suede jacket—and drove into the City.

- *$525. Small room but nice, live with two others. Female preferred.*

This room was inside a smallish white frame house in Glen Park, a working-class district perched on the south side of Twin Peaks. The location was near a BART subway station, and the neighborhood looked safe enough.

I was invited in and given a form to fill out by two unfriendly girls in their twenties. One was a skinny blonde with a bad complexion, and the other—a brunette with greasy hair—was a size 16 at least. Right away I knew it would only work if they were unattached. Unattractive girls without boyfriends like you because they think you'll attract guys and they can have the leftovers. But unattractive girls with boyfriends hate you because they always think you're trying to steal their dorky dates.

I tried to be extra nice and it seemed to be working, but then a guy showed up—the boyfriend of the skeletally thin blonde. He couldn't keep his eyes off me and said I looked like a great prospect. I saw the look the two girls exchanged at that remark and figured it was all over. It was.

- *$575 room with liberal-minded couple.*

This one looked promising as it was in one of those grand old Victorian houses in the Haight-Ashbury district. From the street the colorfully painted house looked charming, with flowering vines growing up one side of the building.

Once inside, I felt like I had stumbled through a time warp and landed in 1965. The place reeked of incense, and some sort of weird snake-charmer music was playing. I expected to see a Buddhist monk or the Dalai Lama walk out of the kitchen. The two liberal-minded people turned out to be a fortyish couple who said they would need to prepare my astrological chart and do a tarot reading. Barrel-chested Carl gravely asked me if I was a Gemini, because Geminis tend to be duplicitous. When I said I was a Scorpio, Carl's eyes lit up.

"Scorpios are very sensual and adventurous." He beamed with satisfaction.

Rhonda, who had a wild mass of wiry brown hair, informed me that they were trained in tantric sex and were looking for a roommate open to exploration and growth.

I put down the tarot cards and fled.

- *$680 room in 3-bedroom amazing flat with view.*

This room was located in an apartment out in the avenues in the heart of the city's fog zone. But there was a splendid view of the Pacific Ocean, even if only from a tiny kitchen window.

The two girls who lived in this apartment looked normal, and the place was neatly furnished in a blend of IKEA meets Pottery Barn. Both girls said they worked in the financial district and asked me where I worked.

I had to admit that I hadn't found a job yet and I had only

just graduated from high school. "I'm getting one right away," I said. "As soon as I find a place to live."

The short-haired brunette frowned and said, "I'm sorry, but we can't take a chance. We need someone who has a job and credit references."

I tried to assure her that I would be dependable, but it was no use.

"We just can't take the chance," repeated auburn-haired Annie. "Our last roommate said the same thing. She moved out while we were at work and still owes us money for rent plus a gigantic phone bill."

After that, I was pretty discouraged, but I reasoned that maybe I was doing things in the wrong order. I decided I should get a job first and then a place to live.

Meanwhile, I busied myself deciding what I was going to keep and what I was going to sell at Saturday's garage sale. I was determined to hang on to a few antiques that my mother had treasured most—especially the china, crystal, and silver that had belonged to my Italian grandmother. I would sell all of the everyday dishes, pans, and other kitchen paraphernalia. I didn't know how to cook anyway.

I rolled up our beautiful Oriental rugs for storage. I also wanted to keep my mother's four-poster bed and its matching dresser, plus the rocking chair from my bedroom—the one my mother had used when I was a baby. All the rest of the furniture had to go. Naturally, I kept the computer and printer—both for my job hunt and for college when I finally made it there. As for the stereo, I had to keep it—you can't live without music, can you? I also kept a couple of boxes with my dolls and other girlie stuff, plus three boxes of my favorite books.

The last thing I packed was a box of our family pictures. I got sidetracked thumbing through them, remembering the days when I was little and my mother had been my whole world. There weren't many photos of Jimmy, but there were lots of snapshots of my mother hugging me, smiling at me, or holding my hand at various ages. My heart ached remembering the days when she would cuddle with me and read to me from my favorite book, *Where the Wild Things Are.* At the part where the wild things begin to dance, together we would scream out the line, "I'll eat you up, I love you so." Now I would give anything to have her hug me and call me her wild thing again.

One picture in particular caught my attention. It showed the two of us on a sandy beach. I couldn't have been more than two, and my mother must have been twenty-five or so. The two of us were standing together in the shallow waves, and I was stark naked except for a lacy white hat, fastened on my head with a chin strap. My mother was holding my hand and smiling down at me with shining eyes and a look of pure love and happiness. She looked so young and pretty at that moment, with her skirt swirling around her legs and her long dark hair ruffled by the wind.

"I'll eat you up, I love you so," I whispered, and I tucked that snapshot into my wallet.

. . .

Once everything was boxed, I e-mailed Brain and asked for help. Thursday night, he showed up with Mike, a boy named

Moe, and a pickup. The three of them hauled my stuff over to Gloria's, and somehow we pushed it all into the back of her garage. To reward them for their heroic deed, Nicole and I grilled burgers and served them with potato chips and chocolate chip cookies. Brain provided some beer, and they hung out until midnight, listening to music and talking about their plans for fall. Everyone was leaving for somewhere.

When everyone finally went home, Stella and I were alone in the half-empty house. That was when it all sunk in. With everyone gone, I couldn't keep busy anymore and pretend that everything was normal. I felt disoriented as I walked through the rooms, remembering happier times. All the familiar objects and talismans of my life were disappearing, and I had an eerie feeling that at any moment, I might vanish too.

Stella was no better. She stalked through the vacant rooms, her tail held high in an affronted manner.

"I'm not too happy about this myself," I told her.

To tell the truth, I felt like bawling again. Where was my mother? Was she punishing me? Did she hate me? This was all so totally out of character for her. I had begun to imagine the worst sort of scenario—my mother murdered by a serial killer. Maybe she was chained up in some dank basement, hoping that someone would come to rescue her. Maybe she had amnesia and couldn't remember who she was and where she came from.

Disappearing like this just wasn't the kind of thing my mother would do, even if she had become involved in some nasty embezzlement scheme. This was real life, not some stupid screenplay where the heroine never suspected that her cupcake-frosting mother was a vampire. There had to be a perfectly logical explanation, but I didn't know what it was, and the not knowing was making me crazy.

My brain whirled around and around like a hamster on an exercise wheel, but I never came any closer to finding an answer. I didn't even know where to begin looking for one.

In my heart, there was always an ache now along with the still unanswered plea: *Oh, Momma, please come home.*

chapter eleven

Nicole slept over so we could spend the evening pricing everything for the sale. Then we stupidly stayed up late, watching a video. We didn't realize that a tribe of garage-sale fanatics would pound on the door at 6:30 in the morning. Eyes half-closed, I staggered to the front door and told them to come back at nine. One old prune with yellow teeth was so rude that I slammed the door in her face.

While a few bargain-hunters hovered on the sidewalk, we pulled, pushed, and dragged stuff onto the driveway and lawn. To set the right businesslike tone, I wore a pair of baggy painter's jeans with lots of big pockets, a blue T-shirt that said *Fashionista*, and running shoes.

We were busy from the minute I signaled that the sale was open. I was glad, because it kept me from noticing who took what and how quickly my possessions were disappearing.

What surprised me most was the number of tightwads who tried to bargain with us. This is California, after all, not Tijuana.

I had anticipated that some of my nosy neighbors would

stop by, and they did. So I wasn't surprised when Cindy showed up, although I thought it was in poor taste. Nicole handled her mother for me. I didn't want to know which of our things ended up in Cindy's clutches.

Around noon, Officer Strobel stopped by to survey the scene and give everything his badass cop stare. He paused long enough to tell me that a woman fitting my mother's description had been arrested in New Mexico as an accessory to some con scheme.

Hope flared up in me for a moment, only to disappear as I realized how ridiculous his statement was.

"What do you mean by 'fitting my mother's description'?" I jeered. "White, brunette, and over forty? You're going to be very busy if you investigate everyone fitting that description. Diane isn't some con artist or an accessory to some criminal gang."

"We have to follow up every lead," he said defensively.

"If you're looking for leads, why don't you find her car? Did it ever occur to you that she may be the victim of a crime? Maybe my mother's been kidnapped."

"We're looking for her *and* her car. But we have no reason to think she's the victim of a crime. Do you?"

I walked away without answering. The police weren't interested in what I thought. They had already made up their minds that my mother was guilty.

. . .

For most of the day we were busy. By three o'clock there were only a handful of shoppers still pawing through my stuff, and my pockets were bulging with cash. Exhausted, I flopped down onto an unsold chair while Nicole went to the kitchen in search of a snack and bottled water. That's when I noticed a silver Porsche Boxster pulling up to the curb on the other side of the street.

A handsome, tanned older man stepped out of the Porsche and crossed the street toward my house. From the tips of his tasseled Italian loafers to his expensively styled silver-tipped hair, this man exuded confidence and money. In fact, he looked more like someone who would have a personal shopper than someone who frequented garage sales.

He walked past everything for sale and stopped in front of my chair.

"Hello, Ashley."

"Do I know you?" I raised my eyebrows.

"No," he said, giving me a brilliant smile. "Your mother kept a photo of you on her desk. You're as pretty as your picture."

I stared at him. "You worked with my mother?"

"I'm Curtis Davidson. I'm sure she's mentioned me. We need to talk."

I groaned. "Listen, Curtis Davidson. I don't have the money, and I don't know where it is. We don't have anything to talk about. You're wasting your time trying to bully me."

"I don't want to bully you, and I don't want to talk about the money. I've been eager to have a conversation with you for some time. There are some things we need to discuss."

Our eyes locked. "What?" I said. "What things?"

Before he could answer, a hefty woman with a sleeping baby strapped to her chest stopped next to him and waved an espresso maker in my face.

"How much do you want for this?" she asked.

"The price is marked," I snarled, moving it out of my face

and pointing to the sticker on the bottom. Then I flashed Davidson a challenging look. "Maybe this gentleman needs an espresso maker."

"Well!" she huffed, jerking it back indignantly. Her baby woke up and started to cry.

Ignoring her, Davidson pulled a business card out of his pocket and pressed it into my hand. I studied it. In elegant, embossed letters it said, *Curtis Davidson III, Partner, Warren Simmons & Co.*

"Give me a call, Ashley. We really need to talk. I've written my private cell phone number on the back."

He walked away down the drive as I stared after him.

. . .

Sunday was less busy than Saturday, but several people returned to buy what they had passed up the day before. By the time we called it quits on Sunday, I had managed to earn a total of $3,500. Of course, it was a pittance compared to the original cost of what we sold. Still, knowing I had more than $3,000 in my purse was the only thing that eased the pain of seeing our beautiful furniture being hauled away to other people's homes. Late Sunday I watched as an ecstatic couple with a young daughter heaved my white wicker bedroom furniture into the bed of their pickup. Again, I had to fight back tears. It used to take a lot to make me cry, but circumstances had changed me into a river of tears. As I watched our belongings disappear, my whole body felt tired and my arms and legs were so heavy that I could barely lift them. In my stomach was an uncomfortable feeling close to panic. What was I going to do now?

. . .

After the garage sale was over, Nicole and I collapsed atop some pillows on the living room floor. As I began telling her about the mystery man from my mother's office, the unlocked front door opened and Tattie walked in.

"Hey!" I said, too tired to get up. "You missed my really big sale." Though we had talked on the phone, I had seen Tattie only once since she had been released.

"I don't exactly have the money to buy stuff anyway," Tattie said. "I hope you got rich." She plopped down next to us and pulled out a joint. "Anyone got a match?"

I pointed toward the matches on the mantel.

"Uh, should you be doing that?" Nicole asked. "Aren't you out on bail or something?"

"Yeah, so what?" Tattie said challengingly. "Are there cops hiding in the bushes?"

I thought it better not to mention that there might be. Instead I asked, "How are you getting around these days without your car?"

"I have to beg for rides," she admitted, making a face. "Anyway, I don't have a license now, so getting my car back wouldn't help me right now. *She* dropped me off."

Tattie always referred to her mother as She, short for She-Devil. Not for the first time, I considered the irony of our three mothers. I wanted desperately to see mine, Nicole wanted to get away from hers, and Tattie hoped her mother would fall down a mine shaft.

"No driver's license! What are you going to do?" Nicole asked. Being without transportation was like slow death in the suburbs.

"It's just one of my many problems at the moment," she said coolly.

"What about the rest—the pills and all that?" I asked.

"I still have to appear before the judge, but I'll probably get probation—first-time offender and so on. I only had enough for personal consumption, not sale. My lawyer says I need to fix my appearance, you know, take out the nose ring and stuff, and appear contrite when I'm in court. You'll have to teach me how to fake being sweet, Nicole."

Nicole squirmed uncomfortably.

"Hey," I said, in a warning fashion. "She doesn't have to fake it. She is."

"Sorry," Tattie retorted, not sounding very sorry at all.

"That's okay, I understand," Nic murmured.

Changing the subject, I asked, "Got any bright ideas for me, Tattie? I have to find a job, pronto."

"A job! From the look of things around here, you should be worrying more about where you're going to live. I'd offer to let you bunk in with me, but She isn't too happy with me right now."

"No problem, I'll figure something out," I said hastily. No way did I want to live in her dirty house or deal with her mother.

"I wish you were still going to Boston with me." Nicole sounded worried. "Are you sure you can't get a student loan or something?"

"It's too late. I checked online. Right now, they're taking financial aid applications for *next* fall, a year from now." I shook my head in dismay. "The only thing I can do is find a job and an apartment here."

"But you should be going to college," Nicole argued. "You're really, really smart. You had a four-point-oh. And look at the way you read all the time."

"I'll get there. I just need to get things under control first. Hopefully, my mom will show up. Maybe I'll be able to join you at BU for spring semester."

Tattie snorted, no doubt at the absurdity of anyone wanting to go to school, and took a long drag off her joint.

"What are you going to do this fall, Miss Tatiana?" I said.

"As little as possible." She rolled over on her back and stared at the ceiling. "My lawyer and my mother are pressuring me to go to rehab. That sounds really dreary. What I'd like to do is take off and go to Europe. I hear you can get really good shit in Amsterdam."

"That's not a very long-term goal. Don't you ever think about the future?" Nicole asked with genuine curiosity.

"Nope," said Tattie. "Life is short, so live it up while you can. It's all shit anyway."

We both were silent at that, Nicole because she didn't believe that, and me because I hoped it wasn't true.

. . .

I foolishly allowed Nic to persuade me to spend that night at her house. Nicole's brothers were sprawled on the living room floor in front of the TV, but there was no sign of Cindy.

Upstairs, Nicole flopped down on her bed and gave an exaggerated sigh. "I'm so tired, I don't even feel like undressing."

I grabbed one of her pillows, tossed it on the carpet, and parked my butt on top of it, elevating my legs on the edge of a chair. "Ah, this feels good," I said, inhaling and exhaling a few times to release the tension in my body.

I looked over at Nicole as she lay stretched out on the bed, her eyes closed. For the first time in a long time, I really looked at her.

"How do you do it?" I asked. "How do you manage to never have any mean or evil thoughts about anyone?"

Her eyes popped open. "Who says I never have any evil thoughts? I have plenty—especially when my mother is nagging me. I'm such a big disappointment to her. I can't be the Miss Popular center of attention she wants me to be. She wants me to be like you, and I can't do it. Sometimes when she's going on and on at me, I tune out what she's saying and stare at a particular part of her body, like her neck. I concentrate, willing her to feel pain there, a pinch or twinge, anything. But it never works. So much for the power of the mind. The only way I'll ever be able to have my own life is by getting away from here." She reached up and began nervously twirling and tugging on a lock of hair.

"Relax, it's only a few weeks away," I said. "And stop pulling your hair! You'll go bald."

Nicole instantly dropped her right hand. "I don't know. I'm not so sure that I should go to Boston now that you can't. I don't want to leave you here by yourself. I think I should stay and go to San Francisco State."

"What *are* you thinking? Just because my life is totally screwed up, you want to ruin your life too? That's really dumb."

Tears welled up in her eyes.

"Listen, I have a shitload of problems right now, and there's nothing you can do about them. You can't bring my mother back, you can't give me a job or a place to live. How does it help me if we're both miserable? For years you've been dreaming of going to school on the East Coast and getting away from Cindy. You'd have to be crazy to throw that away now."

She sniffed and I handed her a tissue from the bedside table.

"Look, I'd love to have you here, holding my hand. I admit, I'm scared about facing all this alone. Everything is totally screwed up right now, but I'll be fine, honest. My mother will come back, and we'll figure everything out."

She didn't look up, just swiped at her eyes with the tissue.

"Come on, I'm tough as old boots, you know that. It's Ashley against the world," I said. "Who are you betting on?"

She finally looked up and gave me a wan smile. "You, you dope. I'm betting on you."

"OK, then," I said, rearranging the pillows against the bed to prop myself up. "You need to toughen up and start thinking about number one for a change. Otherwise, you're going to go through life as a victim with a capital *V*. Everyone takes advantage of you, even me. Of course, you know I do it for your own good."

I heard her giggle at that.

"But not everyone has your best interests at heart. You've got to learn to take care of yourself. You can be a good person without turning into Saint Nicole."

She started to say something, but I wasn't finished.

"I want you to start being selfish. Yeah, once a day you have to be selfish and do something that's good for you, and to hell with everyone else. For one thing, when you get to BU and meet your new roommate, take the best bed in the room instead of saying, 'Oh, go ahead, I don't care. You choose first.' For once, put Nicole first. Do you hear me?"

She was grinning now. "I hear you."

. . .

The next morning, I declined Nic's offer of breakfast and ducked into the shower while she trooped downstairs to mix and mingle with her family over their cereal bowls. When I finally drifted down the stairs, I could hear Cindy and Nicole talking in the kitchen. I hovered on the stairs, listening.

"I don't see why not," Nicole was pleading. "It's not as if anyone will be using my room while I'm away. She wouldn't be in anyone's way, and I'm sure her mother will be back or she'll have found a place by the time I come home at Christmas."

"You're not listening to me, Nicole. I will not have that girl living in my house and sponging off me. She and her larcenous mother have made their beds, and they have to lie in them. Like mother, like daughter."

"That's so unfair. Ashley isn't responsible for all this."

"Excuse me if I disagree, but I think there are some chickens coming home to roost here. She's always been the queen bee, with her great sense of entitlement. I'm surprised that you don't see the opportunity in this, Nicole. This is your chance. You've spent your whole life in her shadow, playing second banana while she becomes homecoming queen or gets the lead in the play. You're just as pretty and just as smart. Now is your chance to shine and show everyone you're the real winner."

"I can't believe you said that. I'm not in a contest with Ashley. I know she can be a little full of herself sometimes, but she has a good heart, and we're like sisters. I've never wanted the same things as her. Why can't you ever understand that? All you ever think about is what you want—you don't care what I want."

I had never heard Nicole stand up to her mother like that before, and I wanted to cheer for her. I settled for accidentally-on-purpose dropping my bag and letting it roll down the stairs with a clatter. All conversation in the kitchen stopped abruptly.

"Good morning," I said brightly as I stepped into their peachy pink kitchen. "Thanks for the bed last night, Cindy. I have to get going now."

Cindy nodded curtly and turned her back on me, while Nicole followed me out to my car.

"I'm sorry about my mother, Ash," she said.

"Forget it. I wouldn't have stayed here anyway. She's never liked me, and she's never going to," I said, and then added indignantly, "I am *not* full of myself."

She smiled. "Oh, no, not you. Never."

As I got into my car, she held the door. "What's next?"

I paused for a moment, thinking it over. "The number one item on my list ought to be finding a job. But I'm curious about my mother's lover-boy boss. I'd like to know what his story is. I think he knows a lot about my mother, maybe even where she is."

"Are you sure you know what you're doing?"

"Nope," I admitted. "But I'm doing it anyway."

Nicole watched me, her eyes wide with apprehension, as I started my car and drove away.

chapter twelve

Monday morning I dialed the cell phone number Curtis Davidson had given me.

"Ashley, I'm so glad you called." His voice was warm, like we were old pals. "Can we get together tomorrow? Somewhere discreet so we can speak candidly."

Yeah, let's be candid, I thought. "Why not today?" I asked.

"I'm afraid today isn't possible for me. Actually, I'm on my way right now to my country retreat. I have to meet someone there, and it can't wait."

"Your country retreat?" I said, my heart beating faster.

"Just a little place I keep up in the mountains near La Honda. Perhaps I can show it to you one day."

"Perhaps you can," I said, my brain buzzing light years ahead. *Maybe sooner than you think.*

We arranged to meet for lunch on Tuesday, and I got off the phone. A minute later, I called Brain and asked him to find out the address of Curtis Davidson's La Honda retreat. He really is a Web wizard. It took him only twenty minutes before he e-mailed me the address: 12046 Deep Ravine Drive.

Next, I called Nicole, but as usual, Cindy was keeping her busy. So I asked Tattie if she'd take a drive with me.

"Sure, why not?" she said.

We drove south on Interstate 280 alongside grassy meadows peppered with oak trees and the glistening water of Crystal Springs Reservoir. The sun was bright in a cloudless sky. I opened the sunroof and let my hair blow in the wind. Tattie leaned back, sucking on a super-sized cola, while Metallica blasted from the CD player until I turned it off so I could explain my mission.

"This Davidson dude was having an affair with your mother?" she asked.

"That's my theory. I want to check out his so-called retreat," I said. "Maybe she's there. I'm going to find out right now."

Four miles later we turned east on Highway 92 and followed the two-lane road as it climbed up into the low ridge of mountains that separates the suburbs along the bay from the farms and beaches on the Pacific Ocean. At the rim we turned south again, onto Skyline Boulevard. Almost immediately the road narrowed, with redwood trees, dense blackberry bushes, and poison oak crowding the pavement on both sides.

Up here coastal fog clung to the top of the forest, blocking the sun and turning the sky the color of congealed oatmeal. The road curved around and between the towering trees. Periodically, we would catch a glimpse of a house before the road twisted away again. I had to slow down and concentrate to keep the Jetta from veering off the highway as the road wound through a long series of corkscrew turns.

Following Brain's directions turned out to be a challenge, since the small lanes that intersected Skyline appeared suddenly and were poorly marked. I almost missed Deep Ravine Drive and had to hit my brakes hard to make the turn onto the narrow side road.

We passed a couple of houses and turned down a driveway next to a mailbox marked DAVIDSON in red letters. I saw his Porsche first, and beyond it, a very modern-looking house perched on a knoll.

I was feverish with a mixture of excitement and dread. If my mother was hiding here, I was about to find out.

"I'll wait here." Tattie leaned back and adjusted her sunglasses. "Don't take too long. The country gives me the creeps."

I jumped out of the car and sprinted down the drive. Crossing a little bridge over a trickling creek, I stepped up to the front door and rang the bell.

A minute or two elapsed, then the door opened and Curtis Davidson III stood there dressed in a V-necked pullover sweater and blue jeans, with bare feet. His jaw dropped and he stared at me in astonishment.

"Ashley! What are you doing here?"

"You said we need to talk," I said, moving forward so he'd step back and let me in.

He didn't. He stared at me without moving aside. "I don't understand. We agreed to meet tomorrow. This is not a convenient time. I can't see you now."

"I couldn't wait," I said. "I'll just take a minute."

"This is not a convenient time," he repeated.

"Why? Aren't you alone?" I said, pushing past him and into the house.

The house was one of those architectural gems you see in magazines, the kind with lots of open space and a mammoth stone fireplace centered between floor-to-ceiling windows. Beyond the windows, I could see a huge deck and steam rising from what looked like a hot tub. Bluesy music was playing and a bottle of wine with two fluted glasses was set out on a granite countertop.

Then I saw her. A woman was seated on the sofa, with her feet tucked up under her. She was wearing a man's dark blue silk robe. She wasn't my mother.

"Hello. Who are you?" she said, biting her lip in surprise, and looking over my shoulder in apprehension.

I stared at her in dismay. She was forty or so, petite and buxom, with bright blue eye shadow.

Curtis came up behind me. "Janet, this is Ashley. Ashley's dropped by, uh, to give me a message. An important message. From my office."

Janet nodded, shaking her improbably white-blond hair.

"Are you the only one here?" I blurted out.

She looked at me with hostile eyes and then said, "Of course. What an odd question!"

Curtis frowned "This is inappropriate. Mrs. Richardson and I are having a business meeting. You need to go. We'll discuss that other matter tomorrow."

Ignoring them both, I marched across the room and peered

into the bedroom. Aside from a rumpled bed, there was nothing to see. No one was there.

Curtis came up behind me, grabbed my elbow, and steered me back toward the door. I didn't resist. My legs moved mechanically while I swallowed hard to choke back my disappointment. At that moment, we both heard the steady honking of a car horn. Tattie was getting impatient.

"Now what!" Curtis muttered in irritation.

I was pretty irritated myself. I felt like a prize idiot. Some girl detective I turned out to be. I wanted to kick Curtis in the shin and run out the door.

"That's for me," I said tightly, and walked out without looking back.

"I'll see you tomorrow." He emphasized the word *tomorrow* as he closed the door.

I climbed back into the car, started the engine, and threw the car in gear. As I sped back up the road in a flurry of gravel, I looked over at Tattie. She was smoking a joint and grinning.

"Well, what happened? Was your mother there?"

"No."

I stomped on the gas pedal as we turned onto the main road. We roared down a short straightaway, then the car skidded on a sharp turn. For one frightening moment we almost swerved off the roadway. I hit the brakes, jerked the car onto the shoulder, and stopped. I put my head down on the steering wheel as I tried to slow my pounding heart.

"Sorry about that," I said, not looking at Tattie.

"So what happened back there?"

"He had someone there all right, but it wasn't my mother. Some blonde with mean eyes named Mrs. Richardson." I pulled my head up and made a sour face. "She was wearing a bathrobe for their *business* meeting."

"So you walked into his little love nest?" Tattie took a drag from her joint and laughed. "That must have been something to see. Oh, wow, I'll bet you scared the life out of him. His penis probably shriveled up to the size of this joint."

I gave her an annoyed look, but then the humor of it struck me and I began to laugh too.

"Mean eyes?" she chuckled. "I'll bet old Curtis isn't interested in her eyes."

I laughed again and started up the car. Slowly, I moved back onto the roadway.

"What are you going to do now?" Tattie asked.

"Well, Curtis isn't hiding my mother there, that's clear. But he knows something."

"Mmmm. Well, if you want, I could seduce him for you," Tattie suggested.

Taken aback, I shot her a look. She was dead serious.

"Thanks," I said. "But I don't think it's necessary. I'm having lunch with him tomorrow. I think I can charm some information out of the old lech on my own."

. . .

The next day I had a hard time deciding what to wear. Should I play the innocent ingénue or sex it up with a tight red dress and three-inch stiletto heels? Finally, I decided on a flowered dress with a low-cut sweetheart neckline and shoes with kitten heels.

I was only twenty minutes late to the restaurant, which, for me, is like being on time. I spotted him as soon as I walked in. No doubt about it, he was handsome for his age and well dressed in an Armani suit with a beautiful blue silk tie. He had the courtesy to stand up as I approached. You don't see good manners like that every day.

A dark-haired waitress appeared almost immediately.

"Two Cobb salads and iced tea," he told her, then added perfunctorily, "Is that all right with you, Ashley? I'm a little short on time."

"Fine," I said as he handed her both our menus.

He turned and gave me a major-wattage smile, with lots of eye contact. I wasn't buying a car from him, so I couldn't imagine what I had done to deserve so much warmth.

"I'm sorry I couldn't talk yesterday. I hope you didn't misunderstand the situation with Mrs. Richardson," he said.

"Oh, no," I said, widening my eyes innocently. "I understand completely. It was very rude of me to barge in like that. It's just that I was so eager to have our talk."

He gave me another warm smile. "You know, you're even prettier than your picture."

I ignored that and got the ball rolling. "So, what is it you want to talk to me about?"

Curtis cleared his throat slightly. "I'm sure you're aware that your mother and I have worked very closely for the past several years."

"Yes," I said, even though I didn't know any such thing.

"Did she talk to you about me?"

"Some," I said cautiously, and took a bite of my salad. If she had, I didn't remember.

He paused, as if to reconsider what he was going to say. I decided to move this whole thing along since he was so short on time.

"I know she's very fond of you."

Of course, I made that up, but I remembered what Phil had said about there being someone else in my mother's life. Curtis was obviously the typical cheating husband. His wife probably played tennis and belonged to the Opera Guild. Or maybe she loved horses more than him. Whatever her story was, I was betting that she didn't understand him.

"I am very fond of her, too. Diane is a delightful woman."

"She is," I said with a little choke in my voice. Totally bogus, of course, but I didn't mind putting on an act for the guy. "Since you and my mother were so close, I'm surprised that you waited so long to call me."

"Of course, I've wanted to get in touch, but the situation called for some discretion. After all, the police might have tapped your phone. And it would have seemed suspicious, or at least imprudent, if I was seen knocking on your door. This unpleasant situation has been very difficult for all of us."

The guy was the complete Yoda of double-talk. "This situation?" I retorted.

He coughed and politely covered his mouth with his napkin. "I refer to the press and publicity and general uproar."

"Not to mention the papers that were served on me."

"Yes, that too." His voice was sympathetic and his eyes were wide open in an unblinking I-have-nothing-to-hide stare that didn't fool me for a minute. "I tried to dissuade the firm from that course of action, but the board was obdurate. I hope you understand it was nothing personal."

He seemed to be waiting for me to answer. I waited for him to go on. This was what playing poker must be like, with each player trying to outbluff the others. I had never actually played poker, but I am an excellent actress after all. I took a sip of my iced tea and gave him another innocent smile.

Finally, he said, "How is she? Is Diane all right?"

"How would I know?"

"You don't have to pretend with me, Ashley. I'm a friend. You can trust me."

I almost laughed. How could he deliver a line like that with a straight face?

He went on. "I've been worried and expecting to hear from her every day. Why hasn't she been in touch with me? Is she angry?"

I caught my breath in surprise but managed to keep from blurting out anything stupid.

"Shouldn't she be?" I retorted.

"No, she shouldn't. I can explain. I need to talk to her, Ashley. You need to persuade her to call me."

"Why do you think I'm in touch with her?"

He gave me a reproachful look.

"I'm not stupid, Ashley. I know that you know where she is and how to reach her."

"And how do you know that?"

He made an impatient gesture. "Your mother would never

disappear without telling you. In fact, the only thing that surprises me is that she didn't take you with her. We both know she's in touch with you, so why are we playing this ridiculous cat-and-mouse game?" He grabbed my hand. "Look, Ashley, talk to her. Tell her to call me. I have to speak to her. I need to know how she's going to proceed."

I pulled my hand away. "It's your fault she's in this mess." It was a question and a statement at the same time.

"Is that what she says? She's blaming me? I think she's being a little bit unreasonable. I seem to recall that your father instigated this whole business and your mother was the perpetrator. I helped her when she didn't know what to do and had nowhere to turn. Perhaps the whole business got out of hand, but she's definitely culpable."

I was suddenly tired and thoroughly disgusted. This patronizing jerk obviously thought I was a complete ditz, but I had his number. Clearly he was deeply involved in whatever had gone on. Jesus, Diane, why were you always such a sucker for these handsome, sweet-talking smoothies?

My face must have betrayed what I was feeling, because he frowned.

"Listen to me. It's in all of our interests if she calls me. Tell your mother that." The look in his eyes wasn't so friendly anymore. He stood up, pulled out his wallet, and put some cash on the table. "Unfortunately, I need to get back to the office. Tell Diane she better not do anything crazy. Because I might do something crazy."

He turned and walked away without another word. I was dumbfounded, but what could I do? Tell him that I'd talk to her? I didn't know where she was, and he obviously wasn't going to believe me.

. . .

Afterward, I couldn't wait to tell Nicole all about the lunch. We sat outside on my deck, discussing the details as thoroughly as we had ever dished the dirt on Mara or the love life of some movie star—and just as pointlessly.

Obviously he and Diane had a falling-out of some sort, since she hadn't been in touch with him. And his worry that Diane might do something crazy must mean he didn't want her to spill the beans. Maybe she even had some evidence with her that implicated him.

But his insistence that I must be in touch with her worried me. He thought she wouldn't go away without taking me or at the very least letting me know where she was. But with every passing day, it appeared she had.

Nicole thought I should turn Mr. Big-Shot Davidson in to the police, but I pointed out that I had no proof. I was sure he was in this mess up to his neck and had probably persuaded my mother to do all sorts of illegal stuff. But it was just my word against his. No one would take the word of a teenager, especially an embezzler's daughter, over a pillar of the community.

What was I supposed to do—break into his office and look for incriminating evidence? Playing girl detective hadn't worked for me so far. This wasn't a game, with me proclaiming Colonel Mustard did it in the library with the candlestick. If there were evidence, Charming Curtis would have already destroyed it or else it would have turned up by now.

He was smug and self-centered, but he didn't strike me as a complete idiot.

"What would be the point anyway?" I asked Nicole. "I'm not a financial whiz or accountant. I can't make heads or tails out of ledgers or figure out if he's cooking the books, even if I found the right ones."

"In the movies, there's always something incriminating on a computer," suggested Nicole. "Where's your mother's computer?"

"She took it with her the day she disappeared. My mother and that laptop were inseparable. If you find it, you'll find her."

She shook her head in befuddlement.

"Why is everything so easy on TV and so hard in real life?"

"Because real life sucks. I don't have any clues to work with. No secret envelope or safety-deposit box to look in. I haven't found any mysterious keys that would lead me to a stockpile of evidence. Nothing."

We looked at each other in dejection.

"There must be *something* we can do," she said weakly. "Someone we can tell."

"Mmmm." I thought about it and sighed. "I suppose I could be a real pain in the ass by calling up his wife and making a lot of insinuations about his being a cheating dickhead. But all that would accomplish is making my mother look like some home-wrecking slut. He would persuade wifey I was a deranged liar or even a criminal. They would either ignore me or, worse yet, tell the cops I was stalking them. Plus, I would totally piss him off, and I didn't like the way he said, 'Tell her not to do anything crazy. Because I might do something crazy.' "

Nicole shivered at that thought, and I didn't feel too great about it myself.

Then I had a stupendous idea. I leaped up and paced across the deck.

"I just thought of something. I could send an anonymous letter to Arthur Warren, the company president, you know, the guy who was quoted in that newspaper article. I could write something like, 'Looking for an embezzler? Maybe you ought to take a close look at Curtis Davidson.' Nothing else, no signature, just a little something to plant a seed and make them think twice about his involvement in all this."

"That's fabulous!" shrieked Nicole. "And you can write *Personal and Confidential* on the outside of the envelope so you can be sure that he gets it."

She jumped up and we started to dance around the deck in glee.

Then, suddenly, Nicole stopped dancing and turned to me with gleaming eyes. "I've just had a *really* fiendish idea. There is something else you can do. I saw it in a TV movie once. This rich guy, a tycoon or something, anyway, he dumps his mistress in a really cruel way. To get even, she *turns him in to the IRS.* For a *huge* reward. You know, hell hath no fury like a woman scorned."

It was my turn to shriek. The idea was so diabolical that I couldn't believe the suggestion had come from Nicole.

"Why not?" I screamed. "Why the hell not? You're a genius. I can't sign the letter, so forget the reward part, but there's no earthly reason why I can't send an anonymous letter to the IRS, hinting that Mr. Curtis Davidson has been a very bad boy."

It made me giggle just to think of the bloodhounds from the IRS pursuing that prick and getting their teeth into his well-groomed hide. Phil had gone through an audit a few years ago, and he had complained about it for weeks. He whined to my mother about the IRS investigators being completely heartless, without a drop of human compassion, just because his bookkeeping was a little sloppy. If Phil, who was Mr. Straight Arrow, had been terrified, I could only imagine what old Curtis would feel, because he obviously had a lot to hide.

I was still smiling the next day when I dropped two anonymous letters into the mailbox.

chapter thirteen

The next two weeks were hell. Finding a job turned out to be even more humiliating than looking for a place to live. No one told me that I was going to have to fill out long applications, answer all sorts of personal (and rude) questions, and be treated as if I weren't quite adequate to sweep the floors. I thought I would be doing someone a favor—that someone would smile and say, "Great. You're just the person we need. When can you start?"

No one did. Instead, they acted as if I should be grateful they were even talking to me.

"Leave your resume and we'll call you," they'd say in a brisk, self-important way.

A resume! What was I supposed to put on it? I had only graduated from high school five minutes ago. I could see it now, *Previous experience: Head Cheerleader, Homecoming Queen, Prom Princess.* Hmm, I had a lot of experience as royalty, come to think of it. Oh, and what about my new skill—Garage Sale Expert?

I didn't see why I needed a resume to be a waitress or sales clerk. When I said as much to Little Miss Priss, who interviewed me at the Gap, she looked as if I had just farted in her face.

"We're not looking for just anyone, you know. We need reliable people who are enthusiastic and have good attitudes," she sneered.

"Wow, it must have been really hard for *you* to get a job here," I said sweetly.

So much for working at the Gap.

References were another problem. Where was I supposed to get job references if I'd never had a job? In the end, I listed Gloria and Phil.

The most annoying thing was remembering how my mother had discouraged me when I said I wanted to be an actress. I even asked her to let me enroll in San Mateo High School, which has a first-rate drama program. But for once Diane wouldn't give in. She said I was too young to face the rejection actors go through. I guess that's what old Jimmy moaned about all the time to my softhearted mother. But I'm tough, a whole lot tougher than my father ever was. While I didn't seem to have the necessary skills for these jobs, I was sure I could act, probably better than half the actresses you see in the movies. When was the last time you saw Drew Barrymore play anyone except herself? I can even cry on cue and without getting all puffy and red-eyed.

All in all, I was beginning to regret having pursued the college prep and honors track in high school. Nothing I knew was the least bit practical. Try getting a job because you're good in French or trig.

The simplest job seemed to require a college degree or special training. I saw a job listing for *Art gallery assistant,* and I imagined myself sashaying around a chic gallery. "Oh, yes, that's one of our newest artists," I'd confide. "You should snap up his work while it's still affordable. That one is only ten thousand dollars."

But they wanted a college graduate knowledgeable about art. That left me out.

Bookstore clerk—now that was more like it; I loved books and reading. As I looked further, though, I saw they wanted someone with a retail background or bookselling experience.

Receptionist—knowledge of Word, Access, and Excel essential. OK, I could use Word, but Access and Excel? No way.

And so it went. I didn't even know what a sous chef was. I'd die before I became a nanny or child-care provider, and I would never demean myself by becoming a burrito delivery driver.

At this point, I just wanted to get a job, any job, so I could get some of the experience that seemed so damned important—so I wouldn't get any more smirks when I admitted that I'd never had a job before.

. . .

Soon I was going to be all alone, everyone was going away in a few weeks. I, the girl voted "Most Likely to Set the World on Fire," was being left behind while everyone else went on to new lives.

Even Nicole had begun shutting me out, though she didn't mean to. For weeks she and Cindy had been racing all over San Francisco, buying the things that every college freshman needs, including a wardrobe fit for New England winters. She had invited me along on their shopping excursions, but I begged off, knowing it would be too painful.

Since junior high I had looked forward to decorating my dorm room, going through sorority rush, and being the center of attention at a series of fabulous college parties. I had poured through and dog-eared back issues of *InStyle* and *Vogue*, imagining the pleated skirts, cashmere sweaters, and cocktail dresses I would buy. None of that would ever happen now. I felt cheated and angry.

Camping in a house without furniture, sleeping on the floor in a pile of blankets, and eating at fast-food places or heating frozen dinners was so depressing that I didn't feel like socializing. Admittedly, I wasn't completely without amenities since I still had the stereo and a small portable TV. But the atmosphere was strange and I felt detached from everyone and everything. For the first time in my life, I would sit alone and listen to all the sounds around me. The whole place had a vacant, transient feel to it, as if the house were waiting for someone or something and I was an outsider who didn't belong. The rooms seemed as lonely and deserted as I felt.

Poor Stella suffered the most. She jumped at shadows and meowed plaintively, as if she were blaming me for all the changes. She didn't know it yet, but bigger changes were in the offing for both of us.

It was just a matter of time before the electricity and water would be shut off. Those bills had mounted to a wince-inducing total since my mother vanished. Gloria advised me to forget about the bills, since they'd eat up all my cash and weren't my responsibility anyway. She called them "uncollectable." I didn't like the idea of turning us into a family of deadbeats, but I was determined not to blow the money I had left.

My cell phone bill was another matter. I used two hundred bucks to bring that account up to date so I could reestablish my communication line. No way could I be without a phone. Putting gas in my tank also required cash now. I discovered the hard way that my car registration and insurance were must-pay items. Of course it was dear old Officer Strobel who brought it to my attention. I was zipping along one morning on my way to get a fruit smoothie for breakfast, when he flashed his red light at me. I pulled over to the curb, rolled down my window, and let out a long sigh as Strobel walked up.

"What now? I know I wasn't speeding. Aren't there any skateboarders or other dangerous criminals you can arrest?"

"Your license and registration please."

Wearily, I reached into the glove compartment and handed them over.

"Your registration expired two weeks ago."

"What?" I grabbed them back and looked. "Well, you've got me. I surrender. Another outlaw apprehended. Congratulations."

"You know, your life might go a lot easier if you knocked off the sarcasm," he said matter-of-factly as he began writing on his pad.

I slumped in my seat, trying not to show how upset I was.

"This is what is known as a fix-it ticket. If you correct this within thirty days, the charge will be dismissed. Do you understand that?"

"Yes," I said, feigning indifference by checking my face in the mirror. "Tell me, Officer. Am I public enemy number one around here? Do you have nothing else to do except wait for me to screw up?"

"That's about it," he said. "All day long, I have nothing to think about except Ashley Mitchell. You know, I could probably manage to have some sympathy for you if you didn't act like a smug little smart aleck all the time."

"I don't need your sympathy," I said angrily.

"Then keep it up, because you're on the right track. Sign here."

I signed and started my car. Then, I just couldn't help tossing off, "Don't ever change, Officer. Stay as sweet as you are."

He just shook his head and walked back to his squad car.

. . .

Ultimately, I did get the ticket dismissed, but only after running around in circles for several days. The DMV was happy to accept my money plus late fees, but then informed me that I had to smog-test the Jetta and provide proof of insurance, costing another $300. All these stupid bills were eating away at my garage-sale profit. It had been so much easier when my mother took care of all this.

Despite my dwindling funds, I decided to pay our health club membership dues. For the past few weeks, I had been working out almost every day. Exercising gave me something to do and a way to release my pent-up frustration. Each day as I pounded away on the bike or treadmill, my mind spun around the same worn grooves without any new ideas. I worried and agonized and accomplished nothing.

Then, within the space of five days, everyone left. Tattie went to a court-approved drug-rehab facility for thirty days. Everyone else left for college. I went to the airport to see Nic off, in spite of my aversion to close contact with Cindy.

Poor Nic was in a state. She should have been on top of the world—I know I would have been, in her place. Yet as she stood curbside, watching her brothers unload a truly amazing amount of baggage, she looked forlorn.

"You better have fun," I mock-scolded her. "Remember, you're doing this for both of us now!"

"Oh, Ash," she said, her blue eyes looking ready for a downpour. "I hate this. I never would have applied to Boston if I had dreamed something like this could happen."

I made a face. "Who could have dreamed this would happen? I'll be fine, and you're going to have the time of your life. Promise you'll e-mail me and describe *everything.*"

"I will," she said. "Every day."

"Really, Nicole, I think you're going to be much too busy to be e-mailing Ashley every day," Cindy interjected sharply.

I ignored her and hugged Nic. "E-mail me whenever you have time. Tell me all about your roommate and your dorm. I'll bet you meet some cool people."

"You'll always be my best friend," she said.

"We'll always be best friends," I repeated, even though I wasn't at all sure that would be true. After all, she would be starting a new life while I was stuck in the same spot without a clue as to how to get out of the hole I was in.

. . .

By Labor Day weekend, I was all alone and feeling extremely sorry for myself. I realized too late that I could have tried to apply for some kind of student loan or grant. To be honest, though, I didn't even know how to begin the process, and it was by no means certain I would get a loan. Would any college consider the daughter of an embezzler worthy of a loan? I doubted it.

For one crazy second, I thought about joining the army or air force. That would give me room and board and even college money eventually. Then I came to my senses. I would hate being ordered around, and as for wearing a uniform—ugh! I could never, ever wear those awful shoes! Nor did I want to go off to Alabama or wherever it is that they send you to boot camp. Anyway, I reasoned that I needed to stay close by in case my mother came back. But just the fact that I actually considered joining the military shows how desperate I was.

Then, a miracle happened. I found a job. Although it doesn't compare to the parting of the Red Sea or the Giants winning the World Series, it seemed nothing short of miraculous. I soon discovered it paid only $8.50 an hour, plus tips. I had broken the code, joined the club, and I was on my way at last.

I had gone to the City to interview for a sales clerk's job at Mick's, a furniture store located toward the ritzy end of Fillmore Street. The furniture is expensive and très chic, just the kind I like. But the interview didn't go well. I could see right away that the guy interviewing me was underwhelmed by my lack of retailing experience. I tried to impress him with my enthusiasm for the furniture, but he blew me off with a "Thanks for coming in. We'll call you when we make a decision."

Dejected, I wandered down toward the cheaper end of Fillmore, looking for somewhere to get a smoothie. That's when I spotted a HELP WANTED sign in the window of a funky-looking coffeehouse called Mad Malcolm's Cyber Café. To be honest, the whole building did look a little mad, painted purple with orange-and-green trim.

I peered in the window and was not impressed by what I saw. The coffeehouse was furnished with a hodgepodge of mismatched furniture, and the customers looked equally odd. This was definitely not my usual kind of place. But maybe that was a good thing—maybe it would give me a better chance of getting the job. Surely people couldn't be standing in line to work at a crazy-looking place like this.

I walked inside and inwardly groaned when I caught sight of the guy behind the counter—he was a pencil-thin, goateed young Asian with a shaved head and a tattoo of a dragon on his arm. If he was the management's idea of the perfect employee, they wouldn't want me. I wanted to turn right around, but I forced myself forward.

"Hi! I'd like to apply for the job," I said with all the sassy self-confidence I could muster. He didn't laugh or sneer or say anything at all, just stared at me, fished out an application from under the counter, and handed it to me. I filled it out and added a bunch of stupid comments about how much I loved coffee (I didn't) and how much I wanted to work there (yeah, right). To show how much I loved coffee, I forced down a latte. Then I went home and forgot all about the place.

Early the next morning, the phone rang.

"This is Malcolm Merriman—from Mad Malcolm's Cyber Café. Am I speaking to Ashley Mitchell?"

"Oh, hello," I said, sitting up in astonishment. I had been half-asleep, trying to muster the energy to face the day. "Yes, this is Ashley."

"Still interested in the job?"

"Of course."

"Can you start right away?"

"Sure," I said.

"Are you flexible? Can you work nights and weekends if I need you?"

"Yes, no problem."

"Right, then. You're hired. Start tomorrow."

I was dumbfounded. "Don't you want me to come in for an interview?" I asked.

"Nope. I'm not looking for a brain surgeon. Making coffee doesn't take a master's degree. As long as you can read and write and have half a brain, I can train you. What I need is someone who can start tomorrow. Nancy didn't give me any notice, just up and left last week to go to Sedona and become an aroma therapist, for Christ's sake."

"I see," I said, though of course I didn't. It couldn't be this easy, could it? There must be something wrong with this job.

"Be here tomorrow at eight AM sharp. No, wait, better make that nine, all right?"

"Uh, sure. Nine." And then the words slipped out before I knew it. It's as if I was channeling Mara. "What should I wear?"

There was a pause and then he said, "You know, for a moment I was tempted to say a clown suit. However, clothes are what I normally recommend."

"I mean, I thought there might be a dress code or uniform," I said, trying to recover my dignity.

"This ain't Starbucks, darlin'. Wear whatever you want. But I wouldn't recommend anything too short unless you want the customers looking up your skirt every time you bend over. Louis said you're a looker."

Taken aback, I answered, "I'll figure it out."

"Fine. See you tomorrow at nine. Bring your Social Security card."

I had a job! I was ecstatic, even though the owner sounded weird. As I stared at my cell phone, I realized I forgot to ask him how much I would be paid. Oh well, it wasn't like I was in a position to turn down anything, no matter how pitiful. And there was one blessing—I was sure that none of my former friends, no one from Burlingame, would ever show up in a place like Mad Malcolm's.

. . .

That night, as I pumped the pedals on the exercise bike, I obsessed about finding a place to live. Whatever my salary was, I doubted it would be enough to rent much of a place, not at the astronomical prices that rentals seemed to cost. It would probably take every penny I earned. How could I find a cheap place to live?

A wild idea began to grow in the back of my brain—a crazy scheme that was born of desperation, but one I thought

I might actually be able to pull off. There was only one roadblock to the plan—it would involve some serious groveling, and to Phil, of all people. I was mortified at the idea, but I didn't see another way. I told myself it would be like acting, only in this case, my role was Little Orphan Ashley.

chapter fourteen

What! Are you nuts? That's the craziest idea you've ever come up with."

Phil paused, wrench raised in midair, to stare at me in disbelief and derision. I had cornered him in one of the station's service bays for Act One, Scene One, of my new play, *Ashley, the Pathetic Beggar Girl.*

Glaring back at him, I remembered why I used to call him Pill behind his back. Then I shifted gears and tried to look both sincere and pitiful. I was wearing my oldest jeans and a gray pullover I never liked, the closest thing I had to rags.

"I know it sounds crazy," I said sadly, with what I hoped was the right amount of pathos. "But what else can I do? I'm desperate. It wouldn't be for long, just till I save some money."

He dropped the wrench on the workbench with a loud bang and let loose with a short, jerky laugh. "You can't be serious. I can't even begin to imagine it. You, of all people, living in a camper. There's no phone service, no stereo or TV, no bathroom, much less bubble baths, you know."

"I am serious, and guess what, my life isn't all bubble baths right now. I'm in trouble and I don't see any way out of it."

Phil ran his fingers through his hair and gave me an exasperated look. "It's illegal, you know."

"Not in a bank-robbing kind of way," I protested. "If it is, it's just a little bit illegal and no one's going to call you on it because no one is going to know."

"People have a way of finding out about these things. Somebody notices or you tell someone and the next thing you know, I've got the cops or the Board of Health around my neck."

"Believe me, Phil, I'm not going to tell anyone. Do you think I want anyone to know I don't have anywhere to live?" I said acidly, and then downshifted my tone again. "I'll make *very* sure that no one notices."

"Ashley, you have no idea what living in a camper would be like. You've never even been camping!"

"What do you think I'm doing now? I have no furniture and the utilities are going to be shut off any minute now. Please, Phil, help me out. I don't want to end up in one of those homeless shelters."

"Come on, Ashley." He snorted. "It can't be that bad."

"Oh, yeah, where can I go with no money, no family, and no job? Maybe you'd like to rent a room for me at the Ritz-Carlton?"

"Your mother wouldn't want you living in a camper behind my station. She'd be horrified. I guess if you're really in a tight spot, you could stay at my place until you're on your feet." He looked as if he couldn't believe that he said it, and I couldn't believe it either.

I sighed. I seemed to be doing a lot of sighing lately.

"At this point we don't know what my mother would want, but she's the one who got me into this mess in the first place. Anyway, I don't think it would be a good idea for me to stay at your place. What would your new girlfriend think?"

Phil shifted uneasily, but didn't answer.

"Look, I'm only going to sleep in the camper. I'll be gone all day and only come back late at night, so no one will notice I'm there. It won't be for long, I promise."

I kept hammering away at him until finally he grumbled, "I've got to get back to work. I'll think about it and let you know."

"When?"

"In a couple of days," he said, turning away. Then he turned back to add, "But remember, I'm not making any promises. I don't think this is a good idea."

I really didn't think he was going to go for it, and I was thoroughly depressed because I didn't have a Plan B. But the next day, Phil astonished me by calling on my cell phone and saying I could try it.

"The only reason I'm doing this is because I know you, Ashley. You won't last a week living there."

"Maybe not," I retorted. "If I don't, then you don't have anything to worry about, do you?"

"You know, maybe this will be a good lesson for you," he said. "Yes, this should be an interesting experiment. I'm going to enjoy watching this."

"Always glad to provide a little bit of entertainment," I replied, trying to keep the annoyance out of my voice. To hell with him, I was tired of being condescended to and treated like a self-centered airhead. He underestimated me. They all did.

But first I had to find a place for Stella. She wouldn't be safe at the camper—what if she got hit by some careless driver pulling into or out of the station? Keeping her locked up inside wouldn't work either; she was used to having a big yard to roam and plenty of butterflies to stalk. The only thing I could do was ask Gloria if she would keep her for a little while.

I spun Gloria a story about how the place where I would be staying didn't allow pets, but that I would find another apartment as soon as possible. Naturally, I didn't tell her about Phil's camper. She probably would have tried to stop me or insisted I stay at her house. I didn't want to deal with her sons or hear daily reminders about what a screwup I was and how Diane had spoiled me.

I told Gloria to take good care of Stella and to not let the boys pull her tail. She's very sensitive about having her tail pulled. She assured me that Stella would be well cared for, and I gave my beauty one last hug. She ruffled her fur and gave me what seemed like a resentful look along with a loud meow. I felt like I was losing my last friend.

. . .

The next night I quietly moved my belongings into the camper. I tried to keep my stuff to a minimum since there wouldn't be much space. I brought bedding, a case full of makeup and bathroom supplies, my iPod, and my mother's blue bathrobe. As for clothes, I brought only the basics: mostly jeans, sweaters, and a few skirts. I packed everything else into the boxes and cupboards in Gloria's garage.

I purchased a few supplies that might be useful, including a flashlight, a couple of candles, bottled water for drinking, and some disposable facecloths for cleaning my face before bed. Being without running water was going to be a challenge.

The camper was parked behind the gas station, snug against a six-foot-high concrete retaining wall, with plenty of room to park my car facing it. The building would block most of my car from the street, although the rear fender and bumper might stick out a little. To a casual passerby, it would look as if my Jetta was one of several cars parked in the station overnight, ready for Phil and Reynaldo to begin work on early the next morning.

When I stepped inside the camper, I was surprised at how small it was. Standing there, I longed to walk out and say, "Forget it. Bad idea." I had to remind myself that I didn't have a backup plan.

At least it was clean. Someone had given it a good scrubbing. To put it mildly, the accommodations were austere. Squeezed nearest the door was a padded bench with a hinged table that could be raised or lowered—my new combination living room/dining area. Overhead were some cupboards for storage. More cupboards were mounted atop the sink, refrigerator, and stove area. I put clothes in all these places since I would be depending on fast-food joints.

At the back of the camper was my new bedchamber: a platform with a mattress on it. The door in the corner opened to a bathroom so small that turning around while inside was next to impossible. But I wouldn't have to worry about that. Without any water or electricity, that teeny bathroom's only purpose was to provide a mirror. I would have to sneak into the station's ladies room and shower at the gym. There was one pathetically small closet. Sleeping and changing was all I would or could do at the camper.

I decided I would sleep in sweats. September and October are usually the warmest months around here, but the temperature always drops at night when the fog rolls in. Dressed in sweats I would be ready for whatever might happen. What if someone walked over and tried to look in the windows? Thankfully, the exterior door locked from the inside. Still, I couldn't let myself forget for one minute that I was sleeping in a flimsy little camper behind a gas station.

Before long, I would discover that it wasn't possible to forget. There's nothing exactly homey about sleeping in an unheated camper behind a stinky gas station. Even late at night I could hear horns honking, tires screeching, and the occasional whine of a fire truck or ambulance siren. I also heard the whistle of the train and sometimes even the jets of the planes preparing for takeoff at the nearby San Francisco Airport. Quite a chorus, all put together. The uninviting atmosphere was not enhanced by the ever-present aroma of gasoline drifting in the air and oozing into the camper. Only a heavy rain washed the smell away and then only temporarily.

That first night, as I sat in that dismal little tin can, the awfulness of the situation finally pierced the cushion of denial I had created around me. This was my new home. My mother was a thief who had vanished without a word, and I might never see her again. I was living on my own like the kind of person I had pitied in the past. My life as a person who was admired and envied was finished.

My chest felt as if a large rock were lodged somewhere below my rib cage, and I had to swallow hard to vanquish the nausea welling up in the back of my throat. Welcome to hell, Ashley, I told myself bitterly. Get used to it. I felt drained and resigned to my imprisonment in this metallic cage. I had only one plan for escape: to create a new life and a new Ashley.

By sleeping in the camper rent-free, I would save enough money to eventually move into a real apartment. I would need at least $3,000 for first and last month's rent plus a security deposit; I already had a good start with the $2,000 left from the garage sale. Accumulating the other thousand might take a couple of months, but I was sure I could endure two months of discomfort to get myself on track.

Meanwhile, I planned to stay away from everyone I knew in Burlingame. When everything was going well—when I had a life, a cute apartment, and was enrolled in college—I'd reemerge as the new, independent Ashley. I'd be on my own while Mara, Scott, and the rest still lived off handouts from their parents.

Looking back I shudder at my optimism. Nothing, not one single thing, went as planned. Luckily, I had no inkling of the disasters that lurked just around the corner.

chapter fifteen

I was fifteen minutes late for the first day of my first job. It had taken ages to find a parking spot near the cafe. Dashing through the coffeehouse door, my hair flying in all directions, I stumbled on the uneven wooden floor in my high-heeled sandals.

"Dammit," I yelped, just managing to avoid the indignity of falling flat on my butt.

As I regained my balance, I saw what was to become a familiar scene: Louis, the thin Asian guy, was manning the espresso machine with a bored look. Standing next to him, Santa Claus was leaning across the counter in conversation with a customer. That's right, Santa, or maybe his clone. Anyway, this fat man had a big belly, a white beard, flyaway white hair pulled back in a ponytail, and a smiling red face. Instinct told me I was gazing at Mad Malcolm.

"She shoved her tongue so far into my ear, I thought she would break my eardrum," said the customer, and Santa laughed uproariously.

That provocative conversation stopped abruptly as I came to a halt in front of them.

"Hi!" I squeaked. "Sorry to be a little late. I had trouble finding a place to park."

"You must be our new serving wench," Santa said. "Welcome to the Madhouse, Cinderella. I'm Malcolm."

"Uh," I mumbled. *Serving wench? Cinderella? Is that supposed to be funny?* "I'm Ashley."

"Of course you're Ashley. I see you took my advice about not wearing a short skirt. Still, you look fetching enough in those tight jeans. A little eye candy never hurts business. Yes, indeedy, you should make an interesting addition to our merry little band."

"Did you say 'the Madhouse'?" I asked.

"That's a name that one of the customers gave this establishment a few years back, and it stuck. It seems to fit, since most of the customers are as deranged as I am."

"No one's madder than Mad Malcolm," contradicted the customer, a tall, husky man of about thirty-five. "Hi, I'm Tom. It's a pleasure to meet you. Your taste in employees is improving, Mal. She looks much more agreeable than Nancy. She tended to be a bit argumentative at times."

"She could be," Mal agreed. "You don't have any strong opinions on doctors or modern medicine, I hope. Your predecessor hated doctors and insisted that they were all in collusion to keep us sick. How about vitamins?"

"Vitamins?" I said. "They're good, I guess. I take a multiple vitamin every day, when I remember."

"One vitamin! My, you will be a change for us all. Nancy took at least thirty a day."

Tom interjected, "She used to tell me this scone was pure poison, all white flour and sugar and chemicals." He took a big, defiant bite out of the scone.

"Atta boy," I said faintly. "Go for the gusto."

Tom grinned at me. He had red hair and a friendly face with so many freckles sprinkled across it that his face had an orange cast.

Malcolm chuckled. "Tom thrives on gusto. Or do I mean bravado? Tom here is the heroic type, a fearless firefighter. We're depending on him to save us all in case of a fire."

"Don't count on me carrying you down a ladder." Tom gave Malcolm a mocking look. "Not unless you lose a few pounds. Now Ashley here, I would carry her with pleasure."

"That's always the way it is with you heteros. Damning a Rubenesque queen to the flames so you can save a slender young maiden."

"Naturally," Tom said. "Why would I save your sorry behind when I can rescue a lovely lady? Besides, I've got my back to think about. Women and children first, that's my motto."

"Heterosexist pig," Malcolm retorted.

I was beginning to catch on. If I was interpreting this banter correctly, Malcolm was gay and liked to tease people, and this place was a madhouse because everyone in it was nutty as a fruitcake.

"The coffeehouse is on the ground floor, so the problem isn't likely to come up," I pointed out.

"Not strictly true. I live in the flat upstairs," responded Malcolm. "Well, it's time to orientate you, dear girl. Tom, go wash your fire truck or make some chili or whatever it is that you do at the firehouse with all those handsome hunks. We have work to do."

"Yeah, duty calls. Tell you the rest later, Mal." Tom headed for the door. "Welcome aboard, Ashley."

Malcolm looked around as if deciding what to do first. "All right then. Now you've met Louis, haven't you? Mister Louis Ling, barista extraordinaire, is hiding behind the steamer. You'll be working with him most mornings."

Louis nodded to me without smiling.

"The kitchen and bathroom are back there." Malcolm gestured behind him as he came out from behind the counter. I was astonished to see he was wearing Bermuda shorts, not a great look for a man of his age and girth. "Let's sit down over here and get the paperwork out of the way. I'll explain things and then Louis can get started with the coffee tutorial."

In between explaining the job requirements and my schedule, Malcolm exchanged hellos and banal chitchat with a steady stream of customers as they came in the door. He acted as if the coffeehouse were his living room and everyone who came in, his guest. At least his conversations gave me a chance to get a better look at my new workplace.

I counted a dozen wooden tables surrounded by mismatched chairs plus an old upright piano in the corner, its top stacked with cups, napkins, and other supplies. In the midst of all this artful shabbiness was a sagging sofa arranged so that it faced the counter and had its back to the entry.

The counter and floor were made of dark wood and the walls were half-covered with wood paneling. Fortunately, it was a corner building, so the place was saved from being a dim cave by two walls of windows. A pair of huge lighting fixtures hung from the twelve-foot ceilings, and tiny white lights were strung beneath and above the counter.

Three computer stations were lined up along the interior wall. A big hand-printed sign on the wall proclaimed the price to be $3 for fifteen minutes and $5 for thirty minutes, 50 cents a page for printouts. Over in the far corner, a rickety three-shelf bookcase was loaded down with dog-eared paperbacks—mostly discarded thrillers and romance novels, I later discovered, plus nonfiction like *You Are Psychic!* and *The False Fat Diet.* Hanging over this sad literary outpost was a massive bulletin board covered with notices of all types and sizes. If you were looking for a lost parrot, math tutor, deep-tissue massage, oil painting of your pet, or workshop for sexually violated men, this was the spot to check.

In Burlingame, coffeehouses use their walls as a kind of informal art gallery, but not here. Every inch of wall space in the Madhouse displayed a collection of demonic wooden masks, many of them carved and painted in a way that looked as if a snake or iguana was eating someone's face.

Malcolm noticed me staring at the masks.

"Aren't they wonderful?" He gestured toward the savage faces. "I adore Mexican folk art, and these ceremonial masks are imbued with the mystical qualities of the ancient Aztecs. I add one or two to my collection every year when I take my annual sabbatical to San Miguel."

"I'm not sure what they're imbued with," I answered, looking up at a particularly grotesque one. "Except that they give new meaning to the expression 'suck face.' "

He chuckled. "They grow on you, you'll see."

Personally, I hoped not.

. . .

My first assignment was to clear tables and wash dishes. Thanks to Malcolm, that song from *Cinderella* where all the mice are singing kept echoing through my brain. Anyway, I managed to finish without breaking *all* the glasses and cups, though I did make plenty of noise.

After that, Malcolm gave me a quick course in ringing up sales on the register, but I felt slow and stupid having to look up each price. I decided to take the menu with me that night and memorize all the prices.

In addition to serving espresso drinks, the coffeehouse had a limited food menu, but nothing complicated. I could handle putting cream cheese on a bagel, heating soup, or warming a slice of quiche in the microwave.

Louis wasn't exactly Mr. Personality, but he was patient when teaching me how to make cappuccinos and lattes. I kept screwing up and managed to burn my hand in the process.

While I fumbled around learning to steam milk properly, Malcolm disappeared for a couple of hours. A steady stream of customers came in and out, a few of them looked normal. Many of them introduced themselves—Isabella, Andre, Roger—until my head was spinning. I wasn't going to remember half their names.

The hours seemed to crawl by, and I was certain I'd never survive the whole day. Maybe it's always that way when you're new and so nervous that you feel like your hands don't work right anymore.

By twelve thirty a steady buzz of conversation could be heard around the room. I was struggling to make a mocha when a tall, wild-eyed man with bushy black hair burst through the door as if a powerful gust of wind had blown him inside. Instead of moving to the counter, he stood in the center of the room and fixed an intense, laserlike stare on each of us one by one, his eyes moving around the room as if he were trying to read our thoughts or souls. He was dressed in a flowing cloak over a dark shirt and pants, and on his head, earphones stuck up like antennas.

"Beam me up, Scotty," I muttered, and shivered.

Stretching out his arms as if he were going to begin an oration and holding a black book up high, the man asked in a booming voice, "Does this book belong to you?"

The coffeehouse fell silent as customers turned and gaped at him. The book he was holding aloft looked like a Bible, but I wasn't sure. I glanced over at Louis, but he didn't say anything to him.

Raising his voice a notch, the bushy-haired man asked again, "Does this book belong to one of you?"

Still, no one answered, although everyone was openly staring at him.

Asking a third time, he shouted, "Does this book belong to any of you?"

Then he whirled around and vanished out the door, slamming it so hard behind him that the window's glass rattled.

The place was quiet for a second, someone tittered, and then people began talking normally again.

"What was that all about?" I said.

Louis shrugged and said, "He's crazy."

Everyone else had resumed drinking their coffee, apparently unperturbed by what had just occurred. I seemed to be the only one who was discomfited by the whole bizarre scene. Clearly I wasn't in Burlingame anymore.

. . .

Around two, Malcolm reappeared, wearing jeans instead of those awful shorts, and sat down at a window table to play Scrabble with some customers. This was a livelier version of the game than I had ever witnessed. In my experience, Scrabble was an excruciatingly slow game that allowed you to paint your nails or read a book while waiting for dull-witted players to come up with words of more than three letters.

Here it was a raucous and highly competitive game involving loud voices, laughter, challenges, and name-calling. The other three players included a twentyish geek in camouflage pants named Jerry, an elderly black guy called William, and a middle-aged woman they all referred to as Mike.

Mike—real name Michelle—was a stocky, no-nonsense type with extremely short silvery hair. I wasn't surprised when a pregnant earth-mother type walked in and gave her a wifely kiss.

Earth Mommy was six feet tall, blond, and looked as if she might give birth any minute. She was accompanied by a small blond toddler. The kid was quite a sight to behold: He/she was wearing a baseball cap, sneakers, and a pink ballerina's tutu over jeans and T-shirt, and dragging a pink feather boa.

I was still giggling at this getup when they came up to the counter.

"That's some costume. Are you a girl or boy ballerina?" I asked.

"I'm a boy, 'course," he said as if I were very, very stupid.

Earth Mommy gave me a look that would have stopped a tank.

"What kind of remark is that? Are you an idiot?" she barked. "Max is very obviously a boy. For your information, playful cross-dressing is a normal stage of any child's development. Children can be permanently damaged if their parents or others"—she raised her voice at this point—"try to impose false gender stereotypes on them."

I flushed bright red, but before I could say anything, Malcolm appeared at my elbow and took over.

"Hiya, Max. How about a cookie? Ashley, give this young man a nice big chocolate chip cookie from his Uncle Malcolm."

I handed Max a cookie, pronto.

"Now, Joyce, Ashley was just joking," Malcolm continued. "Cut her a little slack. This is her first day. She didn't mean to offend you or Max. Did you, Ashley?"

I shook my head vigorously.

He added, "Ashley's just jealous because she doesn't have a beautiful pink tutu of her own. Right, Max?"

Joyce snorted.

"I'm very sorry if I hurt Max's feelings," I said.

Max appeared to have already forgotten us. With his cookie

in one hand, he climbed up on a chair in front of one of the computers. It didn't look as if I had damaged his delicate little psyche.

"Can I get you a hot chocolate, Joyce? On the house." Malcolm was still being conciliatory.

"Let me do it." I moved quickly to the machine.

As I prepared the chocolate, I worried that I might get fired over this. Gender stereotypes? Good grief. I had better watch my step around these people.

At least I was a big hit with Jerry, the nerdy Scrabble player. When Mal introduced me, he stared at me as if I were a movie star. Really, it was laughable. I gave him a nice smile, nothing else, and he started jabbering and making stupid jokes, the kind that are just a notch above "Knock, knock. Who's there?" He might as well have tattooed the word *Loser* on his forehead.

Throughout the game Jerry kept looking over at me and acting like a ten-year-old with his first big crush. He came over to tell me (big yawn) that he was majoring in computer science at SF State, and he kept the Madhouse computers running. He rattled on about computer games and silly sci-fi movies like *The Matrix*. I was polite and didn't say what I was thinking, which was, "Who cares?"

Then Joyce announced she needed to leave. "Max can stay here with you for a bit," she said, and Mike nodded.

"Fine, fine," said Malcolm. "No problem. Ashley will keep an eye on him."

Joyce gave me a warning look in case I was thinking about promoting more false gender stereotypes. I kept my face expressionless, but I was thinking, Oh, great, now I'm a babysitter. What next?

I had just glanced at the wall clock, thinking the hands must be broken because they moved so slowly, when a short elderly woman dressed like a heroine in a gothic novel waltzed through the door. It seemed every day was Halloween at the Madhouse.

I heard her say in a high-pitched voice, "Just stay still, darling. Mommie will give you a treat in a minute."

She was talking into her handbag. I peered over the counter and saw a black nose and dark eyes. A small, wiry, brownish dog stared up at me from inside her bag.

"Is that one of those dogs from the taco commercials?" I asked.

She cooed, "That's Nostradamus. He's a miniature pinscher, and he's my sweet, sweet baby. He's extremely talented, very intuitive, just like Mommie."

An intuitive dog? I suppose that was possible. Dogs always seemed to intuit that I am a cat person.

"I'm Evelyn," she announced, raising her hand and jangling what must have been ten or fifteen silvery bracelets on her right arm. Then she leaned toward me and touched my hand. "You shouldn't worry so much, dear. Everything is going to be all right."

I stared at her, not sure I heard her correctly. "What?"

"Don't worry," she repeated. "You're going to survive all the trials you're going through. I'm a psychic, you know. Perhaps you'd like me to read the Tarot for you one day."

"Now, Evelyn." Mal came up behind her and reached out

to grab one of the brownies on the counter. I had already noticed that he never stopped eating. "Leave Ashley alone. She doesn't need any of that hocus-pocus crap."

"Malcolm's a true Capricorn," Evelyn confided to me, as if that explained everything. "Very conservative and judgmental, like all Earth signs. Fortunately, he's also a dragon."

"A dragon?" I said.

"That's his Chinese animal sign," she explained. "I look at the duality of each person's nature by determining the interaction of his or her Western astrological sign with his or her Oriental year sign. For example, I'm an Aquarius, born in the Year of the Snake. That's why I'm clairvoyant, with strong vision and intuition."

"Does that mean you know things before they happen?" I asked. "When I read my horoscope in the newspaper, it always seems so general it could work for anyone. Or it turns out to be completely wrong."

"Oh, there's nothing accurate about mass media astrology. I do my own charts. I think you must be an Aries? No, you're a Scorpio."

"How did you know that?"

She smiled. "Tell me what year you were born, and I'll tell you what your Eastern sign is. I'm guessing a Year of the Tiger or perhaps Rooster."

I didn't have a chance to answer because Malcolm walked back in, asking, "Does poor old Nasty ever get to walk, Evelyn?"

"Of course he does. But he's really quite happy to ride in my bag. His little legs get tired. And, Malcolm, I've asked you not to call him Nasty."

"Everybody here calls him Nasty because he's a biter," Malcolm mock-whispered to me as he turned to go back to the Scrabble fest.

"He's just shy and doesn't like strangers to touch him," his indulgent owner said. "If you take the time to get acquainted, he's very sweet. Would you like to pet him, Ashley?"

"No, thanks. I'm afraid I'm more of a cat person," I said, keeping my hands clear of her handbag. I already had a burn; I didn't need a bite to go with it.

Just at that moment, a tall, sturdy African-American chick bounced through the door and slammed a knapsack down on the floor by the piano.

"Hey, you must be the new girl. I'm Aphrodite. Everyone calls me Dee. My sister and I work the night shift. How's it going?"

I let loose with a long sigh, then realized I should sound more positive. "Fine. Good." I mustered up a smile, even though I was feeling weary.

"Hey, don't sweat it, girlfriend. The first day is always the hardest," she said breezily. She seemed like one of those upbeat people who can really get on your nerves.

Louis ducked into the back and emerged rolling a bicycle and carrying a helmet. "Tomorrow, dudes," he said, and left.

I was ready to call it a day, but I had another ninety minutes to go. Fortunately, the last hour was the best of the day. Dee and I talked as we worked, and I liked her in spite of the relentlessly cheerful attitude.

Then a tall guy in his twenties walked in and whistled as he stopped in front of the counter. He had a slim build, dark curly hair, lively blue eyes, and a crooked smile, probably because his teeth were a little crooked. No matter, he was the best-looking guy I'd seen all day, and I smiled back at him.

"Well, things are really looking up around here. And who might you be?"

"I might be the new employee. And who are you?"

"Look out for him, Ashley. Patrick's a real bobcat." Dee snickered.

Bobcat? This sounded interesting. Patrick had a killer smile and a lilt to his voice that sounded Irish.

"Fair Aphrodite," he said, rolling out each syllable of her name. "What have I done to earn such disdain from you?" He gave us a delicious grin that could have melted the polar ice caps. "Pay her no heed. I promise I'm as tame as a house cat. The name is Patrick Ryan Rigney."

"I'm Ashley."

"Mmmm, you look like an Ashley. Mal, you old dog, your judgment is improving. Where did you find this rare flower?"

"Get away from her, you Irish devil," Malcolm called. "I don't need you sniffing around my new employee. You'll drive her away with all your bullshit and blarney. Get over here and take over for Jerry. He has to leave."

"Might I have a cappuccino then, Ashley?" said Patrick. "It seems I have to get in the game." He winked at me and walked away.

chapter sixteen

There's no use trying to sugarcoat the whole camper experience. The first week or so it was tolerable. At the end of three weeks, I was tired of it. By the fifth week, I hated it. If I had read about it in a book, it might have sounded like an adventure. As a kid I'd loved reading about the children who lived in a boxcar. But the camper was cold, uncomfortable, and scary. You never realize how important having a home is until you don't have one. I began to have sympathy for the panhandlers sleeping on the streets. At least I wasn't that bad off.

I had developed a daily routine. Each morning I crawled out of my nest, tossed some clothes into my duffle bag, and steered my car to the gym for a thirty-minute workout.

Afterward, I would leap into a steaming-hot shower to enjoy the water as it cascaded over my body. I had never appreciated showers so much. By seven I was dressed and fighting the early-bird workout fanatics for mirror space so I could blow-dry my hair and put on makeup.

After a while, I began to recognize familiar faces among the morning crowd, but I was the only one who showed up seven days a week without fail. I was careful not to get too friendly or make myself conspicuous. But someone did notice. One morning as I wobbled sleepily past the front desk, I was shocked into consciousness by Patti, the girl who checked everyone in.

"Hey, how are ya! You're a little later than usual, aren't you?" she chirruped.

I jerked my head up from my usual stupor and stared at her like a thief caught with the swag falling out of her handbag.

"I couldn't help noticing that you work out every single day," she said.

"Yeah?" I said, my heart pounding, even though there was no way she could guess why I came every day.

She leaned over the counter. "I just wanted to tell you that I admire your dedication. I wish I had your discipline. I've seen you in the workout room, and you've developed great definition in your calves and arms."

I exhaled in relief. "Thanks, I'm very happy with the results I'm getting."

Thinking fast, I confided, "You know, I had a weight problem, so I try very hard to stick to this routine. I'm always afraid if I miss a day, I'll start putting the pounds back on."

"Wow, I'd never guess you were ever overweight," Patti exclaimed, obviously buying the whole bogus story. "What a success story! Maybe we could write about you in our club newsletter."

"Oh, no!" I said hastily. "Thanks, anyway."

"Come on, you'd be an inspiration to our other members."

"No, sorry. I'm very private," I called as I fled toward the women's locker room. For weeks after that, I sped by the front desk as if rapacious timber wolves were after me, but Patti didn't mention it again.

The daily procession of coffeehouse customers began each morning at six thirty. Louis opened, and I joined him at eight. After a week on the job, I was at home standing behind the coffeehouse counter asking, "Single or double latte?"

Malcolm was right—it wasn't brain surgery. I became proud of my new skill at creating mounds of frothy white foam to crown the top of my perfectly prepared coffee drinks.

Louis and I worked together until three thirty, when he was replaced by either Dee or her twin sister, Cassie. Separately or together, the twins worked the late shift six days a week. I left at four thirty, unless it was really busy. At ten o'clock (midnight on Fridays and Saturdays), the doors closed for the night. On Sundays Mal himself opened the place at eight, then I took over at eleven and worked until six o'clock closing.

Saturday was my only day off but I didn't mind. I needed to work a lot of hours so I could earn as much money as possible. I quickly learned that you don't accumulate a lot of cash when you get paid only $8.50 an hour. When I opened my first pay envelope, I went into shock at how much money had been deducted for taxes and stuff. I had to radically revise my earnings and savings estimates. Fortunately, I ate and drank for free at the Madhouse. I've never been a big eater anyway, so a slice of pizza or soup and an apple would do for dinner. I paid for everyday stuff with my tips and plunked my paycheck money into my savings "bank" (a drawer in the back of the armoire inside Gloria's garage).

Malcolm was in and out all day. When he wasn't gabbing with customers, he often went upstairs to work on his novel. Apparently he'd been at it for years, although none of the Madhouse inmates had read any of it. Except Patrick.

Mal and Patrick belonged to the same writing group. The two of them talked about books and writing all the time. I tried to eavesdrop on their conversations whenever possible. I discovered that not only did Patrick have a great smile, he was smart, too. We flirted but he never took it any further.

When the Madhouse was busy, the day would rush by in a blur of coffee and food and boisterous voices. During slow periods, I would check my e-mail on one of the computers. Occasionally, I received one from Nicole. Of course she loved college. I also passed time by reading the newspapers the customers left behind.

At first I just looked at my horoscope and Dear Abby, then skimmed the local news to make sure there weren't any articles about my mother. Little by little, though, I began reading the news articles and the columns. Amazingly, I developed an interest in what teachers refer to as current events. I did it partly to pass the time and partly because I didn't want to seem totally ignorant to the customers.

Getting through the hours at work was easy enough—it was tougher finding something to do outside the Madhouse. I couldn't sit by myself in a dark camper every evening so I had to find places to hang out until ten or eleven o'clock. Staying around the Madhouse was out since it would have looked as if I didn't have any place to go or friends to hang with. No way I wanted to look that feeble.

At first, I explored Fillmore Street. Beyond the mansions of Pacific Heights, Fillmore makes a steep descent into the Cow Hollow and Marina districts before dead-ending at the bay.

When the weather was clear I would walk the street's entire length until I could see the yachts and motor cruisers docked along the shore and the sailboats drifting in the bay, their big sails billowing as they sliced through the steel blue water. If I felt energetic, I would stroll along the green lawn edging the marina, dodging bikers, joggers, and baby strollers until I reached the beach at Crissy Field.

I would dig my toes into the sand, inhale the crisp sea air, and listen to the gulls. An endless parade of people and dogs would walk past me while windsurfers in wet suits maneuvered their boards out in the waves. In the distance huge tankers and other ships passed beneath the rust-orange Golden Gate Bridge, and I wondered if my mother was in Hong Kong or Marseilles or some other exotic port where she would watch that same ship arrive.

As the weather turned chilly, I ventured down Fillmore only as far as Union or Chestnut streets, where I would grab a slice of pizza or see a movie before taking the bus back up the hill to my car.

Doing laundry became my Monday-night ritual, and sometimes I went to Brainwash, a combination Laundromat and coffeehouse. Afterward, I'd stop by Gloria's house to give Stella a hug and pick up my mail (mostly bills). There was never anything from my mother.

On weeknights I could go alone to the movies without being surrounded by couples. It was a great way to use two hours—four if I went to one of the discount theaters with double features. The Clay on Fillmore Street showed foreign and arty independent flicks. Proximity drew me there initially, but I astonished myself by starting to like the oddball films they showed. Once you get used to the subtitles, foreign films can be pretty cool, and they're a lot more inventive than Hollywood blockbusters.

I often went to the library where I could read and pretend to be a college student. I had never really appreciated libraries before—you can stay there for hours without anyone wondering who you are or what you're doing. And no one expects you to buy anything in a library.

One Thursday night in early October, I discovered a new way to spend my evenings. I was killing time in a bookstore near the Civic Center before catching the seven-thirty showing of a French film. As I was browsing through the new fiction table, I noticed a bunch of chairs arranged meeting-style in the rear section of the store. One of the sales clerks was bustling around, and I asked her what was going on.

"We're having a reading tonight," she enthused. "If you're interested, she's starting in a few minutes."

Why not? I had heard Malcolm and Patrick talking about "readings," and here was my chance to find out what it was all about. So I plunked myself down on a chair in the back. The author reading her book turned out to be surprisingly hip and funny. She was so entertaining that I passed up the movie. I almost bought her book, until I found out it was $26.

After that, I started looking for more bookstore events. In one week I heard about voodoo witch doctors, the history of perfume, and two cyclists who pedaled seven hundred miles through Tibet. Soon I found my taste in books radically altered. Before my mother's disappearance, I kept to romances or best sellers about beautiful jet-setters in love and in danger. But life had soured me on fairytale happy endings. Besides, I didn't want to be caught reading trash. One day in the coffeehouse, Malcolm noticed I was reading something called *Forbidden Desire,* and I was totally embarrassed to be exposed as some sort of starry-eyed dimwit.

After that, I picked up a recommended reading list for college freshman at the library and started reading books like *All the King's Men,* which was excellent, by the way. I wanted to be like Jack, the book's narrator, and go to sleep until all my problems went away. One year, two years, it didn't matter. I would have happily slept until my mother came back, however long it took.

On Saturdays I became a relentless seeker of free or inexpensive activities around the city, including museum shows, gallery openings, church concerts, and street fairs. Going to movies and running around town might sound exciting, but to be honest, there were many times when I longed to go home, put on my bathrobe, and relax in front of the TV set with Stella purring on my lap. That's what I missed most, the everyday stuff that you can do when you have a real home.

Each night I delayed it as long as I could, but eventually I had to go back to the camper. I would park my car, make sure no one was watching, and then dart inside. Stealthily I would pull on my sweats and crawl under the bedcovers. Despite my blankets and down comforter, the damp air seemed to seep into my bones. Sleeping in the camper was like sleeping inside a refrigerator, all hard edges and cold air.

All I could do was lie in the darkness, watching the lights of passing cars move across the walls until sleep came. Reading by flashlight was out because someone might notice the light. I felt like a solitary mouse hiding in her hole and quivering for fear a big, evil cat was waiting outside. Fear was my biggest problem. I was terrified of being discovered there alone in the darkness.

Finally I bought a switchblade at the hardware store and hid it under my pillow. Each night before going to sleep, I would grope beneath my pillow until I could feel the cold metal and reassure myself the knife was still there.

chapter seventeen

They want me to take these babies to a pox party. Can you believe it?" Bella announced as she maneuvered a massive stroller through the Madhouse door. With her booming voice, rosy face, and plus-sized body, Bella always seem to explode into a place, rather than merely enter it.

As usual, she was herding three-year-old Stephanie ahead of her while pushing seven-month-old Oliver inside what she called the baby barge. Bella was the live-in nanny for a rich Pacific Heights family, and she stopped by almost daily for coffee and conversation.

"Gracious. What on earth is a pox party?" exclaimed Evelyn. She scurried over to retrieve a drool-covered chew toy that Oliver decided to cast overboard on his voyage to the counter. Along with her nasty little dog, Evelyn doted on babies and children to a degree that I found slightly demented.

"I want a cookie with icing on it," Stephanie requested, looking up with her owlish eyes. "You promised, Bella."

"I did and you shall have one," said Bella soothingly, as she bent to unfasten Oliver from the many straps that held him captive. "A pox party is where you expose children to a child who has the chicken pox. You get your kiddies sick on purpose. Can you believe it?"

"I suppose they want to get it over with." I reached down to give Stephanie her cookie. "I know it's better to have chicken pox when you're young. One of the girls at my high school didn't get it until she was fifteen, and she was so sick that she ended up with scars."

Bella dismissed this notion with an exasperated wave. "No, no, they just want to make sure their travel plans don't get disrupted this winter. I said, 'Why not get the shots?' but they claim they have serious doubts about the safety of chicken-pox vaccinations. I just don't see the sense of it."

She took a deep breath, but before she could get the words out, I said them for her.

"But what do I know? I'm just the nanny," I chanted.

She grinned at me and I grinned back.

Bella had quickly become one of my favorites among the Madhouse customers. Unfortunately, like most of the coffeehouse regulars, Bella had no sense of style. She could have been a knockout if she lost a few pounds, got a great haircut, and bought some new clothes. The right makeup would do wonders for that ruddy complexion of hers. Instead, she didn't even wear lipstick, and her hair hung down her back in a braid.

When I started working at the coffeehouse, I had mentally dismissed Bella and the rest of the crowd as pathetic losers. Bella was frumpy. Evelyn dressed like a gypsy queen. Fireman

Tom favored baseball caps and Hawaiian shirts. And nerdy Jerry wore those camouflage pants every day.

The Madhouse regulars didn't drive Beamers; they drove old Toyotas or rode the bus. They didn't shop at Saks Fifth Avenue or Neiman Marcus and probably didn't know or care who Dolce & Gabbanna were. They didn't go on Caribbean cruises, or fly to Palm Springs for the weekend. None of them seemed to dream of owning a mansion, much less an American Express card.

I considered myself only temporarily poor, while these people didn't seem to have any ambitions and none of them seemed interested in living the lifestyle I sorely missed.

Take the soul sisters, as Malcolm teasingly referred to Aphrodite and her twin sister, Cassandra. They were nursing students who lived with their mother and sang in their church choir. While not typically pretty, they had glowing complexions and strong bodies and were always in training for some athletic event or other. I'll bet the two of them had never read *Vogue* magazine in all of their twenty-five years.

Since none of the employees or customers seemed to share my priorities, I thought it wise to keep my mouth shut. The same couldn't be said for the rest of them. Personal information flowed as freely as espresso at the Madhouse. Male or female, the coffeehouse regulars could outtalk any high school girl or suburban housewife. People shared their life stories even if no one wanted to listen. *Coffeehouse* seemed to mean "confessional" to them.

At first I thought the guys who rambled on and on were hitting on me. But it was women, too, and age didn't seem to be a factor. Young or old, gay or straight, everyone seemed to need someone to unload on.

I was making a latte for this guy—I'd never even seen him before—when he started telling me all about how his bride-to-be had cheated on him with his stepbrother, and her best friend had blabbed, resulting in an all-around family and nuptial meltdown.

After he left, I turned to Aphrodite and said, "What is it about me that makes all these sad sacks want to tell me about their romantic failures?"

Dee giggled and said, "It's not just you, girlfriend. I've heard stories that would curl your hair and make your eyes cross. From women, too, not just guys."

Malcolm overheard us and called, "I'm afraid it's not your obvious charms, girls. It's the venue. In a city like this, people need a place to spend time and find people who will listen when they talk. In a way we're like therapists here. Our little coffee clinic provides a spiritual home for those lonely souls who are short on friends and family in this cold and heartless metropolis."

I understood exactly what Malcolm was saying. All my human contact these days was with people at the Madhouse.

William called out, "Awww, you're making me cry. You wouldn't by chance be writing one of those sappy romances for women, would you, Mal?"

"Poor Willy, you don't have a drop of sentiment in you, do you?" said Patrick. " 'Twas a grand analogy. Where else can you find a kindly listener if not in an asylum? And this is the Madhouse, ain't it?"

"The doctor is in," I quipped. "Ready to dispense coffee and sympathy."

"I'll have some of both," said Patrick, giving me his crooked smile. I couldn't stop myself from smiling back.

But people didn't just pour their personal sagas into my ear. They also asked loads of personal questions—how old was I? Where did I live? Did I have brothers and sisters? I tried to avoid talking about myself, but the more evasive I was, the more questions were asked—it was just like high school! If you avoid answering questions, people tease you about being stuck-up, and the next thing you know, they're making stuff up.

So I lied. I made up answers to the most persistent questions, while trying to stick as close to the truth as possible.

I told everyone that my father died when I was young, and my mother died a few months ago in a car accident (Lie Number One). I claimed to live with my elderly aunt in her house in Burlingame (Lie Number Two). I also said that she was very religious and wouldn't allow me to invite friends over or even take phone calls there (Lie Number Three). Finally, I confided that I had a serious boyfriend named Webb who was away at college (Lie Number Four). In a year or so, when I had saved enough money, I planned to join Webb in San Diego (Lie Number Five).

Now all I had to do was keep all my lies straight.

. . .

Tattie came back from rehab at the beginning of October. She called several times and tried to persuade me to go out with her, but I put her off. I told her about my job at the Madhouse and said I was working a lot of hours—which was true, but not the reason I was avoiding her. If she found out where I was living, the news would be all over Burlingame. Tattie wasn't a gossip, exactly. She just didn't watch her tongue and would disclose the most embarrassing information about herself or anyone else without a second thought. If you complained, she would just shrug and say, "What's the big deal?"

I should have realized that Tattie wouldn't be easily discouraged. A few days after I blew off her last call, I looked up to see her strolling through the entrance of the Madhouse.

"Hey, girl, what's up?" she yelled from the doorway. She was wearing cowboy boots and a cropped leather jacket over an orange minidress that hugged every curve of her amazing figure. Every male in the place whirled around to stare at her.

"Tattie! What are you doing in this neighborhood?"

"I came to see what's keeping you so busy. So this is the place." She walked around the Madhouse, seemingly unconscious of all the eyeballs fastened on her. "Kind of a dump, isn't it?"

"It's all right." I shot her a warning look, but as usual, Tattie was oblivious to the hint. "You look great. Rehab must have agreed with you."

She had grown out her hair to chin-length and it was all one color, plus her eyebrow ring had vanished.

"Don't mention that shithole to me," she protested in a loud voice. "I just survived the longest thirty days of my life. Bor-ring with a capital *B.* No fun, no sex, just meetings and talk, talk, talk. What a drag. Watching TV was all the entertainment there was. The whole time I was there, the only date I had was with my finger."

She now had the undivided attention of every person, male and female, in the place. I was glad that Malcolm wasn't there because he would have rushed over to be introduced. Tattie was definitely Grade-A gossip material.

"It doesn't seem to have hurt you any. You look fantastic," I murmured, hoping she'd get the idea and lower hers.

"Thanks. Don't you love this dress?" She preened, twirling around for me and slipping off her jacket. "I'm going for a sophisticated look these days. Chic-*k*." She drew out the word and made a funny face as she said it. "They want me to look glam at the club."

"What club? Do you have a job?"

"Yep, I'm a working girl now. I've just started a great job. It's easy money, five hundred bucks a night, sometimes more."

"You're kidding," I said. "What kind of job pays that? It must be illegal."

She laughed and did a little mock shimmy. The bald man standing behind her looked like he might go into cardiac arrest.

"No, it's strictly legal. I'm a dancer—an exotic dancer actually. Isn't that a hoot?"

"Oh. My. God." I stared at her with my mouth open. "No way!"

"Way! I'm working on Broadway at the Toys for Boys Club. I dance topless and shake my tits for all the drooling businessmen. If they're extra nice and stuff lots of bills in my G-string, I do a special dance for them, up close and personal. I love it. I feel like a celebrity."

"You must be insane! Tattie, tell me you're joking."

"It is sooooo easy," she burbled on. "I can't believe how

lucky I am. I'm going to buy a new car, a convertible, as soon as I get my license back. And I'm getting an apartment."

"I can't believe this. Your mother must be having fits."

"Nope, she's down with it. She wants to get her hands on some of the money, but no way that's happening. That's why I'm moving into my own place."

She giggled again. "My stage name is Precious. I strut around in this Catholic schoolgirl uniform with knee socks and everything, then I strip down to a G-string. The guys all have their tongues hanging out by the time I'm finished."

"That's disgusting. What's wrong with you?" The words rushed out of me. "You can't do this."

"The hell I can't," she said, starting to look annoyed. "Why are you being so negative? I'll bet I make ten times what you earn in this dump."

"Hey, can I get a double cappuccino?" The bald guy had come out of his Tattie-induced trance to interrupt us.

"Wait your turn," I said. "Or go to Starbucks. Tattie, do you have any idea of the horrible people you'll be dealing with?"

She snorted. "What are you talking about? These people are no different from the hypocrites in Burlingame. I'm taking advantage of my natural assets to make some money. You're just jealous."

"Jealous," I repeated, in true amazement.

"You don't have to be, Ashley," she said coaxingly. "You'd be great at this. I could fix it up for you, and you'd be raking in money too."

"Never," I snapped. "No way. How did you ever get mixed up in this?"

"I was just walking by one of those clubs on Broadway late one night, and one of the barkers—you know those guys who stand out front and try to coax guys inside—well, he said, 'Hey, baby. Wanna job? I'd like to see you dance.' I just laughed, but the next day, I got to thinking about it. So I called up the club and the guy told me to come try out on amateur night. I did and they liked me. Now I'm a star."

"So you dance around nearly naked for a bunch of disgusting old men? What's next? Become a hooker?" I scolded her. "Good luck, Miss Tatiana, because you're going to need it."

Tattie narrowed her eyes angrily. "Who do you think you are?" She spat the words out. "I don't need you judging me. I'm doing great."

We stared at each other for a moment in silence. Then she spat, "Fuck you!" and stalked out, leaving the whole coffeehouse staring after her.

I stood there dazed both by what she'd told me and by my fierce reaction to the news. Maybe I had overreacted. Tattie and I had always gotten along because I never judged her. When had I turned into a goodie-goodie? But a stripper! What was the future in that? She was making a big mistake, and someone had to bring her to her senses. That's what friends are supposed to do, isn't it?

"I think you're absolutely right," said the bald man.

"Keep your opinions to yourself." I growled. "Go sit down and I'll bring you a cappuccino."

I felt disoriented, as if I were a movie heroine watching everyone around me turn into zombies. Maybe someone had put chemicals into the water system, because first my mother and now Tattie had completely lost their marbles. Here I was, lying to everyone and hiding out so I could keep up the appearance of being a normal person while everyone else was flipping out.

chapter eighteen

As October plodded along, I continued looking for some scrap of news about my mother. Nothing ever appeared. Don't ever let anyone try to tell you that no news is good news.

While the newspaper didn't reveal anything about Diane, I felt overwhelmed by the amount of bizarre or lurid or just plain bad news that appeared on a daily basis. Two teenagers were killed in a high-speed car chase. A young boy disappeared on his way home from school. A pedestrian was struck down in the crosswalk on a busy street.

There seemed to be no end to the tragedies that could befall you. Without warning you could be struck by lightning or shot by a madman. Or you could throw your suitcase in your car, drive away, and never be heard from again. Could I, too, disappear beneath dark water without creating so much as a ripple.

At the Madhouse I went through the motions, working and talking to the customers, even laughing and flirting with Patrick. But keeping secrets is hard work. I could never completely relax or let down my guard. I felt as if there were a glass wall separating me from everyone else. On my side of the wall I could observe everyone and everything that went on around me, but I could never break through the glass and be truly part of things.

Earl was the only person I could really talk to. He worked the night shift at the gas station so I couldn't hide my predicament from him even if I tried. Each night, he sat in the station's tiny "office" with a hissing space heater at his feet and collected cash from customers who didn't use credit cards.

When I first moved into the camper, all I knew about him was that he had worked there for a couple of years. I had a vague impression of a stumpy old man who wore a dark cap and a puffy brown jacket. At first I just waved to him each night as I pulled my car behind the station. As I crawled into bed, it was nice knowing that *someone* was out there, at least part of the night.

Then, one Friday night not long after I had gone two rounds with Tattie, Earl knocked on the camper door. I had just stepped inside and knew it must be him, so I opened the door.

"How d'ya do, miss?" he said. "I'm Earl Yankowski."

Up close, I saw that he had the leathery skin and creased face of someone who had spent years in the sun and wind. His gray hair was cropped close to his head, which made his wiry gray eyebrows more noticeable.

"Hi, Earl," I said. "I'm Ashley."

"Pleased to meet you," he said. "I don't mean to bother you, but I saw when you pulled in that your left front tire is real low. You should have Reynaldo fix it tomorrow before you leave. I'd take care of it for you myself, if it weren't for this bum arm."

I noticed for the first time that he held his left arm stiffly as if it were injured.

"Thanks for telling me," I said. "I'll talk to Reynaldo."

"You might want to think about getting some new tires," he added. "Your tread is pretty far gone on all of them. I looked."

"What!" I winced in dismay. "You must be kidding. All of them?"

He nodded confirmation.

"No, I can't be that unlucky. That will cost a fortune."

"It will set you back about a hundred each, including balancing, but driving on them the way they are is just plain asking for trouble. Buying four tires is still cheaper than a funeral," he said. "Phil could help you find some cheap."

I made a face. "I'd really rather not ask him."

"No?" he said. "Well . . . tell you what, I'll see what I can do for you."

When I came home the next night, I found a note from Earl stuck to the camper door. It said: *Go see Chet at Baker's Tires in San Bruno and tell him Earl sent you. He'll give you a good price.*

I did, and his pal Chet sold me four tires for $300, plus tax.

For weeks after that I would occasionally find little "gifts" on my windshield—a coupon for a free coffee at Starbuck's, a toy whistle, a tiny pumpkin, a silly little windup frog someone had probably left in the gas station.

I should have had the good manners to thank Earl right away, but I didn't. I had a bad case of the mean blues or whatever it's called when you feel like both crying and giving someone a good smacking. Rage and hurt had grown inside me until they were like evil twins, first one and then the other poking at me like a sharp stick. I struggled to keep it bottled up. This wasn't what my life was supposed to be like, and it wasn't fair.

Insomnia began to visit me on a nightly basis. I would toss and turn in my hard, narrow bed for hours. A week of sleepless nights had me lurching around like a zombie. By Friday of that week, I climbed into my nest determined to will myself to sleep, but it just didn't work. After an hour, I gave up. I put on my trench coat over my sweats and went outside.

As I stepped out of the camper and walked around the corner of the building, I saw a full moon suspended in the night sky. It was huge, a moon made for yowling. Maybe that's why I hadn't been able to get to sleep. I needed to yowl.

It was almost midnight. Earl was sitting in his chair reading as I walked in. The nasal twang of Willie Nelson singing "Angel flying too close to the ground" was coming from a small radio on the shelf.

Earl didn't seem greatly surprised to see me. He took off his reading glasses, stood up, and got a chair for me so we both could sit in front of his little space heater.

"I wanted to thank you for the tires and the gifts," I said awkwardly. "I really appreciate it. I'm sorry I didn't say something before."

"No problem. Glad to be of help," he answered. "You didn't have to come out here to tell me that."

"Really, I should have thanked you before now," I said, and

then admitted, "Anyway, I'm restless tonight. I haven't been sleeping very well."

"I know how that feels. That's the reason I took this job in the first place. I've always been a night owl so I thought I might as well get paid for staying up."

"What are you reading?" I asked, pointing to the book he had put down when I walked in.

"A mystery—that's the kind of book I like best," he said.

"I don't know why, I never really cared for mysteries."

"They're my favorites. A mystery is like a puzzle that needs solving."

"I've got a puzzle you can solve. Figure out where my mother is and why she did this to me," I blurted out in a bitter voice.

After a moment's silence, Earl said, "You sound like someone who needs to talk. I'm a good listener."

"I don't know what you mean," I answered, and then horrified myself by bursting into tears. I cried until I was drowning in tears. Earl didn't say a word. He just sat there quietly, handing me tissues from his drawer.

Finally, my downpour began to let up.

"This is so stupid and childish," I hiccupped, blowing my nose loudly and then dropping the gooey tissue into the wastebasket beside my chair. "I don't know what's the matter with me. You must think I'm crazy, bawling like this in front of you."

"It's not so crazy. You're hurting," he said matter-of-factly. "It happens to everybody sooner or later, even old coots like me."

I sniffed some more and began twisting and tearing the tissue in my hands.

"Why don't you tell me about it?" he said.

All my defenses were down, and I began hemorrhaging everything I had been keeping inside me. I ranted about my mother and all the drama that had occurred over the last five months. It was such a relief to let it out.

Luckily, it was late, so there weren't any customers to interrupt me. But at one point, I caught a glimpse of a red Mustang pulling up in front of the pumps and I heard a car door slam.

"Wait back there," Earl whispered, motioning toward the service bays, and I ducked out of sight.

After the car pulled away, I came back inside and flopped down into the chair.

"What was that all about?" I asked, raising my eyebrows.

"It's very late," he said. "Human nature being what it is, it's better if we don't put temptation in anyone's way. There are some wicked people out there, and you're too pretty for your own good."

I was touched that he wanted to protect me, especially since he looked more like Superman's crusty old grandpa than a superhero. In fact, Earl looked like someone who had broken a few laws and raised a little hell in his time and that made him eligible to understand my situation. I couldn't talk to normal people with happy families. Someone like that couldn't begin to understand the hole I had fallen into.

Finally, I dried up and wound down. For a few minutes the two of us just sat there in silence, listening to the crackle of the space heater in the corner.

Then Earl surprised me by saying, "Tell me about your mother."

"What?"

"You've told me what your mother has done. Now tell me what she's like."

"What do you mean? She's like a mother."

"Mothers are people too. Describe her. I'll bet you look a lot like her."

I thought about it. "Yeah, we have the same dark hair and hazel eyes, but she's shorter than me and a little heavier. Still, she looks good for her age. I always tell her she should wear clothes with more pizzazz. I love red, it makes you stand out. Diane wears a lot of navy blue. Dull, dull, dull, I tell her."

"So she's the quiet type who cooks and sews and takes care of you?"

"She doesn't sew, not anymore." I laughed at the idea. "She used to knit sweaters for me and make me dresses, but she stopped after I started refusing to wear the goofy little outfits she made. Before Jimmy—my jackass father—died, she cooked a lot, but I'm not a big eater, and I don't want pies and rib roasts and stuff like that. Really, it's just easier to order a pizza or eat Lean Cuisine."

"So what does she do?" He kept feeding me questions.

"Who knows what she's doing now." I paused, thinking about it. "She used to work a lot. She likes to read, mostly romance novels, and dig around in the yard, planting tulips and primroses. She loves flowers."

"She sounds nice."

"She's too nice—that's her biggest problem. She gets all teary when she reads something sad in the newspaper. She buys Girl Scout cookies that we'll never eat because she can't say no to the cute little girls knocking on the door. She's the world's biggest sucker. Anyone can manipulate her, including, no, especially me."

"That's not the worst fault I've ever heard," he suggested, leaning back in his chair and clasping his hands behind his head.

"Maybe not." I grimaced. "When I was little, I thought she was perfect. But as I got older, I saw the stupid way she acted around Jimmy. She was so much smarter and better than him, but she knuckled under to whatever he wanted. I lost respect for her, watching him wipe his feet on her." I broke off. "Why are you asking me so many questions about her?"

"I'm interested. You've told me all the stuff you don't like. Don't you think it's a good idea to remember the good things too? Tell me what you liked about her."

"There's the niceness, I told you about that. And she believes in good manners. I'm not talking about etiquette and using the right fork, I mean not calling people names or being rude—that kind of manners."

I smiled to myself, remembering. "She's sort of a neat freak too. She straightens up the magazine racks while she's waiting in line at the supermarket. She always says you should leave a place better than you found it. Once we went on a picnic and she picked up trash—not just ours, but the stuff that other people had left behind. I told her that she couldn't clean up the whole world and she said, 'But I can try.' "

My voice trailed off as all the memories came back to me. I wasn't feeling angry anymore, just exhausted and sad.

"So did your mother do all this to you out of meanness, or did she just make a mistake?"

I sighed. "Of course, she just made a mistake, a really big mistake. I know she loves me and didn't mean to ruin my life. But she did. And where is she? Why doesn't she come home?"

"Sometimes coming home is the hardest thing to do, baby doll," Earl said. He stood up and rubbed his bad arm. "Anyway, it's time to close up. I should have shut the station a half hour ago. I'm an old man and I need to go home."

I stood up too and gave him a wan smile. "Thanks for giving me a shoulder to cry on."

"Anytime, anytime. My life isn't that exciting, so I'm happy to hear about yours."

I chuckled, said good night, and went back to the camper. That night I slept like a baby who had worn herself out throwing the world's biggest tantrum. Apparently, hysterical outbursts and crying jags are better than sleeping pills, because I felt amazingly calm and rested the next day.

After that, I began to wander out for late-night conversations with Earl once or twice a week. I didn't always do all the talking. Over time he managed to get a word in edgewise. I learned that he grew up in Nevada and had traveled the world in the merchant marine. He'd married and been divorced twice. Now he lived with his daughter, a single mom with two kids, a few miles south in San Mateo.

Earl didn't watch as many movies as I did, but he liked to read, so we talked a lot about books. He liked to describe the elaborate plots of spy novels and thrillers to me, and I would tease him that all those conspiracies gave him a suspicious nature.

"Nope, I'm not suspicious, just watchful," he replied. "We all need to be watchful. The world can be a surprising place."

"Surprising!" I hooted. "It's shocking and confusing and downright loony. I used to think I knew everything, and now I don't understand one damn thing about life or people, even my mother, the one person I thought I knew better than anyone. It scares me."

"Don't worry. Old Earl will keep an eye on you till you get it all figured out again."

"My hero!" I giggled, giving him an affectionate smile. "Earl, why are you so nice to me?"

He snorted as if to dispel any notion that he was nice. "Please, I'm no hero. Just ask my daughter. I wasn't around much when Teresa needed a father, and she got into a whole lot of trouble. She married a real dirtbag, and now she's trying to bring up two kids alone. Maybe you're my way of payback—you know, fixing my karma or whatever they call it. What goes around, comes around. One of these days it'll be your turn to help someone."

"I'm a mess! How could I help anyone? I feel like I have one foot on a banana peel."

In fact, I had been worrying lately that Phil might decide to toss me out of the camper. I felt sick to my stomach at the very thought of moving out of my hidey-hole. Much as I hated it, at least I knew what to expect and how to cope. What if some worse disaster lay in store for me when I moved on?

Sleeping in the camper wasn't so frightening when Earl was around. He chased away the bogeymen, and I appreciated the fact that he never offered me any fake sympathy. Instead of giving advice, Earl liked to offer up what he called platitudes. He collected memorable quotations from the books he read and had an appropriate one for every occasion. "Forgive your enemies, but never forget their names" was one he particularly liked. Earl said that one came from President Kennedy.

Another favorite was: "We are what we pretend to be."

I argued with him about that one, contending that pretending to be smart didn't make you smart.

"Well, now, maybe that's true," he mused. "But doesn't it make you smarter than pretending to be dumb?"

"I don't know about that. It seems to me that for centuries women have succeeded by playing dumb. Look at Marilyn Monroe."

"She pretended to be dumb and that made her dumb or else she *was* dumb," Earl answered. "A smart woman doesn't kill herself over some love affair gone wrong. Learn from her mistake. There's no man worth killing yourself over."

"Don't worry," I assured him. "I'm way smarter than that."

During another late-night visit, I told Earl about how I wanted to live like a normal person.

"Describe a normal person for me, baby doll. I don't think I've ever met one," Earl said. "There's an old saying . . ."

"Not another old saying," I groaned.

"Yup. Are you listening?" He grinned at me. "The only normal people are the ones you don't know very well."

chapter nineteen

I rolled over, groaning as I slammed my knee against the hard metal back of the camper's sleeping platform. Rain was hammering the roof and I shivered at the sound. The rumbling of cars and trucks surging down the streets signaled it was time to get up.

Although eight weeks had elapsed since I began living here, I still loathed waking up in the cold camper. The past week of nonstop rain wasn't helping my mood. Not only was I sick of the soggy weather, I was just plain tired. Three nights in a row I had stayed up late gabbing with Earl. Now my lack of sleep was catching up to me.

By the time I got to the coffeehouse, I was admittedly grouchy. I lurched around the place trying to keep up with the chaos caused by the early-bird coffee crowd. It was a relief when the pace finally slowed. Then, as I bent over to pick up a dirty cup from one of the coffeehouse tables, I felt a hand on my back.

Snap! The elastic from my bra made an audible noise as it cracked against my bare skin.

I flinched and whirled around. Jerry was standing there, grinning at me. I reached over and slapped his computer-geek face.

All nine or so of the people in the Madhouse stopped what they were doing to stare at us.

"It was just a joke," Jerry mumbled.

I grabbed the dirty cup and marched past him to the counter, then turned back to hiss, "Save your junior high school tricks for someone else. And stop watching me all the time."

From the corner I could hear Mal laughing, of course. Mal always enjoyed any drama unfolding in his establishment.

Jerry flushed red and sputtered, "What?"

My lip curled at the sight of his stricken expression. Didn't the guy have any pride?

"Look, I know you watch me, and I want it to stop. It's extremely annoying."

"Jerry, my boy," Mal drawled. "Your obvious appreciation of our lovely Ashley seems to be having a detrimental effect on her disposition."

"I'm not watching you," Jerry denied without conviction, then added, "At least, well, it's just that you're so . . . interesting."

I snorted. "Yeah, I'm a regular Einstein. I'm sure you're watching my mind. News flash, Jerry: You're not my type."

"You hear that, Jerry? Don't expect any mercy or sympathy from this girl," Mal interjected. "Fill us in, Ashley. Tell us all about your type of man. What is the way to Ashley Mitchell's heart?"

Mal's wisecracks were like a sudden splash of cold water in my face.

"I don't think that's anything I want to share," I said, giving

Mal a stern look. I turned to Jerry and lowered my voice. "I don't want to be a complete bitch, all right? Just give me a break. Keep your hands, your eyes, and your practical jokes to yourself."

Jerry nodded sheepishly and looked down at his feet. He muttered, "Sorry," and fled out the front door.

Both Mal and I stared after him, me in chagrin and Mal in amusement.

"Uh-oh. Maybe I overreacted," I said.

"Don't worry," Mal retorted. "Jerry is embarrassed, but he'll get over it. The lad is a computer genius, but he's socially challenged. You had every right to call him on his inappropriate behavior. However, try not to make a practice of driving paying customers out of the coffeehouse."

"Like we could drive Jerry away with a stick," I said, smiling at the absurdity of it. Mal chuckled and picked up his newspaper to resume reading.

I stood there a moment and then darted into the tiny restroom. I paused to look in the mirror, staring at Ashley Mitchell—bitch, barista, and love object for dorks.

At least part of my outburst had been frustration that Jerry, rather than Patrick, was enamored with me. The charming Irishman seemed immune to my charms. He flirted and joked but never asked me out. At least no one knew about my infatuation. Mal had a sort of radar about that kind of thing, but so far he hadn't caught on.

A few days after my skirmish with Jerry, I overheard a conversation that gave me some insight into Patrick. Malcolm and Patrick were talking about their writing class. William was there as well, but Jerry wasn't in the coffeehouse and that allowed me to move close enough to eavesdrop.

"That piece you read on Tuesday was your best ever, Mal. I could practically taste the malt whiskey sliding down my throat," Patrick said.

"Thank you, dear boy," retorted Mal with a pleased smile. "As you are a master of sensory description I consider that a real tribute."

"So this guy really writes?" interjected William, leaning over to gesture with his thumb toward Malcolm. "I thought he was slinging the bull."

"That's the sign of a good storyteller, William. As my dear departed mother used to say," quipped Mal, "if a liar repeats a story often enough, he begins to believe it himself."

"You know, Mal, we hear a great deal about your dear departed mother," William said. "What about your father? Like all the rest of us, you must have had one."

Malcolm raised one eyebrow. "Not to hear my mother tell it. She liked to pretend that she did it all by herself. When I was growing up, both sex and my father were verboten subjects. He vanished before I was born, never to be heard from again. Maybe he was gay. Or maybe she drove him crazy. She often had that effect on me. At least I never had to endure the cliché of the outraged father who rejects his gay son."

"Fathers have expectations," Patrick said. "At least you didn't have to worry about letting yours down."

"What's the matter, Patrick? The old man doesn't like having a skirt-chasing, poetry-quoting n'er-do-well for a son?" William jeered.

"My father's a doctor, and he wanted me to study medicine or science, not history."

"You studied history?" said Mal in surprise. "I didn't know that. I would have thought, with your gifts and love of poetry, you would have pursued writing and literature."

"Ah, well, what is history except true stories? Some are exciting, some are dull, and most defy logic. But they're all human and complicated. And they don't have the tidy, predictable endings that fiction gives you. I figured studying literature would teach me to write just like the other fellows, while studying history would give me insight into people and events."

Patrick leaned forward, absently running the fingers of his right hand through his hair. "My dad claims history just shows people making the same mistakes without learning a damn thing from the past. He believes that only scientists truly change the world for the better."

"What about writers? What about Shakespeare and Dickens and all the great poets?" I interjected myself into the conversation without being invited.

"Ah, but did they change the world or merely record what happened? I'm not saying that I agree, I'm just repeating my father's view of it all. I love words, not empirical data. I don't have the knack for scientific research."

"Still, I envy you your relationship with your father," mused Mal. "I always thought it would have been nice to have a normal family."

"*Normal* isn't the word I'd use to describe my tribe," said Patrick.

"I have a friend who says that the only normal people are the ones you don't know very well," I said.

Both Mal and Patrick chuckled

"I think your friend may have something there," Patrick said. 'I never know how to define normal."

"I do," Mal said with an emphatic air. "Normal is what I approve of or what I do. Everything else is abnormal or, at the very least, in very poor taste."

At that moment, the phone rang, and I moved behind the counter to answer it. A woman's voice asked if she could speak to Patrick Rigney.

"Just a minute," I said.

Malcolm raised an eyebrow quizzically. I said, "It's for Patrick. A woman."

Patrick and Mal exchanged a look, then Mal said, "Tell her he's not here."

I repeated his words into the receiver and hung up.

"It was Jeanne and she wants you to call her."

"Oh, God, will that woman never leave off?" groaned Patrick.

"You've no one to blame but yourself," Mal scolded him with a mocking air. "My dear boy, you are your own worst enemy. You let these situations drift along and suddenly find yourself ensnared in romantic catastrophe."

"Hold on. I'm an innocent man. I never made a pass, much less a commitment of any sort, to Jeanne. I never proposed or discussed marriage with Caitlin. As for Lynda, well, I'm only human. But I start out having a little frolic with a girl, and before you know it, she's saying she loves me and is making plans. I've never pretended I was a marrying man. What more can I do—wear a sign?"

"Maybe you should." Mal stood up and walked over to refill his coffee cup. "You smile at them, flatter them, quote poetry, and otherwise get their love-starved hearts fluttering wildly. You're every woman's dream—just like the hero of a romance novel. No wonder they start weaving romantic fantasies about you. You need to belch, scratch your privates, get sloppy drunk, and stay glued to the sports channel. In other words, be the typical unattached American male."

William snorted. "Yeah. Start wearing a baseball cap and calling every girl 'Babe.' They'll run away screaming."

"What you're *supposed* to do is tell them the truth *before* they begin weaving fantasies!" The words burst out of me.

The three of them stared up at me in amazement.

"Whoa," Mal started to protest, but I kept right on talking.

"I hate people who lie and then claim they're trying to protect you," I sputtered. "They're the worst kind of cowards because you end up being more hurt than if they'd just been honest in the first place."

"You sound as if you've had personal experience with this problem, Ashley. Care to elaborate?" Mal added in obvious amusement.

"No!" I said tartly, then took a deep breath and added in a calmer tone, "I'm not talking just about boy-girl stuff. It applies to any relationship. It could be your mother . . . or . . . or anyone who's important to you. Lying to keep people from being mad at you is really only protecting yourself. Even if you want to tell them the truth, in the end it could be too late."

"Listen to her," William interjected, "she's pretty smart for a sweet young thing."

"I'm not all that sweet," I said.

"No, you're not, are you?" Patrick flashed his crooked grin, making my pulse gallop. "But you're probably right. Maybe I have caused harm by drifting along and not making myself plain. I'll take your advice. I wouldn't want you thinking I'm a pathetic dog who needs a kind word and a pat from every passerby. I can take a kick now and then."

"Careful," Mal warned him. "Ashley here sounds as if she'd be happy to administer a few swift kicks."

They had no idea. I'd be happy to give him a few good kicks, and a few kisses, too.

chapter twenty

Fog often creeps over the Golden Gate Bridge and oozes across the water until the bay and Alcatraz Island are swathed in a fluffy white blanket. Sometimes, though not often, the fog will move inland, twisting and creeping up the hills and through the streets until everything is swallowed up in it.

It was late on a Friday night when I drove toward Burlingame through a heavy, inland-floating fog. Everything had a dreamlike quality, and all the other cars on the road seemed to appear and then disappear into the mist. The gas station was an oasis of light in the dense vapor. As I pulled my car in, I waved to Earl and went straight into the camper.

For once, sleep came easily. I don't know how long I had been asleep when my dream morphed into a delusion that I was back home in my white wicker bed. Stella was scratching at my door. *Scratch, scratch. Rattle, rattle.* "Go away, you crazy cat," I started to say, and then suddenly I was wide-awake.

It wasn't a dream. Someone was rattling the door latch to

the camper, and it definitely wasn't Stella. Someone was trying to get inside.

I didn't move—I couldn't. I just stared at the handle as it twisted back and forth in the darkness, too frightened to even take a breath. My heart pounded so loudly I thought it was audible. *Who was out there?* I knew it couldn't be Earl because he would have knocked. Earl would have called my name.

In blind panic I thrust my hand under my pillow for my knife. As I groped wildly for the familiar cold metal handle and flipped it open, I sliced my forefinger on the sharp edge. A scream welled up in my throat and I bit my lip hard to smother it. My finger throbbed in pain and I could feel blood oozing out of the cut.

Bam! The unknown invader jerked the door *hard,* trying to force it open. The door shuddered, but it didn't open.

The darkness seemed heavy and oppressive, almost a physical entity threatening me. I tried to control my panic, putting one hand against my mouth while I clutched the knife in the other. I thought my heart would explode out of my chest.

Bam! The door shuddered again.

Bam, bam, bam, bam, BAM! The invader frantically tried to open the door. It took all my willpower to keep from screaming in terror.

Then the noise stopped.

I listened, willing the invader to go away, still constricting my breath for fear of being heard. I thought I heard shoes scraping on the cement. I stayed frozen on my bed, waiting and listening. Three minutes passed or maybe five. It seemed like an eternity. A car engine started and I heard a car pull away. It was so quiet I could hear the faint buzz of the station's fluorescent lights.

Still, I waited, like a rabbit in its hole, too terrified to come out and make sure the hound had left for good. All the time I kept wondering, Where is Earl?

Finally, I got my courage up and crawled out of the sleeping compartment. I peeked out the camper window. All I could see were halos of light circling the station's floodlights amid the dense fog.

I quietly slipped on a raincoat and thrust some shoes on my feet.

Gently I unlocked the door. The *click* as the lock opened sent an electric shock up my spine.

My heart thumping, I stepped outside. The damp air made everything look hazy.

"Earl?" I called out in a low voice. There wasn't any answer.

As I crept toward the front of the station, I saw that something was holding the door to the men's room open. A shoe?

I walked over and gingerly pushed on the door. Earl was sprawled on the tile floor, not moving, a bloody gash visible on the side of his head.

"Earl," I called, struggling to keep my terror under control. "Oh, God, Earl! Can you hear me?"

I knelt and touched his neck. He was still warm. But he didn't answer or move. I darted around the building and into the office to call 911.

"I need an ambulance right away." I was close to hysteria.

"At the Shell Station on El Camino and Burlingame Avenue. Hurry! Someone's hurt."

"Is this a police emergency or a medical emergency, ma'am?" The operator answered me in a calm voice.

"I—I d-don't know." I was stuttering. "Both. Earl is bleeding and I don't know what happened to him. Please, you have to hurry."

"I'm dispatching an emergency vehicle now to your location. They'll be on the scene in five minutes," she said. "Try to remain calm. Is the patient breathing?"

"I don't know. He felt warm, but his head is bleeding."

"Is he conscious?"

"N-no," I stammered. "Please hurry. I'm scared."

"It's going to be okay. Try to stay calm, miss. What's your name?"

"Ashley," I said.

"It's going to be all right, Ashley. Who is injured? Your boyfriend? Your brother?"

"A friend," I said.

"How old is your friend?"

"Old," I said. "I don't know—about seventy."

"Do you know what happened? Did he fall or could he have had a heart attack?"

"I don't know, I don't know." I was gripping the phone receiver as if it somehow were holding me upright. "I think someone may have hit him."

"Take it easy, Ashley. Try to stay calm. Can you check his breathing and see if his airway needs clearing?"

"How do I do that?" I said doubtfully, but before I could move, I heard the sound of a siren. I dropped the phone to dash outside. A fire-department rescue truck pulled up in front.

"He's around here," I motioned as two men in heavy black-and-yellow jackets jumped down from the truck. Laden with equipment, they rushed around the corner toward the men's restroom. One of them went inside and crouched beside Earl.

"He's breathing, but it's shallow," I heard him call to his partner, and I almost collapsed on the pavement from relief.

In the distance I heard a second siren, and within seconds a police car pulled up. Out of it jumped my old tormentor, Officer Strobel.

He looked at me, then walked over to talk in a low voice to the paramedics.

"Will he be all right?" I interrupted them. "Is he going to be okay?"

"They're going to transport him to a hospital as soon as an ambulance gets here," Strobel said. "Why don't we get out of their way?"

His hand closed on my arm like a vise as he led me into the office. The cash drawer was hanging open. It was empty.

"What happened here, Ashley? Was there a robbery?"

"I don't know," I gasped. "I was looking for Earl and I found him in the men's room, just lying there with his head bleeding. I don't know if he fell or if someone hit him. I was afraid he was dead. He's not going to die, is he?"

"They're taking good care of him. But I need you to tell me who did this. What were you doing here at this hour? How do you know Earl?"

I started to cry, and Strobel half led, half pushed me into a chair.

"I need a handkerchief," I mumbled. He rummaged through the desk and pulled out a box of tissues. As I wiped at my tears and blew my nose, my brain whirled, trying to come up with a credible story about why I was here. I didn't want to tell Strobel that I slept in the camper if I could help it.

"All right, can you tell me what happened now?"

I nodded and began, just slightly bending the facts. "I stopped by, you know, to see Earl. I didn't see him in the office when I pulled in, but I thought he was in the back or something. After I parked, I was walking past the men's room and I saw him lying there. When I realized he was unconscious, I called 911."

"What about the cash drawer?"

"I didn't even notice it until now."

"So you didn't see anyone here? No cars were pulling out as you pulled in?"

"No, I didn't see anything. No one was here."

"Did you touch anything?"

"Earl. And the phone. Maybe the desk when I called."

"The cash drawer?"

"No, I told you, I didn't notice it was open."

"Good, maybe we can get some prints off of it."

I thought of the hand yanking on the camper's door latch and then thrust it out of my mind. I wasn't going to bring the camper to his attention, no matter what.

"What happened to your hand? Is that Earl's blood?"

I looked down at my hand. It was bloody from the knife cut. I stared at it without answering.

"Tell me why you're here, Ashley. This is an odd hour to make a social call. Why did you park your car in the back?"

"Earl's a friend of mine," I said. "I stop by sometimes to talk to him. He likes me to park back there, out of the way."

"You and Earl are friends?"

"Yeah," I retorted. "Why is that so hard to understand? He's a nice old man. And you know very well that my mother's boyfriend owns this gas station. I know everyone who works here."

Suddenly, I thought of Phil.

"Oh, God, I better call Phil and tell him about this."

"Yeah, do that. Tell him we need him to come down here," he said. "I'll find out how Earl is doing. What's his last name?"

"Yankowski," I said. "He lives with his daughter and her kids in San Mateo. I don't know the address."

Strobel nodded and went back to confer with the firemen. I dialed Phil's number. Luckily, he answered right away, and I told him about Earl as well as the story I had concocted for Strobel. He said he'd be right down.

By the time Phil got there, the ambulance had already left with Earl in the back. I sat in the office, listening to Strobel question Phil about the amount of cash that might have been in the drawer. Finally, I interrupted them.

"Listen, can I go to the hospital? I'm worried about Earl."

Phil stared at me as if I had suddenly grown a second head or third eye, but he didn't say a word.

"All right, go ahead," Strobel said. "Just leave me your address and phone number so I can get in touch if I have more questions."

I gave him Gloria's address and the number of my cell phone.

"I'd like a word with you, Ashley," Phil finally spoke up.

"I'll come by here tomorrow, after I find out how Earl is doing," I said, giving him a look that I hoped said, *Keep your mouth shut.*

As I turned to leave, Strobel said, "You know, it's lucky you stopped by here tonight. He might have bled to death before someone found him."

I shuddered and walked away.

. . .

At the hospital, no one would tell me anything because I stupidly admitted that I was a friend and not a relative. Some officious clerk kept asking me whether Earl had any insurance. As if I knew! She couldn't seem to think about anything except whether they were going to get paid, never mind that someone's life was in jeopardy. I told her so in a scornful voice, and we took turns glaring at each other. I grudgingly gave her Phil's phone number but refused to stop badgering her about Earl's condition.

I must have worn her down because she disappeared into the back and a nurse emerged to tell me that Earl was stable and I should go home.

Minutes later the insurance queen returned to her chair and began shooting hateful looks at me from behind her desk. Just to make it clear she wasn't driving me away, I lingered in the waiting room, enjoying their hard little chairs and fluorescent lights for a few more minutes as I debated where to go.

Finally, I went back to my car and drove around aimlessly. It was almost two in the morning—too late to check into a motel. Anyway, without a credit card, no one would rent me a room.

Every muscle and joint in my body ached all of a sudden. I needed to lie down somewhere, anywhere. I drove through the dark, foggy streets and somehow ended up in front of Gloria's house. I parked at the curb and stared at the darkened windows. No one stirred. I couldn't wake them all up, and what would I say if I did? I gave up, slumped over on the front seat, and fell into a deep, dreamless sleep.

. . .

I woke up to the banging and clanging sound of the garbage truck. Stiff and dazed, I sat up and looked at my watch. It was nearly seven. Soon the whole neighborhood would be peering out their windows and wondering whose car was parked outside. If Gloria spotted my car, she would come out to interrogate me. I didn't feel any more prepared to answer questions today than I had last night. I quickly started my car and drove back to the gas station. Everything looked normal, and Phil's truck wasn't anywhere in sight.

Bolting inside the camper to grab some clothes and makeup, I was back out in seconds. Still, Reynaldo managed to waylay me as I was throwing stuff into the backseat of my car.

"Hey, Ash-lee, Phil is looking for you. He wants you to call him right away."

"Yeah, I know. I'll call him."

"We were robbed last night, while you were gone?" He made the last part sound like a question.

"Do you know how Earl is?" I asked.

"Phil talked to the hospital. Earl had a concussion and bruised ribs, but they let him go home. Maybe his guardian angel was watching over him last night."

"That's wonderful," I said with real relief, feeling as if an immense weight had been lifted off my chest. I could breathe normally again. Maybe everything really would be all right. I moved into the driver's seat. "I have to hurry or I'll be late for work. Tell Phil I'll call him later."

I lied, of course. Saturday was my day off. I didn't know where I was headed, but I didn't want to talk to Phil yet. He would want me to move out, and I had to figure out how to persuade him to let me stay. As frightening as staying in the camper now seemed, being tossed out was even more terrifying. Surely I could get a better lock for the door or maybe even a heavy metal chain. Phil *had* to let me stay. Where else could I go?

chapter twenty-one

After a quick shower at the health club, I called Reynaldo to get Earl's home address. I needed to see for myself that he was all right, and find out exactly what story he told the cops.

Earl's place turned out to be a small frame duplex in the "less expensive" section of San Mateo. Still, the building was painted a friendly yellow and the yard was tidy. I knocked on the door and heard him call, "It's open."

As I opened the door, I saw him propped up on a tweed sofa watching a rerun of *Law and Order.* He was pale and had a bandage on his head and another on his chest. "Hey, you don't look too bad," I said. "Are you sure you didn't fake an injury just to get a little time off?"

"Hello, baby doll. Not too bad for an old guy who just got his butt kicked, eh?" he retorted. His voice was more raspy than usual. "I'm feeling no pain thanks to the pills they're giving me. Especially now that you're here to talk to me."

"I was worried about you," I said, lightly touching the

unbandaged side of his forehead and smoothing back his wiry gray hair. "Where's your daughter?"

"I told her not to miss work. She'll be back later. I expect Phil will stop by too."

I sat down in the chair next to the sofa.

"So, what happened last night? That was the single most terrifying night of my life."

"I was pretty terrified myself, with that punk kid waving a gun in my face. I didn't know if it was loaded or not, but I wasn't taking any chances. He helped himself to free gas and the money in the drawer, then tried to lock me in the bathroom. When my back was turned, he thumped me good with his pistol. I'd like a chance to thump him back."

"He tried to open the camper door. Do you think he knew I was in there?"

"He did?" Earl thought that over for a moment. "No, he couldn't have known you were there. It was a slow night, not much money in the drawer, probably less than a hundred. He must have been after anything he could lay his hands on. He had a kind of wild-eyed look, like he was on drugs."

"Who was it? Did you know him?"

"Nope," Earl said, shaking his head for emphasis. "Never saw him before. The police already asked me all that and everything else under the sun. He must have come in off the freeway in the fog and probably took off the same way. I doubt he'll be back."

"I hope not. I never want to go through that again. What did you tell Strobel about me?"

"Don't worry, I figured you wouldn't want Teddy to know that you were staying in the camper. I told him you stopped by now and then to brighten an old man's night."

"And he believed you?"

"Seemed to. Why not? It's the truth, more or less."

Relieved, I sank back into the chair. "Now all I have to worry about is Phil. He wants to talk to me. I'm afraid he's going to make me move out, and I'm not ready to leave yet."

"You do need to move. Living at the station is dangerous. Of course, nobody gives a hill of beans for my opinion, but I've never understood why Phil let you stay there. I'll hate to see you go, but you need to find somewhere safer to live."

"I know, I know. But not yet. Would you talk to Phil for me? I know you can persuade him to let me stay just a little longer."

He sighed and shook his head. "I'll talk to him. After all, you saved my life. Teddy said I might have bled to death if you hadn't found me. These scalp wounds bleed something fierce."

"You're too tough to die," I joked. "But what's all this 'Teddy' stuff? Strobel's a jerk."

"Oh, Teddy stops by the station now and then. He's a good guy who wants to make the world safe from evildoers, and that's not a bad ambition for an officer of the law. I admit he's a bit overeager at times and a stickler for going by the rules. Still, his heart is in the right place."

"I find it hard to believe he has a heart." I sniffed.

"Don't be too hard on him. He sounded as if he admired you," Earl teased me.

"Oh, please. Now I know you're out of your head. They

must have given you too much medication. That guy has never given me anything except a hard time."

"Is that a fact? I think you might be missing something there."

I just shook my head. We both fell silent for a moment, as the familiar sounds of screeching tires and slamming doors serenaded us from the television.

I stood up. "Well, I better get going. Do you need anything?"

"Naw, I'm fine. Just stay away from the camper until I get things fixed up with Phil. I'm expecting him to stop by any time now. I'll talk to him."

"I'll make myself scarce for a day or two," I said.

After I left Earl, I wasn't sure where to go next. Finally, I went back to Gloria's house.

As I pulled up to the curb, Stella leaped off the porch railing and dashed across the lawn toward my car. When I opened the door, she looked up at me and began yowling her welcome or complaints, I wasn't sure which.

"Hello, Fat Cat," I murmured as I lifted her in my arms. "How's my beauty?" I stroked her silky fur and she meowed energetically, telling me all her problems. At least Stella hadn't forgotten me.

"I missed you too," I told her as I walked to the front door and rang the bell.

The door flew open and Gloria's two demons stared at me from behind the screen door. Then the younger one, Matthew, darted away and I could hear him yelling, "It's her. It's her."

Good grief, you'd think I was the Wicked Witch of the West.

"Hello," I said politely to the older one—Daniel.

Gloria's head appeared in the doorway leading to the kitchen and then she walked toward me, her slippers slapping on the floor.

"Her name is Ashley and you know it," she said. "Hi, Ashley. I see you've found Stella already."

"She came running up to my car. She's never done that before. I think she misses me."

Gloria lifted her hand to smooth back her flyaway hair. "I'm sure she does. These two stinkers don't understand that you need to be gentle with a cat. A tiger would be a better pet for them."

"We want a tiger! We want a tiger!" Matthew started chanting at top volume. I tried not to wince.

"What brings you over today? Are you taking Stella with you?"

"I wish! No, I stopped by to . . ." I hesitated for a moment, on the verge of dumping all my problems in her lap, but then I just couldn't do it. "To see what was happening and pick up my mail."

"Come in. Have some tea, or maybe you like coffee now that you're working in a coffeehouse?"

"Tea's fine." I followed her into the blue-and-yellow kitchen and sat down at the table, still clutching Stella.

Gloria bustled around, removing cereal bowls and the remainder of what obviously had been breakfast. The table was sticky from sugary cereal and spilled milk.

"Boys, go watch cartoons. I want to talk to Ashley."

At first they ignored her, squirming around us like Apaches circling the wagon train. Finally, they left when they found no entertainment value in our conversation.

"How's the job going?" she asked.

"Fine." I stifled a yawn. It had been a long night. "It's an eye-opening experience. Some of the customers are a little bizarre, but I'm getting used to them."

She put a steaming cup of tea in front of me. "Listen, before I forget, I wanted to tell you we're going to Denver for Christmas. You're welcome to join us."

"Thanks, Gloria, that's nice of you, but I have to work." I had been avoiding even thinking about the holidays.

"What will you do for Christmas?" she asked.

"I've already been invited to have dinner with a friend," I lied.

"Oh, good," Gloria said in obvious relief. "I was worried that you might be alone. Anyway, I'm glad you stopped by. I've been asking around about Curtis Davidson."

Back in September I'd told Gloria all about my conversation with dear old Curtis.

"Who have you been asking?" I stirred my cup, watching the white sugar crystals disappear into the murky liquid.

"You know how it works. Someone always knows someone. There are *no* secrets in the suburbs, at least not for long. As it happens, a good friend of mine serves on the Coyote Point Museum Board with Mrs. Curtis Davidson III, otherwise known as Claire. She and Claire went to school together, and they've been close for years. And another friend lives next door to the office manager at Warren Simmons."

"So what has your network of informants told you about Claire and her hubby?" Stella jumped up into my lap and began to wash her front paw.

"Boys, turn that volume *down*!" Gloria screamed. She took a sip of tea before resuming our conversation in a normal tone.

"For one thing, Curtis is skating on thin ice these days at the company. The office manager told my friend that they've been going through his files, expense reports, and job records with a microscope. Maybe your anonymous note has something to do with that. But the word is out that the other partners are sick of him anyway. Apparently his work ethic isn't that great and hasn't been for a long time. He disappears for hours and spends more time out of his office than in. He claims he's on sales calls and at job sites, but he's been spotted several times at bars during the day. There's also talk about a woman who seems to require hours and hours of his advice about the hypothetical building of an addition to her house."

"Wow, Diane could really pick 'em," I said in disgust.

"Diane isn't the only one who fell for his line of baloney, believe me. He must be quite charming because Claire didn't marry him for his money. Her family made a fortune in San Mateo real estate after World War Two. She's the one with money, and she keeps an iron grip on her share."

"Smart woman. Does she know he cheats on her?" In my lap, Stella purred as I stroked her soft orange fur.

"She'd have to be blind, deaf, and dumb not to—and she's not any of those things from what I hear. She must have been tired of his philandering, because they separated about a year ago. But they're back together now, at least in public. As for what their relationship really is, who really knows what goes on in anyone else's marriage?"

She stood up and peered around the corner to see what her brats were doing. Nothing dangerous apparently, because she sat back down.

"I hope she throws him out, and the company does too," I growled. "But I don't know if any of that will help my mother, even if she comes back."

"I don't know either," Gloria said, staring into her cup. "I just don't know."

We both fell silent, thinking about my mother. I looked down and noticed the milk carton on the table in front of me. A child's picture was on it with the words *Missing* and *Reward.*

"Hey, do you think I could get my mother's picture on one of these?" I said, tapping on the carton.

Gloria didn't crack a smile at my feeble joke. She just reached across the table and squeezed my hand. I squeezed back.

. . .

The only place I could find to stay for the next few days was a youth hostel. I knew from listening to customers that there were several local hostels where a bed would cost about $20 a night, no credit cards required. I decided to try the Emerald City Hostel, near the club where Tattie worked.

Anxious to mend our relationship I had left a couple of messages on Tattie's cell phone since our blowup, but she hadn't returned my calls. After all, she had come to my rescue when everyone except Nicole had shunned me.

The hostel was on the second floor over a street-level restaurant and an adjacent porn shop. I walked up a narrow stairway to the lobby and waited at the desk while a moon-faced dweeb behind the counter had a conversation (if you can call it that) with a bug-eyed freak who needed to see a dentist.

"This seems like a cool place, dude," said the freak. He was wearing a tank top, probably so everyone could admire the tattoos covering his arms.

"Yeah, it's cool. You meet a lot of cool people," the clerk said, nodding vigorously for emphasis.

"That's cool." The tattooed freak nodded back. As their heads bobbled, both of them stared at me, as if expecting me to comment on the relative coolness of it all.

"You know what I think would be really cool?" I said. "If I could check in before the century ends."

Their heads stopped bobbling, and in unison, they glanced at each other, probably thinking I was a she-bitch from hell.

"Well, catch you later," the guy said. The clerk nodded.

"Stay cool, dude!" I called as he turned away.

I registered and paid for three nights in cash. The place had a decidedly let's-wear-Birkenstocks-and-burn-incense kind of ambiance. I soon discovered the sleeping quarters were only slightly more luxurious than the camper. The women's dorm was sparsely furnished with bunk beds and foot lockers for storing your gear—and nothing else. The bathroom resembled a girls' locker room.

On the plus side, the place was a lot warmer than the camper and had a spacious lounge furnished with couches, tables and chairs, a pool table, and a big-screen TV.

Settling myself down in one of the chairs, I called Tattie's number. She didn't pick up. I left a message telling her I was at the hostel and wanted to talk to her. Then I looked around, ready to enjoy the novelty of relaxing in a warm room and watching television like a normal person. Of course, *Fear Factor* wasn't my choice and the other three people watching were strangers, but still, it felt almost homelike.

After I'd spent two hours watching bad TV, Tattie appeared in the doorway to the lounge, a vision in a pink suede jacket over a form-fitting black strapless dress.

"Hi!" I said awkwardly. "I'm glad you stopped by."

We moved to the far corner and sat down in a couple of chairs arranged around a table.

"I left you several messages," I said. "Are you still mad at me?"

"Oh, I got over it." She stared down at her hands and began chipping the crimson nail polish on her left thumbnail.

Diving right into the deep end, I asked, "How's your job going?"

"There's no business like show business," she answered.

"I'm sorry I overreacted about it, but you took me by surprise and I was worried. But you look fine."

She straightened up and looked me in the eye at last. "Actually, the job isn't as much fun as it used to be," she admitted.

"Oh."

"I quit yesterday. You know me, I get restless. No big deal. I just got sick of the creeps, and management was always on my ass about something. Be on time, be nice to the customers. Do this, do that. Who needs it?"

"So what are you going to do?"

"I haven't decided yet," she said. "I know some people heading to Puerto Escondido for the winter and I might go along. Lots of surfing and good shit down there. You should come too."

"Be careful." The words escaped my mouth before I could stop them. "I mean, I've heard that it's really bad to get caught with drugs down there. Mexican prisons are supposed to be real hellholes. Anyway, what happened to Amsterdam?"

"I'll do that eventually. I don't like to overplan."

I shook my head in wonder. "You really amaze me. You do exactly what you want and to hell with what anyone else thinks. I wish I could do that."

"Don't!" she said abruptly. "I got to this point the hard way. You can't even imagine all of the shit I've had to endure."

I was surprised at her tone. I hadn't seen a serious Tattie very often. "I know, your parents drinking and all that. It must have been tough."

She snorted. "Please. Drinking was just the tip of the iceberg. The Mad Russian introduced me to the 'joy' of sex at the ripe old age of twelve. He was drunk, of course, but he knew exactly what he was doing. I had a good figure even then. When I told the She-Devil, she tossed him and all his clothes out on the lawn. But she blamed me. After that, she made sure I was never alone with any of her boyfriends. As if I was interested in any of the losers she dates!"

My mouth fell open in shock. "Omygawd, Tattie. I had no idea. I can't imagine . . . you should have had him arrested and sent to prison."

"I survived." She pulled a cigarette out of her purse and lit it. "Could have been worse. At least I didn't have to go into foster care or some juvi home. Maybe he did me a favor. I found out how to use my assets at an early age, and I intend to keep using them until I don't have them anymore."

"Maybe you should talk to someone—you know, a therapist."

"What for?" she snorted. "Crying in some shrink's office once a week for the next five years isn't going to fix anything. He's the one who needs fixing. Castration would be my therapy of choice."

Canned laughter erupted from the television across the room.

"Hey, you can't smoke in here!" the guy from the front desk yelled across the room at us.

"Then I'll go someplace where everyone isn't such a tight-ass," Tattie shot back at him, blowing a big cloud of smoke his way. She turned back to me. "What are you doing here, anyway?"

"It's a long story. I'm just here for a couple of days." I avoided her eyes because I didn't want to tell her about the camper.

"Yeah?" she said, eyeing me with a shrewd look. "I tell you all about the Mad Russian's banging me, and you can't tell me why you're staying in a hostel?"

"Really, it's not that big a deal. I couldn't stay in my place for a couple of days and this seemed as good as anywhere."

"You're being very mysterious."

"I don't mean to be. It's just that my place isn't so great. But I'm looking for a better apartment and then I'll have you over. I promise."

"Sure," she said. "Are you still working at that dump, the Nuthouse or whatever you call it?"

"Yes. I like it." As I said it, I realized it was true.

"Whatever," she said, and reached down with both hands

to pull up her strapless top, which was inching downward in a losing battle with gravity.

"I've gotta go. I always need a little cock and tail on a Saturday night. I don't suppose you want to come out with me tonight?"

"No, I'm wiped out. Another time."

"Yeah, sure."

"I mean it. I'm not into partying right now, but I still want to hang out with you. I need all the friends I can get. I'll never forget the way you came to my rescue when everyone else was treating me like I had leprosy."

She laughed. "We lepers have to stick together, don't we? Okay, girlfriend. I'll call you." She blew me an exaggerated air kiss, then disappeared down the stairs to the street.

A week later I was back living in the camper when Tattie left a message on my cell phone saying she was off to Puerto Escondido.

chapter twenty-two

Another rainy Wednesday. It was seven o'clock at night and I had come to the City Lights bookstore in North Beach to hear an author read his book about the San Francisco earthquake. After the reading, I was working my way through the crowd toward the door when I found myself face-to-face with Patrick.

"Hello, darlin'. When I spotted you sitting there, I couldn't believe my eyes. I had to come see if it really was you." Patrick grinned down at me.

"Why wouldn't it be me? Did you think I couldn't read?" Actually, I was thrilled to run into him like this, but his arrogant tone annoyed me.

"I was sure you *could* read, I just didn't know you *did,*" he said. "You don't look like someone who would be interested in geology."

"For your information," I protested, "I'm interested in all kinds of things. I don't really think you know me well enough to guess what I'm interested in."

I brushed past him and started out of the bookstore. He followed me.

"True enough," he said, falling into step beside me. "But you look like a girl who would go in for *Bridget Jones's Diary* or *Pride and Prejudice.*"

"There's nothing wrong with either of those books," I retorted. "I like a good love story. I suppose you're too intellectual for books like that."

"Not at all. But someone warned me recently about creating false expectations and romantic fantasies, so I'm trying to stay clear of anything that smells of romance."

I sniffed at that remark, and he asked, "How is it that you know so much about romance at your young age? How old are you anyway? Twenty-one? Twenty-two?"

Ignoring his question, I said, "What does age have to do with it? Are you worried I might develop romantic fantasies about you?"

"Not you," he laughed. "You're a hard-hearted girl who already knows all about my misdeeds. Aren't we just having a friendly conversation?"

He continued to walk beside me, asking, "Where are we headed?"

"I don't know where you're headed, but I'm going home," I answered. Truthfully, I wasn't ready to go back to the camper, but I didn't have a destination in mind yet.

"It's way too early to go home," he said. "Let me buy you a pint."

"No, thanks, I don't drink," I said. Realizing that sounded way too prudish and not wanting to admit that I wasn't old enough, I hastily added, "I mean, I don't feel like having a drink tonight. Maybe a cup of coffee, I suppose."

He steered me down Columbus Avenue to one of the sidewalk tables outside Caffé Greco and fetched us both cappuccinos.

"So, what did you think of the author?" he said. "Have you read his book?"

"Not yet," I answered. "I'll probably have to wait until the library gets a copy."

"You can borrow mine," he said. "Have you read his other book, on the madman who helped write the *Oxford English Dictionary*?"

"No. A madman wrote that dictionary?"

"Yep, one of the contributors was a genuine murderer, from America no less. You Americans are a pretty violent lot."

"Yeah, right. Ever heard of Jack the Ripper?"

"He was English."

"What about all those Irishmen shooting and blowing each other up?"

"That's in the North," he said. "I'm an Irishman from the Republic, where violence these days usually amounts to a pub brawl over a woman. We're all dreamers, liars, and poets—or fools."

"And which are you?" I asked.

"All of the above, my girl, all of the above. So tell me about yourself." He gazed at me with intense interest, and I noticed again what blue eyes he had. "Apart from the odd fact or two, I don't know anythin' about you except that you work at the Madhouse and you're a very pretty girl who likes to read."

"There's not much to tell."

"Come on, now. Tell your Uncle Pat all about it."

"It's a sad story, Uncle Pat," I said, imitating his Irish brogue. "I'm a penniless orphan working to earn my daily bread. All I have in the world is my little red Jetta and a cat named Stella."

"I see," he said. " 'Tis a sad tale indeed. Both your parents passed recently?"

"My father died when I was fourteen, but we didn't get along anyway. My mother died a few months ago. So I'm all alone."

"Except for the cat named Stella. Nice name, that."

"It means star in Italian."

"Are you Italian?"

"On my mother's side. My father was Irish, or so he always said. Mitchell is an Irish name, isn't it?"

"Yes, indeed it is. So we're compatriots. That means we have to stick together, you and I."

The two of us chattered away for a couple of hours. I lied through my teeth whenever he asked me about my background but it was fun to talk with someone who actually read fiction. Scott and the boys I knew in high school never read anything that hadn't been assigned by a teacher except *Playboy* or *Sports Illustrated.*

I told Patrick I was planning to enroll in college soon.

"So what's holding you back, girl?" he asked.

"Money, Uncle Pat. No one works at the Madhouse because they're rich," I answered. "I've been doing some research and I should be able to take a couple of night courses starting in January. Next fall I hope to get a student loan and go full-time."

"At San Francisco State?"

"I'm not sure," I said. "It all depends."

"On what? A boyfriend? A pretty girl like you must have a fella or two."

"Not exactly," I said, and changed the subject. "Tell me about Ireland. Is it beautiful?"

"That it is! There's nowhere like it on earth. Of course, you have to get used to a wee bit of rain," he said, turning his brogue up a notch.

"How much is a wee bit?"

"Nearly every day," he said, and we both laughed.

"Are you from Dublin?"

"No, I'm from Wexford, a little town where the River Slaney flows into the Irish Sea. Like all of Ireland, Wexford has Norse roots and a dark, sad history at the hands of the English. Cromwell sacked the town more than three hundred and fifty years ago, but we've not forgotten."

"America didn't even exist then. As a country, I mean. My ancestors must have still been in Ireland, getting sacked along with yours." *Oh, God, I'm beginning to babble.* I stopped myself by asking him another question. Guys always like to talk about themselves. "What did you do in Wexford?"

"Grew up, went to school, the usual. My family's still there. Like any reasonably bright, ambitious lad, I went to university in Dublin and stayed there, working as a busker and a bouncer and writing the odd piece. All Irishmen are half in love with America. I was lucky enough to get a visa when I wanted to visit America. So here I am."

"I know what a bouncer is," I said, "but what's a busker?"

"A street performer—I play the guitar and sing a little."

"Wow, I'd love to hear you sometime. What sort of music do you sing?"

"All Irishman learn to sing Irish folk songs and ballads in our cradles. Do you know Irish music?"

"No. Everything I know about Ireland, I've learned from the movies."

He smiled at that. "So you like movies?"

"I love them," I said. "I go at least once or twice a week."

"What's your favorite film?" he asked.

"Oh, there's so many." I thought about it for a few seconds. "I really loved *Sliding Doors* with Gwyneth Paltrow, but I guess *Breakfast at Tiffany's* has to be my all-time favorite. I love Audrey Hepburn."

"You like old movies?" he said. "Me too. You should watch *The Quiet Man* if you like films about Ireland. *The Dead* is another good one. What do you think of film noir?"

"Mmmm, that sounds like black-and-white movies, and I think they're boring."

He shook his head at me in pity. "Oh, you ignorant girl. Some of the best movies ever made are black and white. You haven't lived until you've seen some of the film noir classics. I tell you what: *Out of the Past* and *A Lonely Place* are playing at the Roxie on Friday. Mitchum and Bogart, two of the best. I'll take you. You need educating."

I agreed to go to the movies with him. Maybe it was reckless, but I was sick of being alone and going everywhere alone. Table for one, please. One ticket, please. I had been the loner, the loser, the ghost, and I was tired of feeling invisible.

. . .

I was very excited about my "date" with Patrick. At least, I hoped it was a date—it wasn't exactly clear. I had never actually "dated," the way I understood the concept from the olden days. My high school crowd traveled in packs and went out in groups. Only toward the end of an evening did couples get together in corners and cars and other isolated spots. Scott and I had been a couple, but we had never gone on a date for a movie and a milk shake like those dopes on *Happy Days.*

For the last few months I had been too busy adjusting to my new circumstances to worry about hooking up. My experience with Webb would definitely be worth repeating with the right person, but I hadn't had the time to do any shopping. Not just anyone would do. My romantic fantasies revolved around a sophisticated and intelligent guy who knew about poetry, literature, and art, and looked good wearing a tuxedo.

While Scott had been way cute and his family had plenty of money, I had never considered him husband material. No way was I going to spend a lifetime watching basketball games and surfing tournaments. And I didn't plan on ending up with some boring banker or lawyer whose idea of a good read was the *Wall Street Journal.*

I pictured my future husband as an intellectual—a writer or poet or maybe a film director. He wouldn't care whether the 49ers or the Raiders won the Super Bowl, and he would never, ever think farting was funny.

I wasn't stupid enough to imagine that Patrick was "the one." Sooner or later, he would be moving on. But in the meantime, he was attractive, well read, and didn't say "dude" five times a minute.

At the Madhouse the next day I felt a little apprehensive about how he might behave toward me. He was as friendly and flirtatious as ever but didn't say a word about our chance meeting or our plans for Friday night at the movies. I was relieved. The last thing I wanted to do was become the center of any Madhouse gossip.

Hugging my secrets to myself had become a habit. I feared the disapproval or pity that exposure might bring. More than that, I was afraid of admitting that my mother wasn't coming back.

. . .

By the time Friday arrived, I was finding it hard to remain cool about my "date" with Patrick. We had agreed to meet outside the Roxie Theater at six thirty sharp. I didn't bother to change my clothes after work—that would have sent a signal that I wanted to impress him. But I did pull my hair out of the ponytail I wore at the coffeehouse so that it hung loosely to my shoulders. Then I unbuttoned the top button of my shirt to show a little cleavage. As Tattie would say, I intended to use all my natural assets tonight.

The Roxie turned out to be a run-down movie house in the rougher section of the Mission. It was surrounded by ethnic restaurants, secondhand stores, and other graffiti-covered buildings. As I walked toward the theater, a black man with a bandana on his head went past me, spinning and hip-hopping to his own music.

Outside the theater I saw Patrick waiting with a cigarette in one hand. He was wearing jeans, a black turtleneck, a black leather jacket, and boots—in other words, he looked dangerous and totally yummy. Even the cigarette didn't put me off, although I had always sworn I wouldn't hook up with a smoker.

Once inside, I discovered that the interior of the movie house was not so bad. The movies were good, too, even if they were in black and white.

As we walked out, Patrick said, "Let's get a bite to eat, shall we?"

I nodded agreement.

We walked to a tapas restaurant called Andalu. After we settled into a corner table and ordered, Patrick stretched out his legs and asked, "So what did you think of the films?"

"I liked them," I admitted. "Especially the Mitchum guy. The other movie was pretty dark and had an interesting twist to it, but I just don't get Bogart as a screen idol. And the women were annoying. You had to sort of admire Kathie. She played helpless, but underneath she was ruthless and determined not to be controlled by anyone. But the other chick didn't *do* anything, just looked beautiful and got a lot of massages. Suddenly she's in love and starts cooking and taking care of her man. Then—hello!—she starts to think that he's a murderer. Maybe all that housecleaning stuff made her flip out."

"Spoken like a true woman of the twenty-first century," he tweaked me. "Are you saying you don't want to cook and be some bloke's little woman?"

"Not like that. I don't want anyone bossing me around and

expecting me to mother him. Is that what you're looking for in a woman?"

"Like most men, I want it all. A woman to take care of me who's beautiful, intelligent, and passionate."

"Sounds like two women to me."

He grinned and drawled, "So, tell me all about this boyfriend of yours in San Diego."

For a second, my mind went blank until I remembered the lie I had told about Webb. Maybe this was a good time to unravel that particular part of my tangled web.

"Oh, him," I said carelessly. "There's not much to tell. He's a great guy, but it's so hard to maintain a long-distance relationship. We didn't pledge undying love or eternal fidelity to each other."

"That's good," Patrick said, leaning back in his chair. "You're a bit young for pledging undying anything."

"I'll be a year older very soon," I said mysteriously.

"Me as well," he said, then added with a mock leer, "What's your sign, darlin'? I'm a Scorpio. We're supposed to be very sexy devils, if you believe all that malarkey."

"I'm a Scorpio too."

"Now what are the odds of that? I'll be precisely a quarter of a century old on November nineteenth."

"My birthday is the twenty-second," I said. He raised his brows at me as if in a question, and I added, "And 'old enough' is all I'm saying."

"I thought women didn't start hiding their age until at least thirty," he protested.

"I'm getting an early start."

"We'll have to celebrate our birthdays together," he announced. Just then, the waitress plopped our plates down in front of us, so nothing more was said about age or birthdays.

It was nearly one when he walked me to my car. I was parked in an alley—not dark exactly but not floodlit either. After I unlocked the door, I turned around to say good night and hopefully get kissed. But he gently pulled me against him, one hand in the small of my back and the other resting slightly on my shoulder. We stood there, inhaling each other. He felt great and smelled wonderful, like soap and leather.

All my nerve endings were tingling, and I realized that somehow he had gotten control of the situation. That wasn't what I was used to at all.

"You're so lovely," he whispered with his cheek lightly touching my hair. "You know I fancy you, don't you?"

Then just as quickly, he released me, and called, "Drive safely" as he walked away.

Unkissed and off balance, I got into my car and drove back to the camper, to enjoy a night of pleasant dreams for once.

chapter twenty-three

On Monday Patrick strolled into the coffeehouse around eleven and we both pretended that nothing had happened between us. I was careful not to pay any special attention to him, yet I was aware of every movement he made. At one point, I looked up to see him staring at me with a half smile on his face. I walked over to the table where he was sitting.

"Did you want something?" I asked. "Another cappuccino?"

"That would be grand," he said.

As I reached over him for his cup, my breast lightly brushed his arm. With that brief touch, the air between us seemed to become charged with electricity. I froze for a moment, then moved away.

When I caught Malcolm's eye, I realized he had noticed.

He didn't say anything right away. But the next day, when the place was half-empty, Mal invited me to sit down and have a cup of espresso with him.

"How do you like working here?" he began.

"Great," I said, thinking that only a fool would tell her boss any different.

He must have realized the same thing because he chuckled. "Like you'd say anything else." In a falsetto, he added, "Mal, you're an idiot and the customers are all cracked."

I smiled but didn't say anything, not sure where this conversation was going.

He went on. "We probably seem like a bunch of eccentrics and lost sheep to you. Let's face it, you're different and everyone here knows it. You look like a girl who took a wrong turn on her way to Neiman Marcus."

I started to argue, but he cut me off. "Don't get me wrong, I'm happy you're working here. You're smart, you've got a lot of energy, and you don't take any guff from anyone. But we both know you don't really belong here."

"But I do. No one could be more of a lost sheep than me right now."

Mal patted my hand. "Okay, dearie. We're happy to have you in the flock. But, please, listen to a piece of friendly advice. Patrick is, well, he's very attractive. If I were younger and he were gay, I'd chase after him myself. But he's not for you. He's too old, for one thing."

At my look of protest, he wagged his head. "Hey, I'm your boss. I know exactly how old you are."

"I'll be nineteen in two weeks," I interrupted.

"Listen to you! Eighteen or nineteen, Patrick is six years older than you in age and a lot more than that in life experience. He's not going to settle down in the suburbs, drive an

SUV, and raise two point five children. The man is an adventurer and a womanizer, with a girl back home in Ireland and half a dozen scattered between here and there."

"Come on, Mal. Don't you think I know that?" I teased him. "I'm way too young to settle down, much less have kids."

"Of course. But you should be dating fresh-faced, beer-swilling college boys, not Irish bad boys with literary ambitions and a trail of broken hearts."

"Bad boys—now that sounds promising," I jibed. "Things are so dull in the suburbs. No one I know has ever left a trail of broken hearts."

He laughed. "Maybe I overdid the purple prose. Hell, I'm a fool for even trying to warn you. You're gonna do what you wanna do, whatever I say."

I gave him a teasing look. "Relax, Grandpa. Times have changed." I stood up and paused to add, "Have you ever thought that I might break *his* heart?"

"Maybe you will." Mal smiled back at me. "Maybe I'll just sit back and watch all of this unfold."

Not if I can help it, I thought. Whatever happened with Patrick, I didn't intend it to be a source of entertainment for the Madhouse inmates.

. . .

Another Friday night and I was singing along to the radio and playing poker in a gas station with a seventy-year-old grandfather while trying not to think about an Irishman with a crooked smile.

"You can't sing and play poker at the same time. You have to watch what's going on," Earl scolded me, reaching across the desk to tap on my cards. "If you don't, you might as well not play. The easiest way to win at poker is to sit across the table from folks who are drunk, tired, or just not paying attention."

"Sorry," I yawned. "But we're just playing for fun right now."

"You said you wanted to learn how to win. To win, you have to work at it and concentrate. The player who isn't distracted or drunk will win your money because he was paying attention."

I sat up straight in my chair "All right, I'm paying attention. Remind me, is it a flush or a straight when all your cards are diamonds?"

He let out a long sigh, shaking his head. "You know, I think I'm going to call. Let's see what you've got."

I spread my cards out on the desk and Earl chuckled. "You've got a pretty good hand there. That's a flush. But I've got something better."

He deftly fanned out his cards. Four queens. "These ladies beat your flush, I'm afraid."

"I think I see why you made a lot of money at poker." I sighed, and grabbed a potato chip to nibble on.

"It takes time, baby doll. Like anything else in life, it doesn't come without effort. Luck is for suckers. Poker is a game of strategy. When the cards are cold, you fold, and when the cards are running your way, you throw money into the pot. The secret is to study your opponents and figure out what they're thinking while you make sure they don't have a clue about what's on your mind."

"I'm good at acting," I said. "For sure, I'd be good at bluffing."

He shook his head. "Bluffing is an advanced skill, and it's hard to get away with. Most people give themselves away and don't even know it. I knew a man who always licked his lips when he was bluffing."

I stretched and yawned again. "Wouldn't you love a beer right now? I would."

"Don't look at me. I don't drink and I don't give alcohol to teenagers."

"You don't drink? Ever?" I said in surprise.

"Can't," Earl said.

"Does it make you sick—I mean, throw up?"

"The stuff makes me drunk, crazy, and sick. I had a bad problem years ago. Almost killed someone in a fight over nothing—nothing!" He shook his head in wonder at his own stupidity. "So I gave it up. Promised myself I'd never touch another drop, and I haven't."

"And you just quit, without going to meetings and all that? You really are a tough guy."

"I guess AA works for most people, but it wasn't for me. I believe in being fair and respectful of others and taking responsibility for your own behavior. But I have problems with religion and folks who want you to believe what they believe. I've especially had trouble believing that making love could be a sin."

"Me too," I agreed, and then added, "Making love. No one I know calls it that."

"You kids talk worse than half of the men I used to ship out with." Earl frowned. "Potty mouths without a clue as to what you're saying. You don't have any idea what love is."

"Have you ever been madly in love?" I asked.

He chuckled. "Madly in love? Well, I guess so. Madly in love or lust. Sometimes it's hard to tell."

"How do you know the difference?"

"Well, there's a fair amount of lust in love, or should be. But when you're in love, you want to be with that person and talk to her, not just do the horizontal hula with her." He stared at my face. "Are we talking in generalities here or is there something you want to tell me?"

"I'll let you know," I said, smiling a little at his protectiveness.

"You remind me of an article I read about the moose in Yellowstone."

"I remind you of a moose?" I said, mystified. "Is this another one of your goofy platitudes?"

"Nope. It's a true story. Fifty years ago the wolves and grizzlies were shot and chased out of Yellowstone. For a long time, the moose didn't have much to worry about. A couple of years ago, the wildlife experts reintroduced wolf packs. But those moose were so dumb that they didn't even try to get away. The wolves just had to walk up and make the kill. Quite a few moose died before they wised up and learn to take off in a trot when the wolves showed up. They had to *learn* to become watchful. Don't learn everything the hard way, baby doll. Listen to your uncle Earl."

"Don't worry," I promised. "I'll be watchful."

. . .

Saturday, Patrick left me a phone message saying he was playing that night at an Irish tavern and did I want to drop by? You bet I did. Deciding what to wear wasn't easy, but I finally chose tight low-rider jeans and a navy top that let my toned midriff show. Plus boots and a raincoat, of course. The rainy season had begun early this year.

He said the music began at nine, so I arrived at ten, not wanting to seem overeager. I had to show my phony ID to get in, but it wasn't a problem. If the guy at the door wondered what an Elizabeth Castillo was doing at an Irish hangout, he didn't ask.

The place was noisy and crowded. I managed to snag the lone empty stool at the crowded bar and ordered a soda. Patrick was onstage, along with a fiddler and another guitarist. I was impressed with his playing. At one point he gave me a wave and a wink. I felt a little self-conscious amid all the boisterous groups of friends. Before long, two guys sitting next to me offered to buy me a Guinness. I laughed and declined, but they persisted.

When the music stopped, Patrick put down his instrument and made his way toward me, stopping to talk to people along the way.

"You're breaking my heart, beautiful," pleaded one of the guys, trying to persuade me to go with him and his buddy to another bar.

Just then Patrick walked up to us. "Get away from her, you horny bastards," he said, stopping in front of me and taking my hand. "Shall we get some fresh air then?"

"Sure," I said, not bothering to point out the rain. I grabbed my coat and headed outside. We strolled silently down the sidewalk toward no particular destination.

"I enjoyed your music," I said finally, mindful of my manners.

"Did you? Good." His tone was matter-of-fact, as if his mind was elsewhere. He looked at me and began to laugh. "You're drowning, girl. I'm an ejit to drag you out here in the wet. Let's duck under here."

We stopped under the awning of a closed appliance store and he lit a cigarette.

"I'll be going back to Ireland soon now," he said.

My heart dropped. "When?"

"In a few weeks," he answered. "I'll be spending Christmas with my family and then I'm going off to Spain for a bit. A friend has a job for me there, teaching English, and I'll have time to work on my book."

I turned my back to him and looked out at the rain. I didn't know what to say except, *Don't go! Don't go!*

"I made these arrangements months ago," he said. "And my visa is expiring."

"I understand," I answered. "Still . . ." My voice trailed off.

"Still," he echoed, tossing away his cigarette. He shook his head. "You weren't part of the plan."

I turned around and we stood silently looking at each other. He had such deep blue eyes and a nice mouth, too. What I wanted must have been written on my face, because he pulled me to him for the kiss I had been longing for. And what a kiss it was. My knees went weak, and I kissed him back with enthusiasm.

"I've been thinking," he whispered into my neck, making all the little hairs on the back of my neck bristle. "We should have that birthday celebration before I leave."

I just held my breath, afraid to move from this sweet spot.

"A friend has offered me his cabin in the mountains near Lake Tahoe. We could drive up there on the weekend."

"Would your friend be going?" I asked.

"No way." He answered. His hand had found its way inside my raincoat and was lightly caressing the skin of my bare midriff. I longed for him to move his hand farther down. "Just the two of us."

I considered the idea for a millisecond and then said, "We can take my car."

The next day I went to the free clinic on Haight Street and got a prescription for birth control pills. Was I really ready to begin a sexual relationship with Patrick? Damn right I was!

chapter twenty-four

Lust Lessons: Your Guide to Toe-Curling Good Sex
Make Him Quiver with Desire: 7 Erotic Trigger Points
12 Hot Bedroom Tricks to Try Tonight

With a stack of women's magazines in front of me, I plowed through these articles and several more before the big birthday weekend at Lake Tahoe. I wasn't all that experienced, but I didn't want Patrick to know that. All the magazines said men want sexually confident women, and I was determined to be as confident as possible.

To be honest, the more I read, the more intimidated I felt. Impressing him with my prowess seemed like a whole lot of hard work. Some of the stuff they described seemed gross, like swirling your tongue along the inside of his armpit. Wouldn't that taste a lot like deodorant? Other sexual acts seemed to require gymnastic skills. I may have been a cheerleader, but I wasn't a contortionist. How was I supposed to orchestrate all these moves and be multiorgasmic at the same time?

As for tapping my inner dominatrix, I wasn't sure I had one. I really didn't want to get all involved with dildos and whips and vibrators. I couldn't imagine pushing him down, ripping his pants off, and devouring him like an animal in a sex-crazed frenzy. I didn't think I could talk dirty either—certainly not while concentrating on everything else I was supposed to be doing. The whole thing sounded ridiculous.

If that wasn't enough, one article discussed problems that could occur "when he's got an aircraft carrier and your dock space is only big enough for a dingy." I wasn't sure about the size of *anything.*

By the time we left for Lake Tahoe Friday evening, I was suffering from equal amounts of anticipation and apprehension, if not outright terror.

. . .

Lake Tahoe lies in a valley high in the Sierras, along the border separating California and Nevada. Though it is surrounded by forest and snow-covered peaks, most of its shoreline is jammed with resorts, vacation homes, and motels. I had been to Tahoe many times over the years, usually staying at the vacation home Nicole's parents used to own on the lake's north shore.

Patrick and I were scheduled to leave as soon as I finished Friday's shift at the coffeehouse. Malcolm had given me Sunday off, though I didn't tell him why I wanted it.

I had suggested meeting Patrick at his flat, but he told me to pick him up at the Bus Stop, a sports bar on Union Street where his friend Eoin bartended. I couldn't find a parking space, so I stopped at the curb outside the bar and honked.

Patrick appeared in seconds with a small gym bag in one hand. I hopped out to unlock the trunk.

"That's all you're taking?" I said, smiling broadly.

"How much do you need for a weekend?" he asked.

I opened the trunk to show him, and he laughed at the sight of my two bulging suitcases.

"That's more than I brought with me to America. What would you be carrying in those bags?"

"Clothes, of course, and shoes . . . and *things.*"

It began raining as we crossed the Bay Bridge. The two of us jabbered away, totally oblivious to the downpour. Patrick told me about Ireland and his family and his ex-girlfriend Caitlin.

"Where I come from, you go to a dance, kiss a girl, and she's your girlfriend. The whole town has the two of you married before long. It took me a long time to break free from that."

"How did you do it?" I asked.

"In the end, by leaving," he said. "It was the only way. So long as I was there, everyone had expectations, even though I never even thought of asking her to marry me."

"Couldn't you just tell them?"

"Would they listen? They only hear what they want to hear, my mother in particular."

I told him all about growing up in Burlingame and Nicole and Scott, even Webb. But I didn't tell him the truth about my mother. If I had told him the whole pathetic story about Diane and the missing money, he would have felt sorry for me. This weekend was all about romance, not true confessions.

As the highway began to climb the foothills of the Sierras, the rain turned to sleet. By the time we reached Emigrant Gap, the pavement was covered with snow and a huge sign proclaimed that chains were required at Donner Summit. We drove back about fifteen miles till we found a service station doing big business in the sale of chains. Patrick gallantly forked over the $55 so that we could proceed up the wet, slippery highway.

We chugged along at a merry twenty-five miles per hour, with the chains noisily slapping the road. Even at such a slow speed, the snowy road was difficult to manage, and we passed several cars that had skidded into snowbanks. I began to worry that we would end up stranded along the highway.

Two hours later we arrived at his friend's cabin. The driveway was covered with a foot or more of snow, so we wedged the car up against a snow drift and plodded to the door, sinking deep into the powder with every step. I was so cold that I didn't care about anything except getting warm.

Patrick immediately started a fire going. The place was a cozy A-frame furnished with a lot of rustic birch-log-type furniture. The sofa was upholstered in blue denim, with a Navajo rug underneath. In the bedroom a king-sized bed was covered with a big red-and-blue comforter designed to look like an Indian blanket.

We found a stereo, a big-screen TV with a DVD player, and a sizable collection of movies. There were board games, snowshoes, skis, and even a small sled. The cabin had everything you might need to entertain yourself in a winter wonderland.

We didn't use any of it. In fact, we barely got dressed all

weekend. All my article reading and worrying about sexual expertise had been pointless. Patrick proved to be an expert in the bedroom, and I was a very willing student.

He didn't pounce on me the minute the bags were inside, but we were cold and the obvious way to warm up was to remove wet clothing. That led to a great deal of kissing and caressing. We had plenty of time and he didn't rush me.

Since we hadn't thought to bring any groceries, we were forced to eat canned soup, tuna, and other supplies foraged from the cabin's cupboards. But Patrick proved to be something of a cook—he even made biscuits. Finding something to drink was easy. The cabin's owner maintained a large supply of beer, soft drinks, and California wines.

Late Saturday I woke up to the sound of clattering in the kitchen. I could smell the aroma of wood burning in the fireplace mixed with the odor of something delicious cooking. But I was too sleepy to investigate and fell back asleep, only to be awakened a couple of hours later by the sound of Patrick's voice singing "Happy Birthday."

I sat up to see him standing in front of me, holding a birthday cake glowing with candles. He had borrowed my car to go to the store and baked a cake while I was asleep. Being served a birthday cake by a deliciously naked man has to rank at the top of the chart of any girl's most unforgettable experiences.

"I only had ten candles," he said. "But I didn't know how many to put on, did I?"

"Nineteen," I said, sitting up and winding the sheet around me.

He almost dropped the cake. "You're only nineteen!"

"Yes. What's the problem?"

"The problem is I'm a bloody cradle-robber," he groaned.

"Don't worry. I'm potty trained and everything," I said. "I'm very precocious."

"That you are," he agreed.

I reached over, swiped a bit of icing from the cake, and licked it off my finger.

"How is it?"

"Yummy," I said, taking another swipe at the icing and holding up my finger. "Want a taste?"

"Indeed I do," he said, licking my finger, and minutes later we were at it again. Much, much later I asked him, "How did you get so good at this? Caitlin?"

"Caitlin! My God, I would be standing at the altar with a shotgun to my head if I spent a weekend like this with her. No, you inspire me," he said.

"Yeah, sure. Try again," I snickered.

"It's true. Word of honor," he said, running his finger down my spine in a delicious way. "As you are well aware, there have been a few other romantic encounters before you. When you do a bit of traveling, you meet a girl or two along the way. Dublin girls are nice and English girls too, but you American girls are especially congenial."

"Congenial." I smiled at that. "That's a nice word. I'm sure you've known lots of congenial girls."

"Let's not spoil the weekend by talking about that. Let's enjoy being here and forget about everythin' else. I'm mad about you, even if you are a mere babe. I should give you a spanking for not telling me how old you are." He gave me a light smack on my bare bottom. "I would have struggled a bit harder to keep my hands off you if I'd known you were so young. But I imagine you could convince a monk to renounce his vows."

"You're definitely not a monk," I said, turning over and reaching up to pull him down to me. "So I tempt you?"

"You've been making me crazy for quite a while. But I'm leaving and you seemed . . ."

"What did I seem?"

"Oh, I don't know. Vulnerable, I suppose. I didn't want to take advantage of that, but I have," he said ruefully. "You may end up hating me for it."

I winced inwardly. Vulnerable was definitely not how I wanted to come across.

"I'm a big girl and I can take care of myself," I protested. "It's been a very good birthday, believe me. It can't always be this good, can it? I think we must be very special together."

"That we are, my girl. That we are," he murmured in my ear.

It turned out that I didn't need the suitcases of clothes and shoes I had brought with me. I didn't wear any of them. By the time we left on Sunday afternoon, I was sore but blissfully satiated. I was also truly happy for the first time in months.

chapter twenty-five

On the Monday after our weekend at Lake Tahoe, Patrick came into the coffeehouse around nine. I couldn't stop smiling at him. Luckily, no one noticed, as business was brisk and the inmates were especially rowdy.

Midmorning, Tom began regaling a group of regulars with the latest installment in his absurd love life, which should have been subtitled "Looking for Sex in All the Wrong Places."

"I've been keeping an eye on the dating Web sites for you, Tom," said Mal, pointing to the computer screen and then reading from it. "Here's a good one. *Baseball-loving Brunette. DWF.*"

"Divorced white female," Tom translated.

"Pretty, buxom, well educated. I can tell good stories and use big words. Seeking compassionate, thoughtful man of means 30 to 45 for intellectual, emotional and physical relationship. No heavy drinkers."

"That lets Tom out," hooted William. "He wouldn't understand big words."

"But I'm full of good stories," Tom answered.

"She already knows good stories, she doesn't need that," I objected. "Besides, a fireman is not a man of means."

"Close enough. You have to know how to read these things," explained Mal. " 'A man of means' equals 'must have job.' No panhandlers or bums. 'Compassionate' means 'someone who doesn't kick dogs and knock down old ladies.' "

"And 'buxom' means 'weighs two hundred pounds,' " said Tom.

"Only losers or married men on the prowl use the personals to find a date," William growled.

"My sister's friend Lisa met her husband online," protested Jerry.

"And he'll be out of prison next year," quipped Tom, and everyone howled with laughter.

"Have you ever noticed that it's always a friend of a friend, never someone you really know?" I said. "I think that story falls into the urban legend category."

"Nope, not true," Malcolm retorted. "I actually met Todd that way."

That silenced us. Todd was Mal's former boyfriend, the one he still mourned five years after his death from AIDS.

Tom said, "How about you, Ashley? Where did you meet your boyfriend?"

I was startled, then realized he was referring to my mythical boyfriend, Webb. "The time-honored way—in school," I said, making sure I didn't look at Patrick.

"Girls like Ashley don't have to seek out men," Malcolm said, giving me a sardonic look. "They fall out of the sky at her feet, don't they, dear?"

"That's right," I replied. "I have to wear a helmet to keep from getting clobbered when they land."

At that moment, Bella marched through the door with Stephanie and baby Oliver. Bella was wearing a shaggy-looking yellow coat that came down to her hips. Poor girl, she had chosen the wrong moment to wear her "new" coat. She might as well have been wearing a bull's-eye as far as this unruly bunch was concerned.

"Bella, sweetheart, when did Big Bird die?" said Malcolm. "Why didn't anyone tell me?"

"Hey, Bella, I think you're molting," William called out.

Jerry made a chirruping noise before adding, "Have a heart, Bella. Give it back. Think of poor Big Bird standing there on Sesame Street, shivering."

"Shut up the bunch of you." She made a face at them. "This coat was a bargain. Mike sold it to me for only eight dollars."

"I have one word for you: Refund," Tom hooted.

Bella appealed to me. "What do you think, Ashley?"

"It's very, uh . . ." I searched for the right word and, after mentally discarding *loud* and *hideous,* said, "cheerful."

"Yes, isn't it?" She beamed. "And it's very warm."

Just then the door burst open and the wild-eyed man with bushy black hair stampeded through it.

As usual, he was wearing earphones hooked up to a CD player. As usual, he asked in a booming voice, "Is this your book?"

As usual, we all just stared.

Again he yelled, "Does this book belong to you?"

Then Malcolm jumped to his feet and strode over to him.

"This has to stop, pal. We're all tired of this routine. Go *away*!"

Mal tried to stare him down, but the bushy-haired guy wouldn't make eye contact. He began waving the book in Mal's face.

Pushing the book away, Malcolm said, "You know, I've always wondered what you listen to," and he grabbed the guy's earphones, put them on his own head, and listened intently.

The bushy-haired man went berserk, tearing the earphones off Malcolm and knocking him to the floor. Bella screamed as Malcolm fell. Tom and Patrick simultaneously surged up from the table to help him.

With his earphones in one hand and the book in the other, the man bellowed, "Satan! God will punish you for your crimes!" and stormed back outside.

"That wacko is dangerous," I said, coming out from behind the counter. "You should call the police."

"Never mind." Mal sat back down at the table, assuming a nonchalance that I doubt he felt. "We can't call the police every time some lost soul comes in armed with a book. Anyway, I imagine we've seen the last of him."

"The Book Man is one inmate that the Madhouse can do without," snickered Jerry.

"I should have ignored him. It was stupid to get him worked up like that," said Malcolm, and then he added with a laugh, "This is one of those moments when I wish we served alcohol. Oh, well, let's play Scrabble and forget all this. Sorry, Bella, if the children were frightened. Ashley, give young Stephanie a free cookie."

Young Stephanie had been watching the whole thing in wide-eyed wonder.

"I just have one question, Mal," said Patrick. "What on earth was the guy listening to?"

"Talk radio," suggested William.

"Bible-thumpers," said Tom.

"Al Green," I said, tongue in cheek.

"You're all wrong," proclaimed Mal. "He wasn't listening to anything. There was no sound of any kind coming out of his radio. Anything that guy was hearing came from his own head."

. . .

Before Patrick left the coffeehouse, he managed to pull me aside and whisper, "I want to see you tonight."

"Sure," I said, relieved that he wanted the same thing I wanted.

"I'll take you out to dinner when you finish work," he said. "Meet me down the street at the Elite Café when you get off."

We smiled at each other and he left.

I saw Mal's eyes on me. The man must have the place wired or something, he was so tuned in to everything that was said or done around there.

"We're going to miss that boy, aren't we?" Mal murmured.

"Yes," I said, avoiding discussion by turning away to busy myself clearing a table.

Before we went to Tahoe, I knew Patrick would be going back to Ireland soon, but I hadn't focused on exactly how soon that would be. I was crazy about him and didn't want him to go. Some girls would have tried to worm some sort of promise out of him. But that's not my style. While I didn't want him to leave, a girl has her pride. These days, that's about all I had. All I could do was act as if my heart weren't breaking. But it was.

Patrick was sitting at the bar staring into a glass of Guinness when I walked into the Elite. The café wasn't serving dinner yet, so I sat down at the bar beside him.

"Would you like a drink?" he asked.

"Nothing right now," I said.

He shook his head. "Our timing is definitely off."

"I just had a coffee," I said. "I'm not thirsty right now."

"I wasn't meaning the drink. I was talking about us."

"Oh, us."

"There's no way I can stay."

"I know that."

"But you'll miss me, won't you?"

"Of course," I said evenly.

"It's probably for the best that I'm leaving. I'm really a selfish bastard, you know." He grinned. "As many a lass has told me time and again."

"It's nothing to brag about."

"I'm not bragging, but I'm not apologizing for it either. I'm just admitting the truth to you."

"So, go, Mr. Selfish. Have a nice trip." I kept my voice light.

"Mind you, I have plenty of other bad habits, too."

"I'm sure you do."

"I leave my belongings strewn about everywhere. I'm opinionated. I smoke too much. And I spend far too much time at the pubs with my pals, drinking beer and having a bit of craic."

"Crack?" I said, startled.

"Not dope," he said with a laugh. "*Craic* is having a good conversation with your mates. Talking is one of the things the Irish do best."

"So why are you telling me this?"

"I don't want you pining for me after I've gone."

I gave him a scornful look. "Seems to me you should have included conceited as one of your faults. Don't worry about me."

"Good. That being said, I'd like to spend some time with you between now and when I leave on Thursday."

Instead of answering him, I asked, "Don't you like it here? People from all over the world fight to get here and become citizens. Why not you?"

"I'm Irish," he said. "Ireland will always be home for me. I like America, and San Francisco is grand. But it's not the only grand place in the world. I have been looking forward to Spain. And I've a yen to go to Australia too. I'm not ready to plant myself yet. What about you? Don't you want to travel and see the world?"

"Of course. I have to straighten some things out first, and I want to go to school."

"And then? What do you want to be when you grow up, my girl?"

"You'll laugh," I said.

"No, I won't," he said. "Not unless you're going to say film star—" He broke off at the expression on my face and started laughing.

"See, I knew you would," I said. "But not film star. Actress. Actor, I guess. That's what Julia Roberts and all the rest call themselves. I suppose the word *actress* is sexist."

"Well, you definitely are pretty enough to be an actor or film star or whatever it's called," he conceded.

"I can act, too," I said indignantly, thinking that he had no idea how every day was a performance for me. "The high school drama teacher said I had talent and presence. I can sing and dance, even play the piano. But my mother hated the whole idea because my father, the *act-tore*, never got anywhere. I don't think he was any good at it, or else he didn't have the stamina for it. I have plenty of stamina. I want to major in liberal arts in college and then gradually ease into theater and drama."

"So what's stopping you?" he said.

"Lots of things," I said. "Money being the main one. When my mother, uh, when she was gone, everything fell apart."

"Isn't it time you pulled it back together?" he said matter-of-factly.

"Yes," I said slowly. "I guess it is."

He grabbed my hand and began tracing the lines on it with the tip of his finger. "You'll work your way through this and come out on top."

"Thanks," I said as tears prickled at the corners of my eyes. I shook my head to make them disappear. "I will. I'm a lot more grounded than I used to be. There's nothing like learning the hard way."

"Ah, experience is always the best teacher," he said. "If you survive it."

"I have so far. I've changed so much in the last few months that my own mother probably wouldn't recognize me."

"I admire you for it. So many people can't change. I hear

fellows say, 'Oh, that's just the way I am,' as if they have no control over what they do or say. That's bloody nonsense. Moving on to a new place isn't all that easy, mind you, unless you're willing to adapt. It's been a struggle to keep going, keep moving, keep me eye on the goal."

"What is the goal?" I asked.

"It's different for everyone. For Patrick Rigney, it's seeing my name on a book in a bookshop window. And not just any book, but one I can be proud of and makes my father proud."

I smiled. Patrick probably was a selfish skirt-chaser, but I couldn't imagine having a conversation like this with any other boy I had ever known.

"You'll do it. I know you will," I told him.

He gave me one of his crooked smiles and lightly ran his finger down my cheek. I felt a shiver all the way down my spine.

After dinner Patrick persuaded me to go back to his place for the night. It wasn't a hard sell. I spent the next three nights in Patrick's bed.

Thursday morning we woke early and lay silently, holding each other as daylight gradually illuminated his room. After we dressed, I watched him stuff the last of his belongings into his pack.

"There's a sock on the floor in the corner." I pointed to it without moving to pick it up.

He glanced over at the orphaned sock and shrugged. "We'll leave it for the mice."

"Sure. Why not?" I said, struggling to keep from sighing or getting teary. My heart was in the pit of my stomach, and I felt a little light-headed. At moments like this, it takes a good actress to hold it together. I could have won an Academy Award.

Together we walked downstairs and stood on the sidewalk, waiting for his ride to appear. Both of us studied our shoes as if we had run out of words.

Finally, still looking down at his boots, Patrick said, "So you're sure you have my e-mail address?"

"Yes, I have it."

"I'll be expecting to hear from you and to hear you've started school." He looked up then and ran his fingertip lightly across my lips. "Who knows, one of these days you might be thinking of taking a holiday in Spain or even Ireland and decide to look up your old friend Patrick."

"Who knows," I echoed, unable to say more because of the large lump lodged in my throat.

The airport shuttle pulled up to the curb, and we moved toward it. Patrick hefted his baggage into the back and turned to me.

"This is it then," he said, pulling me to him. Our last, deep kiss went on so long it made my knees weak. A final squeeze to my hand and he climbed into the front passenger seat. He gave me one of his crooked smiles, the shuttle pulled away, and he was gone.

I walked to where my car was parked and slid into the driver's seat. *Snap!* Just like that, my big romance was over. Oddly enough I didn't feel like crying or anything. You'd have thought his departure would have sent me right over the edge. I guess you can get used to bad things happening. Or maybe it was because I had a little microscopic atom of hope inside of me—a hope that it wasn't completely over between us. Patrick could come back. I could go to Spain.

As I drove to work that morning, for the first time in weeks, my thoughts turned from Patrick to my mother. As I thought about her, the little atom of hope inside me seemed to shrink. My mother was the one thing in my life that seemed more elusive than ever. As each day passed, it seemed less and less possible that she would ever return.

. . .

The following Thursday I went to Gloria's for Thanksgiving dinner. I appreciated that she included me, but to tell the truth, I ached for my mother. All I could think about was the way things used to be. While I forced down Gloria's cornbread stuffing and pumpkin pie, I kept wondering if this was how holidays would go from now on.

Just that week there had been a story in the newspaper about an eighty-one-year-old woman with Alzheimer's who has disappeared at the Dallas airport. The attendant escorting her took her eyes off the old lady for a few moments and she was gone, vanished, beamed up to a spaceship maybe. Neither the airport security nor the Dallas police had been able to find her. If the police couldn't find a little old lady at an airport terminal, no wonder they couldn't find my mother.

Diane had been gone seven months now. I had stopped expecting my mother to reappear at any moment, although I still hoped. I liked to imagine that she had amnesia and one morning she would snap out of it. I liked to daydream about that day. I would hear my cell phone ring and hear her voice on the other end. She'd tell me how she suddenly remembered everything and longed to see her beloved daughter. I would tell her how sorry I am about the fight and every mean thing I ever said or did. I would promise to be a better daughter from now on. I'd tell her, "I'm so sorry, Mom. I love you."

I always ended my daydream there, without letting thoughts of the missing money or the police ruin it. All I cared about was having my mother back, hugging her, and feeling her arms around me again. All I wanted was to hear her say, "I love you, Ashley."

chapter twenty-six

during the four months I had been residing in the camper, I tried to avoid running into anyone I didn't want to see. That included most of the residents of Burlingame and all of my old school friends. But one Saturday morning my luck finally ran out. I was filling my tank at Phil's station when a silver BMW sedan pulled up to the pump ahead of me. I was dismayed to see Nicole's mother in the driver's seat.

As Cindy climbed out of her car, Reynaldo appeared and immediately began filling her tank. She didn't say a word to him. Instead, she flounced over to me with the supremely self-assured air of an aristocrat ready to squash an inferior under the heel of her pointy-toed pump. I steeled myself for a barrage of rude questions.

"I trust you're paying for that gas," she said, brushing imaginary lint off what looked like a sealskin jacket. I could see a huge diamond-and-sapphire ring glittering on her third finger—an engagement ring?

"Do you know of another way?" I answered in tones dripping

with sarcasm. "Hello to you, too, Cindy. I see you get service even in a self-service station."

"I *always* get special service here," she said. "So, Ashley"—she looked me up and down as if appraising me for a price markdown—"how's our little camper queen doing these days?"

I stared at her, my mouth open in shock.

She smirked at me. "You know, I like to picture you using a gas station bathroom every day. Do you ever worry about all the germs that might be in there? After all, you never know who used it last."

"How—," I began, and then stopped.

"How do I know? Philip told me, of course." She snickered. "In fact, he didn't want to let you move in, but I convinced him it would be a valuable experience for you. You needed to be brought down off your high horse."

Philip. Why would Phil tell Cindy? There could be only one reason—she was Phil's new girlfriend—my mother's replacement.

"Phil-lip," I repeated. "And you. I might have known."

"But you didn't, did you?" She laughed again, clearly delighted with herself. "We've been seeing each other almost a year now. Philip coached Mark's soccer team, and we would see each other at practices and games, share pizza with the boys afterward. It didn't take him long to realize that I could give him what he wasn't getting from your mother. Diane was too busy for him—busy stealing money as it turns out."

I stared at her smug face and longed to slap it until I made her lip bleed.

"You're seeing the owner of a gas station? Isn't that quite

a comedown for you?" I sneered. "Your ex-husband was a corporate executive, a big man on Montgomery Street."

"Philip is an entrepreneur. He makes plenty of money with this station. He may be a little rough around the edges, but I'm taking care of that. All my friends think he's very good-looking. I call him my Marlboro Man. Anyway, the boys are crazy about him, and he's so much better with them than their father is. They hardly see Walter anymore."

"Does Nicole know about this?"

"Not yet, but don't you worry. She'll get along with Philip just fine. I'm sure he'll love dealing with my sweet Nicole after being around you. He told me once that you had only three facial expressions—pouty, sulky, and sullen.

That one stung, but I didn't give her the satisfaction of knowing it.

"Maybe I wasn't always as nice to Phil as I should have been, but at least my mother isn't a bitch like you," I spat back at her. "Poor Phil, he doesn't know what he's getting into. I pity him when he finds out what you're really like."

Pointing one of her bloodred nails at me, she retorted, "He knows very well what he's getting, and he's very happy with it, Little Miss Smartass. I'm not an embezzler. I'm not a freeloader living in a camper. You know, maybe you've sponged off him long enough. I'll have to talk to Philip about that."

She walked off, got into her car, and gave me a spiteful little smile as she pulled away. I raised my right hand and gave her the finger.

After she left, I started wondering if she'd told Nicole where I was living. Then I realized she couldn't have. Two days ago Nicole had come home for the holidays and left several messages on my cell phone. I hadn't called her back because I didn't feel like pretending everything was just fine while she chattered about all the fun she was having in college. If Nicole knew where I was staying, she wouldn't have called. She would have pounded on the camper door, looking for me.

. . .

After filling my tank, I drove to Gloria's house. Gloria and her family had left Friday morning to spend the holidays in Denver with her husband's relatives. She had suggested I might want to stay there and keep an eye on things while they were gone. I leaped at the chance. It seemed like a golden opportunity to stay in a warm house, sleep in a regular bed, watch television, and otherwise live normally for a few days.

I parked in the driveway and scooped up Stella, who was sunning herself on the front step. Together we went inside and curled up on the sofa to watch TV. After the program ended, I went into the garage where all our furniture and belongings were stored. I wanted to add another $100 to the secret stash I kept hidden in the oak armoire. Counting it reassured me that I was making progress toward an apartment of my own. At my last count I had about $3,400. I would need every penny if Cindy persuaded Phil to kick me out of the camper.

The door to the armoire wasn't properly latched, but I didn't think anything of it other than to mentally remind myself not to be so careless. Then I pulled open the little drawer where I kept the cash and looked inside.

The drawer was empty.

I reached in, scraping my fingernails on the wood and clawing the back of the drawer as if the cash were invisible and I could make it materialize with my touch. My money was gone! I couldn't believe it. It had to be there. I must have moved it to another drawer. Maybe I dropped it. Frantically, I searched the entire armoire, then knelt down to search the floor around it. No money. Nothing.

My brain was reeling from the shock. It had taken me nearly six months to accumulate that money. Now it was gone. How could this happen? Someone must have taken it . . . but who?

Gloria, I thought, trying to control my rising panic. Of course, Gloria must have found it and taken it into safekeeping for me. But wouldn't she have mentioned it? I smothered that doubt and told myself that she forgot in the frenzy of preparing for the trip.

But what if Gloria didn't have my money? My mind came up with all sorts of wild scenarios. What if her husband had taken it, and spent it all? He could claim he never took it, and I would be totally screwed. Or what if some random person like the gardener or a neighbor borrowing a shovel had come across it and helped himself? What was I going to do? I was helpless without that money. This wasn't some stupid Monopoly game. I didn't have the will or energy to go back to *Start* and save it up all over again.

I tried to stand up again, but my knees started shaking. My stomach flip-flopped, and I felt dizzy, as if I had just stepped off the carnival's Tilt-A-Whirl.

Over and over I kept thinking, Please, please don't let this happen to me. I am really, really sorry for every awful thing I ever did. Please don't let this happen to me.

. . .

I staggered through the next two days in a sick-hearted daze, telling myself that Gloria had the money. I tried calling the number Gloria left me, but no one answered and no one returned my messages. I tried to convince myself that it would be all right. In five days she'd be back and would fix everything. But in the deepest part of my brain, a small, ugly voice kept whining, What if she can't? What if it's gone for good?

For the first time, I started to think about chucking it all and joining Tattie in Mexico. If hard work and thrift didn't work, what was the point of trying? Getting crazy on drugs and alcohol seemed the only option left. Oblivion beckoned like a warm, cozy blanket.

Sunday night I finally reached Gloria. She apologized for being out of touch.

"Ashley, Merry Christmas! How are you getting along? Any problems?" she chirruped warmly.

"The house is fine, but I have a big problem, Gloria."

"What is it?" Her voice changed and her customary sharpness emerged.

"I never told you, but I've been putting money in the armoire in the garage for safekeeping . . . you know, squirreling away my savings. When I checked two days ago, it was gone."

"Gone?"

"Disappeared, missing, not in the drawer where I left it. I was hoping you had it."

"No, I don't know anything about it," she said slowly. "How much money are we talking here?"

"Over three thousand dollars."

She groaned audibly. "Have you lost your mind? Keeping that kind of money hidden in the garage?"

"I was trying to keep it hidden like you said, so my mother's company couldn't take it away from me."

I heard her groan again and that only increased my panic.

"If you didn't take it, then where could it be?"

I was talking faster and faster now, and my words turned into a howl of despair. "I don't know what to do. I need that money. God, what will I do?"

"Calm down, calm down. I'll talk to Richard and we'll figure out what happened. No one's been in the garage that I know of, so the money has to be there somewhere. We'll get it straightened out when I get home. Don't let this ruin your Christmas."

Oh, sure, like my Christmas was going to be so jolly anyway, I thought as I hung up the phone.

The last thing I wanted to do was deck the halls and make merry. But I had already promised to join Earl and his daughter's family for dinner. And if I didn't go there, what would I do? Drinking eggnog in the camper while I brooded didn't seem like much of an alternative.

So I had Christmas dinner with Earl's family. Earl's daughter, Teresa, was petite, with long brown hair and kind eyes. I was surprised to see that she was half-Mexican. I don't know why I was surprised—after all, half of California is Hispanic—but Earl had never mentioned it. All he ever told me was that she was bringing up twelve-year-old Jack and fourteen-year-old Melissa on a bank teller's salary along with occasional child support payments from her ex-husband.

The whole family was nice to me, even teenage Melissa, and I recalled with embarrassment how sullen I had been at fourteen. Earl beamed with pride, and I found myself wishing I had a grandfather and a family of my own.

chapter twenty-seven

Business at the Madhouse was slow, the days seemed to drag by while I waited impatiently for Gloria to return. I was just going through the motions behind the counter one afternoon after Christmas while Louis unloaded some supplies in the kitchen. Mal left, saying he was going to the bank and to run some errands. But I suspected he was really going to take a nap.

I wished I could nap myself as I was suffering from a scratchy throat and a killer headache. I had self-diagnosed these symptoms as a bad case of the blues. I longed to lie down and dream of a blue-eyed Irishman with a crooked smile.

By four o'clock only a handful of customers were scattered around the coffeehouse. A young guy wearing a knit cap sat at one of the computers, and two teenage girls were giggling at one of the window tables. At a table toward the back Jerry was reading what looked like a comic book. He was ignoring me and vice versa.

Then Bella burst through the door, pulling Stephanie and pushing Oliver in the baby barge. Stephanie immediately ran over to the five-foot-tall Christmas tree Mal had placed in the front corner between the east- and north-facing windows. The tree looked dry, no doubt due to the dozens of colored lights that had been blinking on its branches for the past month. After examining the gift-wrapped boxes under the tree, Stephanie brought one of them over to the counter.

"Who is this present for? Why haven't they opened it?" she asked.

"I don't know, Steffie," I said wearily. "You'll have to ask Mal when he comes back."

"Put it back under the tree, love, and tell me what you want," Bella said, shrugging off her fuzzy yellow coat and throwing it across an empty chair.

I watched while Bella spent the next few minutes trying to coax Stephanie into taking a muffin instead of a cookie. That's why I didn't notice when the wild and woolly Book Man slipped through the door.

I glanced up only when I heard the guy at the computer say, "Stop that, dude. Are you crazy?"

To my amazement, the Book Man was marching around the coffeehouse, flinging liquid everywhere from a jar he was carrying. He looked like a priest splashing holy water on a pagan temple.

"Hey," I shouted. "What are you doing?"

Ignoring me, he continued to throw liquid all over the old sofa, the Christmas tree, and then Bella's yellow coat.

"My coat!" Bella shrieked, grabbing up her yellow fake fur.

Without saying a word, the man began striking matches and throwing them on the tree and the sofa. Both burst into flames. Then he tossed a match toward Bella. It set her coat ablaze.

Bella screamed and dropped the coat.

I yelled, "Are you crazy? Louis. *Louis!*"

As I scrambled under the counter for the fire extinguisher, I could hear the wild man chanting, "God punishes evildoers. The Lord Jehovah cleanses your sins in fire."

Louis slammed through the kitchen door, took one look at the scene, and grabbed the extinguisher from me. He darted across the room, but the Book Man knocked him down. Louis hit his head on the floor with a loud *crack.* The extinguisher went skidding across the floor.

With what seemed like superhuman strength, the Book Man turned and dragged the burning sofa toward the front door.

Bella hadn't stopped screaming. Both Stephanie and the baby joined in. I rushed over to retrieve the fire extinguisher, but the Book Man grabbed it first. He tossed it into one of the computers, knocking it off the table and shattering the monitor.

Out of the corner of my eye, I saw the customer at the computer dashing toward the door. As he pushed past the burning sofa, he knocked the Book Man sideways against the flames. It looked to me as if the Book Man's sleeve caught fire. Still, he didn't stop chanting.

Then someone—it had to have been Jerry—moved toward him. They began to grapple with each other. Was Jerry trying to get past him or to subdue him? So much smoke and noise filled the air that I wasn't sure. The fire was spreading fast, and smoke obscured my vision. I could hear grunting coming from somewhere and a thumping noise.

Suddenly I realized that we all needed to get outside.

"Come on, Louis! We need to get out of here!" I knelt and pulled on his arm. He managed to stand up. I gave him a shove toward the counter and he tottered toward the kitchen. As I turned back toward the others, Bella charged forward in a mad dash to get to the blocked front door. She rammed the stroller into my shin, almost knocking me onto my knees.

Wincing in pain, I grabbed her and shook her. "Forget the stroller! Just take the baby out! Get the baby out of the stroller and go out the back way. I'll bring Stephanie."

Obediently she reached down and fumbled with the stroller straps, but she was too panicked to work the safety catch.

"I can't, I can't. The belt is stuck!" she shrieked.

I ran behind the counter, grabbed a knife, and sawed on the straps until they broke. In one motion I scooped up Oliver and thrust him into Bella's arms.

"Go out through the kitchen!" I said, looking around frantically. *"Now!"*

I glanced toward the windows. Dimly I saw the two teenage girls still frozen in their chairs, too frightened to move.

"Come on!" I screamed at them. "You have to go out the kitchen door!"

They stared at me with blind eyes.

I ran over to them and pulled on the nearest girl's arm. They both shot up as if I had suddenly broken the spell. Their chairs clattered to the floor.

"Go! Go!" I said, pushing them toward the kitchen door. They stumbled through it.

I whirled around to grab Stephanie. She wasn't there. Oh, God, did she go out with Bella or was she still in here?

"Stephanie, *Stephanie!*" I yelled. "Come on, baby. We have to get out of here."

The smoke had become so thick that it choked me. I grabbed the wet, dirty cloth we used to mop up spills. Holding the rag to my mouth, I dropped to the floor and looked around wildly. Then I caught a glimpse of something or someone under the table closest to the counter.

I crawled over to the table. My arms banged against the legs of the furniture as I reached out frantically. Then I felt something. It was a leg. Then I grabbed her shoulder. Her soft little body was curled up into a knot and twisted between the chair and table legs. I knocked the chair over trying to pull her out. She whimpered in terror.

"It's Ashley, Steffie," I said, fighting to sound calm. "Please come out. Let's go find Bella."

She went limp and I pulled her into my arms. Half carrying, half dragging her, I crawled toward the kitchen, banging my knee on the counter as I moved around it. I stood up, still clutching Steffie, and we burst into the kitchen. I stumbled over the boxes that Louis had been unloading and kept going. We staggered through the gaping door and burst out into the fresh air.

I collapsed on the curb, still holding Stephanie in my arms. We both were coughing and sobbing. From fear. From smoke. From relief.

"Is the bad killer gone?" Stephanie whimpered, looking up at me with a tear-streaked face.

"Yes, he's gone," I said. "We're safe now."

"I want my mommy," Stephanie cried.

"Me too," I mumbled. "Me too."

"Are you okay?" someone asked me. I couldn't answer. I was still fighting to get myself under control. Sirens screamed in the background and a fire truck pulled up to the corner of the building.

A fireman in full gear ran up to us. "Is anyone still in there?" he asked urgently.

"I'm not sure," I said.

He dashed inside through the back door.

I pulled Stephanie to her feet. "Let's go find Bella and your brother."

We managed to get to the front of the building, veering out into the street to avoid the hoses. Bella stood next to an ambulance watching a paramedic doing something to the baby.

"Stephanie!" Bella shrieked and ran to us. I could see her hands were shaking, and her usually ruddy face was pale. "Thank God you're all right. Jesus, Mary, and Joseph. I've never been so scared."

"We're all right," I told her, looking down at Stephanie's tearstained face. "Steffie is fine, aren't you?"

Stephanie nodded, but she looked far from fine. The pupils of her eyes looked like pinpricks, and her tiny legs trembled. I knelt down to steady her.

"How's Oliver?" I asked.

"He's seems all right. They're just looking him over as a precaution," she said. "It's just a precaution."

"Stephanie needs to go home, Bella. You should take them both away from here."

"I'll get a cab just as soon as the paramedic checks out Stephanie." Bella grabbed my shoulder and whispered fiercely in my ear, "They're going to fire me, I know they will. They'll fire me for putting the children in danger."

"Take it easy, it's not your fault. The important thing is the kids are safe. I really don't think they'll want to fire the nanny that saved their children."

She hesitated. "But really I didn't save them, you did. You got us out of there."

"We did it together. As far as I'm concerned, you're a heroine," I said. "Now take them home. Stephanie looks ready to collapse."

Bella pulled Stephanie up into her arms, hugging her as she carried her over to the paramedic's truck.

I stood up, turned around, and gazed at the surreal scene before me. There were firemen and hoses everywhere. Traffic was stopped along both Fillmore and California streets. Dozens of gawkers stood on both corners, watching the melodrama unfold before them. The light was fading, or maybe the smoke made the sky look so dark. The whole scene was like something being broadcast on the evening news.

In the midst of the chaos, I saw Tom gesturing to another fireman. I couldn't muster the strength to walk over to him. Instead, I wearily sank down onto the curb. Seconds later he pounded across the sidewalk and grabbed my arm. "Are you all right, Ashley?"

"Yeah. Where's Louis?" I asked. "And Jerry? Did everyone get out?"

"Louis has a sore head, but he'll be fine. What happened here, Ashley? How many people were inside?"

I tried to get my brain working. My head felt thick and I seemed to be moving in slow motion. "Let's see. There was Louis and me. Bella and the two kids. Jerry. Two girls I didn't know, but they ran out the back door ahead of me. So I know they're all right. And a guy using the computer. I'm sure he made it out the front door because I saw him knock the crazy guy into the sofa. Counting the crazy Book Man, that's nine. No, ten, isn't it?"

"You're not making any sense. What Book Man?"

"You know, the one with bushy hair, who always comes in screaming about the book. He came in spraying some kind of liquid, gasoline maybe, all over the sofa, the tree, everywhere, and set fire to it all."

"*He* set the fire? Well, that explains why it went up so fast," Tom said. "Mal's going to be furious that he was at the bank and missed the whole thing. He would have stopped that guy in his tracks."

"I'm not so sure he could have. It happened so fast," I said. And then, my head cleared and I realized what he was saying. I grabbed his arm. "Oh, God! Tom, I'm not sure Mal went to the bank. He might have gone upstairs to take a nap."

"What! They said no one was up there!" Tom exclaimed,

and then he yelled, "Larry! Upstairs!" as he dashed over to the metal security gate blocking the doorway to the stairs. They hammered at the security gate with axes.

I stood there watching as the purple paint blistered across the side of the building and the smoke swirled and twisted up into the sky.

The security door finally fell sideways. Tom and Larry bounded up the long staircase. It was amazing to see how quickly they moved wearing all the heavy gear.

Louis came up alongside me, and we waited anxiously as the seconds elapsed. Finally, they came hurtling back down the stairs, carrying Malcolm between them. A paramedic surged forward and clamped an oxygen mask on Mal's face.

Other firemen crossed in front of us, wheeling a gurney. The person on the gurney wasn't visible. Jerry? The Book Man? Whoever it was, he was badly hurt. Or dead.

"There's one more," I heard a fireman say.

I couldn't watch anymore. I walked across the street and sat down on the curb. My legs felt weak and my throat ached. I looked down at my hands. They were grimy—from what, I wasn't sure.

I don't know how long I sat there before Louis joined me.

"Mal's breathing," he said. "They're taking him to the hospital for observation. Smoke inhalation."

"What about Jerry?" I whispered.

"He didn't make it. Neither did the nutcase who started this."

Jerry was dead? I couldn't quite comprehend it. Suddenly, a wave of nausea hit me. I felt ashamed that I'd never liked him. The guy had been immature, sure, but he wasn't a bad person. Maybe he could have been the next Bill Gates. He would never have a chance to grow up, find a girlfriend who appreciated him, and accomplish all the things that he might have accomplished.

Someone put a blanket around me, but I shrugged it off. I heard Tom say, "Maybe you should go to the hospital, too, Ashley. Just as a precaution."

"*Precaution* is a popular word today. You know, you don't really hear that word very often, do you? I always used to think of it in connection with condoms. Now it will always make me think of fires."

"Ashley, you're in shock," he said, wrapping the blanket back around me.

"No, I'm fine, I'm really fine. I just don't know what to do because I can't leave," I said.

"Why not?"

I looked at him dully. "Because my purse is in there," I said, pointing to the blackened interior of the Madhouse. "With my car keys inside."

"Forget your keys. The building's a total loss. You'll never find them in there. You shouldn't be driving anyway. Let me call someone for you."

"There's no one to call," I answered. "How pathetic is that? I can't think of anyone to call."

chapter twenty-eight

"No, no, *no*!" A voice was moaning and it woke me up. Then I realized the voice was mine. I sat up on the camper bed, my heart pounding as if I had just been chased by a horde of devil worshippers. It was still dark. I grabbed my watch and looked at it. 3:06.

My skin was damp and my throat and chest ached. I pulled off my sweat-soaked nightclothes and crawled back under the blankets naked. My head throbbed and I squirmed uncomfortably under the covers, too disturbed to get back to sleep.

I had been dreaming that Tattie and I were driving along that mountain road to Curtis Davidson's country place. My Jetta moved like a rocket along the curvy stretch of highway. Tall, dark trees lined both sides, and the road looked like a twisting tunnel with no end in sight. As the car careened around corners, the seat belt cut sharply into my collarbone and left breast. The car picked up speed, going faster and faster into the darkness. I frantically pressed the brake pedal. But the car didn't slow down. Horrified, I looked over at Tattie. She grinned at me from the passenger seat. She took a long hit on the joint in her hand, held it in, and then blew the smoke out toward me. I stared at her in shock. But she just laughed and reached out her hand to give me the joint. I waved it away wildly, and the lighted joint flew out of her hand, onto the car seat. I looked down to where it landed and saw smoke billowing up. I took my hands off the steering wheel and fumbled to grab the burning joint. The car swerved off the road and rolled over and over and over and over and over and over.

That's when I woke up.

I lay there, shuddering from the memory of my nightmare. Only a few hours had passed since I left the smoldering ruins of the coffeehouse. Tom had called an emergency locksmith for me, but two hours elapsed before I finally had a new ignition key. Fatigue plus a stabbing headache and my worsening sore throat had drained my energy. It took all my strength to drive myself back to the camper. I crawled straight into bed and for a few hours I slept like someone in a coma.

But after my nightmare, I tossed and turned. Yesterday's headache continued to pound inside my skull. My throat was so sore I could hardly swallow. Around seven thirty I pulled myself up and tried to follow my usual morning routine at the health club. Within minutes of mounting the exercise bike, I began coughing and felt too light-headed to continue.

I went to Walgreens, bought some over-the-counter cold medication, and returned to the camper. Reynaldo paused and stared at me as I pulled behind the station. The whole day was misery. My headache didn't let up while my cough turned into a honking, chest-searing rumble that made my lungs hurt.

I didn't have enough energy to do anything or go anywhere. Collapsed on the sleeping platform, all I could do was sleep fitfully and cough and dream.

I dreamt I was an alien creature and my skin was made of fire, only to wake up with my skin burning. I tossed off all my blankets and half my clothing. Minutes later I was shivering and pulled everything back on. My whole body ached, and I coughed so violently it left me gasping for air.

I lost track of time. I knew it was still daylight, but I had to use the toilet and I didn't care who saw me. I staggered out of the camper and over to the ladies' room. Reynaldo called to me as I walked by. I didn't respond—I had no energy to spare for thinking or talking.

Back in the camper, my coughing went on and on. The pain in my chest became sharper, and the coughing made my throat constrict and my stomach heave. I was gagging and struggling for breath so that I didn't even look up when someone came into the camper.

Then I heard Earl's raspy voice.

"Are you okay? Ashley? Are you sick, baby doll?"

I couldn't answer. Just breathing was hard enough without trying to talk. Each breath I took brought a searing pain.

Earl gently put his hand on my forehead. I looked up at him, but he seemed slightly out of focus. My eyes burned from the exertion of all the coughing.

Everything that happened after that was blurry. Over my head I heard Earl's voice and then Officer Strobel's talking about me. I heard the words *delirious* and *can't breathe.*

Earl said, "She's hotter than a pistol."

I wondered for a moment if this is what it was like to die. In your last moments of life, maybe all you listen to is the rhythm of the air going in and out of your lungs.

"Let's go," Strobel said, leaning over and lifting me up, still twisted inside my blanket. He carried me outside the camper. The cold air and the bright lights of the gas station made me blink. Above them the evening light was fading. In the distance I could hear the usual roar of traffic along the street.

Strobel put me down onto the backseat of a car, and Earl climbed in next to me.

"You're going to be all right, baby doll," Earl said, pulling me so that I rested against his shoulder.

I was too exhausted to reply. The car twisted and turned through the streets. As Strobel drove, he muttered something unintelligible under his breath. A couple of times Earl said, "Take it easy," but I didn't know if he meant me or Strobel.

Then we stopped, the car door opened, and people appeared. All at once there were hands touching me, pulling at me, propelling me along on a gurney as if I were a turkey on my way to the Thanksgiving feast. Bright lights shone in my eyes and I was told to open my mouth, open my eyes, do this, do that. I wanted to push them away as they poked and pinched at me from all sides. Insistent voices kept asking me questions that I didn't want to answer.

"Ashley, can you hear me?"

"Are you in pain, Ashley?"

"Do you know where you are, Ashley?"

"Ashley, have you eaten or taken any medication in the last six hours?"

They kept repeating that last question over and over but I couldn't think, I couldn't answer.

I felt a hand, a woman's hand, gently brush back my tangled hair, and I whispered, "Momma?"

"Do you want us to call your mother?" someone asked.

"Yes," I said. "I want my mother."

After that, there were voices in the background and more prodding, more coughing, but my mind went spinning away from me.

I woke up in a hospital bed with an IV in my left arm and plastic oxygen tubes hooked inside my nose.

A woman in a pale green smock came in and fussed with the plastic bag hanging on the hook near my head.

"My chest hurts," I said.

"I shouldn't wonder," she answered. "You had a collapsed lung. Your doctor will come by later and explain. Would you like some water or chicken broth?"

I shook my head and closed my eyes again. Some time later I reopened them when another woman wheeled a cart next to my bed and expertly thrust a thermometer into my ear. As the woman took hold of my arm and began to attach a blood-pressure cuff, I noticed someone sitting in the chair at the foot of my bed. It was Nicole.

"Nic," I said foolishly. "What are you doing here?"

"So you still remember who I am. I was beginning to wonder." She walked over to the other side of my bed and took my hand in hers. "Why didn't you return my calls, you jerk?"

I waited until the temperature taker finished and left the

room. "I was going to. It's just that . . . there's been a lot going on."

"No kidding. I can't believe you've been living in Phil's camper. Why didn't you let me know? I would have helped you. I would have borrowed some money from my dad for you."

"I know," I said. "But it wasn't your problem. Anyway, I didn't move into the camper until after you left town."

"You could have called me. All those letters and e-mails and not once did you think to mention where you were living! I feel so bad that you had to go through that."

I could see tears glistening in her eyes. "Well, I'm fine. See?"

Nicole chuckled. "Bronchitis and a collapsed lung. Yeah, you're the picture of good health."

I took a good look at her. She was glowing and had a new air of self-confidence that I had never seen before.

"It's really good to see you. You look wonderful."

"Thanks," she said, bending over and showing me her scalp. "Look, no hair loss. Can you believe it? I don't twist and pull my hair anymore. I'm completely cured."

She paused and then giggled. "Well, almost completely cured."

"That's great. How did you do it?"

Nicole gave me a sideways smile. "Getting away helped a lot. From my mother, of course, but it turns out that I had to get away from you too."

I winced. "Ouch!"

"I didn't mean it like that," she said hastily. "It's just that you've always protected me. Juliana, my therapist, said I needed to learn to deal with my own problems instead of relying on you to rescue me. I leaned on you too much."

"You're seeing a therapist? Since when?"

"Well, I never told you—I never told anyone. I had a hard time adjusting to college and being on my own. I didn't want to admit how hard it was. Everyone there seemed smarter and more self-confident than me. I thought I was going to go completely crazy if I didn't talk to someone. Then I found Juliana through the dean's office. She's really helped me see that I could do it alone."

I just looked at her, not sure how to respond.

"But I've missed you a lot," she added, her eyes shimmering again. "We're together again, and it's my turn to help you. When you get out of here, you're definitely not going back to that camper. You'll come home with me. You're my best friend and that's where you should be."

"No. Never. I don't want to be anywhere near the happy couple," I said fiercely.

She was silent for a moment. "So you know about that?"

"About Cindy and Phil?" I managed a shaky laugh. "Yeah, she couldn't wait to rub it in my face."

"I'm sorry, Ash. I had no idea."

"Don't worry about it. I was pretty clueless myself, and not just about that. But I've learned to take care of myself too, and I'll figure something out. It's just that I had some money saved to rent a place and—"

"And you still have it!" said Gloria as she strode into the room carrying a vase full of my favorite red roses.

"I do?" I tried to sit up but couldn't.

"Yep, every penny of it. It's all there."

"Where was it?"

Gloria looked a little sheepish at that question. "The boys took it. They had it hidden in their toy box."

"You're kidding," Nicole interjected as I stared dumbly at Gloria.

"Nope. They followed Ashley into the garage one day and watched her take the money out and count it. To them it was like play money. They took it and played with it, then hid it just like she did. Believe me, they know better now."

Gloria said the last sentence with such emphasis that Nicole and I exchanged glances, both of us wondering what she did to them.

"Then everything really will be all right," I said with relief. Then a dark thought hit me. "What about the hospital bill? This must be costing a fortune."

"I've talked to your boss, and he told me about the fire. Your doctor feels that smoke inhalation caused or contributed to your condition, and Malcolm says his insurance will pay your hospital bill."

"You talked to Malcolm?" I said in wonder. "You have been busy. I guess I'm confused. Didn't you just get home from Colorado?"

"Two days ago. Phil called me right after you were brought here," she answered.

"You've been here since yesterday morning," Nicole chimed in.

"I have?" I said.

"You have. Where do you want these?" Gloria waved the vase of roses she held.

"Right there," I said, pointing to the table at the foot of the bed. "So I can see them. Thank you, they're beautiful."

"They are nice," she agreed, rearranging them slightly. "Who are the rest of them from?"

Only then did I notice three other flower arrangements, all of them oversized flower-shop deliveries.

"I don't know," I said in amazement.

Nicole picked up the cards and read one to me. "*To our little heroine. Get well soon. Mal and the Inmates.* Sounds like a rock group," she laughed.

The second one was from Phil, Earl, and Reynaldo, and the last card was the most astonishing of all. It was signed *Ted Strobel.*

"You see?" Nicole said. "There are a lot of people who care about you."

I turned my head into the pillow so Nic and Gloria wouldn't see me cry.

. . .

Over the next two days I had more visitors, including Earl and his granddaughter, Malcolm, and Bella. When Phil showed up, we both avoided the topic of Cindy.

After talking about the weather and the gas station and my car needing a tune-up, Phil cleared his throat and said, "About the camper—"

I interrupted him. "I don't need to stay there anymore. I'm

going to stay with Gloria a few days and then find a place in the city."

"That's good," he said with obvious relief.

"I want you to know that I'm very grateful to you for letting me stay there."

Phil avoided my eyes and said, "Well, I'm feeling a little guilty about that, after you ended up in here. Your mother—"

I interrupted him again. I did not want to discuss my mother with Phil ever again. "That's not your fault. I am truly grateful to you for letting me stay. I don't know what I would have done if you hadn't helped me out. Thank you."

"You're welcome," he said, looking me in the eyes for the first time.

"There you are. Even in here you're still a glamour-puss." Malcolm's voice boomed so loud they could probably hear him at the nurse's station. Behind him I could hear Bella's giggle and see Tom grinning at me.

As the three of them thundered into my room, Phil gave me a wave and slipped out the door.

chapter twenty-nine

Sunday morning Officer Strobel strolled into my hospital room, dressed in regular clothes instead of his cop's uniform. It was only 8:15, but I was wide awake because the woman in the next bed had been whining nonstop for the last hour about how the nurses didn't understand the tremendous amount of pain she was suffering.

"Hi!" I said in surprise. "Thanks for the flowers. Have a seat."

"You're welcome," he said and sat down.

After an awkward silence I hesitantly asked if he had brought me to the hospital.

"Yeah, Earl called me. I took one look at you and knew you needed to get to a doctor right away. Ever since the robbery, I'd been keeping an eye on the gas station, so I had already figured out you were living in the camper," Strobel said, shaking his head at me in disapproval. "I was going to speak to Phil about it. Living there was a really dumb idea."

I started to bristle and then he added, "Still, I have to admit you've got guts. I thought you were just another spoiled, selfish Burlingame brat. But, in spite of that big chip on your shoulder, you've got courage."

I didn't know whether to be flattered or offended by his remark. I decided not to waste my energy getting mad.

"I wouldn't call it courage," I admitted. "I just didn't have any choice. It was sink or swim after my mother disappeared."

"I see a lot of teenagers sink like stones. They're used to their parents buying them whatever they want, so they think they can buy their way out of any situation. They perpetrate all kinds of offenses, get caught, and find out—surprise—there are some things money can't buy."

"You know, it's funny, I never hear anyone except a cop—I mean, officer of the law—use the word *perpetrate,*" I tweaked him.

He flashed a quick smile, but kept on ranting. "All of the kids around here have this sense of entitlement—as if the world owes them something and they don't have to work for anything. They get handed it all. Life is one big party for them. They think they're exempt from the rules that the rest of us have to live by."

I held up my hand to stop him. "Excuse me, but I don't think it's all their fault. *Somebody* has encouraged them to think they're special and exempt from the rules, you know. Anyway, where did you grow up that's so different?"

He gave me a sheepish grin. "Oh, I grew up around here, just like you. But my parents taught me some values."

"Poor Strobel," I said lightly. "Did Daddy give you values instead of a nice new car or a stereo?"

"I have a first name, you know. It's Ted."

"All right, Officer Ted. We'll agree that you were raised better than the rest of us. How about having a little sympathy for those who weren't so lucky?"

He recrossed his legs and leaned back in the chair. "Well, I have to admit it's not *all* upbringing. Some people survive and turn out to be good citizens in spite of the worst sort of home environment. Others cross the line and end up in the gutter no matter how much love and money Mommy and Daddy give them. An awful lot of people are just plain weak. If they never have to face anything too difficult, they remain law abiding, but the minute a situation turns ugly, it's impossible to know how they'll react."

"That's a very cynical view of the world you've got there, Ted."

"Cynical? Maybe," he said. "But I've learned it the hard way, one day at a time. I'm happy to see that you can take care of yourself and stay out of trouble when things get tough. I wasn't too sure for a while there. You started running with a bad crowd—"

"A bad crowd! What do you mean?" I interjected.

"That Krylov kid. She's a disaster waiting to happen."

"Tattie's all right. She's been a good friend to me," I retorted.

"You don't need friends like that," he said.

"I think I can decide that for myself," I said icily.

We both fell silent. Then I said in a tight voice, "Well, thanks for stopping by. I appreciate everything you've done for me."

He shuffled to his feet, walked to the end of the bed, and

stared down at me. "So, what are you going to do now? You can't go back to living in the camper."

"I'm making other arrangements."

"Good," he said. "I'm glad I was wrong about you. And I'm pretty sure you're going to be fine."

For the next twenty-four hours, all I did was think about my future. The hospital would be releasing me sometime tomorrow, and Gloria had invited me to stay with her family until I was fully recuperated and had found a place of my own. But that was only a short-term solution. I had kept everything on hold while I waited for my mother to come back. But I couldn't keep waiting for something that might never happen. Nicole had gone back to school. Tattie was partying in Mexico. Patrick had left with a fair-thee-well. The Madhouse had gone up in smoke.

As far as I could see, I had only three options. I could become a total outlaw like Tattie, but comfort and safety are important to me. I wasn't cut out for living on the edge. Option two was to just drift and see what happened, but that hadn't worked well so far. That left Door Number Three: I could try to create the life I wanted. The inmates of the Madhouse seemed to embrace this philosophy—Mal especially. The coffeehouse functioned as both his business and his social life, with writing as his hobby. He had carved out an existence that worked for him.

The question was, what did I want? College seemed like the best place to start. Tattie claims you can learn more by living life then you'll ever discover sitting in a classroom. But I wanted to sit in classrooms with other kids my age and discuss the meaning of life and Descartes and Tolstoy. I just had to figure out how to make it happen.

. . .

Two days later I was sleeping in Gloria's combination guest room/office/den with Stella at my feet. Despite my intention to sleep late, my internal alarm clock seemed to be irrevocably programmed to dawn. Maybe it was for the best since Daniel and Matthew bounced out of bed early and created enough mayhem to wake the dead. By eight I was dressed and drinking green tea with Gloria while her boys maneuvered action figures in a galactic battle on the floor beneath us. We weren't really talking about anything in particular when Gloria suddenly cleared her throat and announced, "Ashley, I owe you an apology."

"Don't worry about it," I said. "It wasn't your fault the boys hid the money. I shouldn't have left all that cash in the garage. Let's just forget about it."

She squirmed in her chair. "Well, thank you, but that's not it. It's something else."

I looked at her, mystified. She sighed and absentmindedly rubbed her forefinger across a tiny chip on the rim of her teacup.

"This has been bothering me for a while now. I need to apologize for stampeding you out of your mother's house—your house—last fall. There wasn't as big a hurry as I let you believe. You could have stayed a few weeks or even months longer before the bank foreclosed. I never imagined you would end up in a place like that camper."

Her face flushed and her mouth twisted in a self-deprecating grimace. "To be honest, I blamed you for what happened. I thought it served you right to have to move out of the house and fend for yourself. I was so judgmental. I should have been concentrating on what a bad friend I was instead of what a bad daughter you were. What if you had died? I would have never forgiven myself. As my best friend's daughter, you deserved better from me."

I looked at her in amazement and then I reached over to grab her hand. "Don't. There's no need for you to feel guilty. Some of it *was* my fault. My mother got herself in a huge mess and I was too wrapped up in myself to notice. I've wished a thousand times that I could go back and change things. All I want now is for her to come home so I can make up for all the awful things I said and did."

I sighed, one of those long sighs that goes on forever. "Besides, we both know that there's no way I could have kept the house and paid the bills. I had to move on sooner or later. It's been hell at times, but I've learned to appreciate my true friends and you're definitely one of them."

Gloria sniffed and wiped the corners of her eyes.

I pretended not to notice and shifted my gaze toward the window, weirded out by this new, emotional Gloria. I much preferred the sharp-tongued version.

"Maybe I should make some pancakes," she said, regaining her normal, brisk voice.

"Don't do it for me," I said, still looking out the window. "Uh-oh, I think I see Stella stalking some robins. I better go out and chase them away."

With that, I dashed outside so I wouldn't cry too.

. . .

Except for the noise her boys made, I enjoyed my stay at Gloria's. No more leaping up at dawn and racing to the health club. No more killing time at book readings, coffeehouses, or in libraries. I slept, read, and watched television. Nicole came over several times to hang out, until she had to go back to school. Every few days I stopped by the gas station to chat with Earl.

The weather was consistently rainy, as Januarys tend to be around here. When the sun finally appeared, I decided to make the most of it by driving into San Francisco and going to my favorite spot, the beach at Crissy Field. Along the way, I parked on Union Street to dart into my favorite pizzeria for a slice.

On my way back to the car, I couldn't help noticing a spectacular teal-blue silk dress with a lacy black overskirt in the window of one of the more expensive boutiques. I stopped to admire it, even though I knew I didn't need it and couldn't afford it.

As I reluctantly turned away from the store window, I bumped into a girl walking along the sidewalk with two friends. They were talking and laughing in loud voices and carrying shopping bags from all the expensive shops. With a shock I realized one of the girls was Mara.

"Ashley!" Mara shrieked in surprise. "How *are* you?"

Just the person I didn't want to see. Ever.

"Mara, hi. I'm fine. How are you?"

"*Exhausted,* just *exhausted,*" she gushed, shaking Armani Exchange and Bebe shopping bags at me. "We're on a mission. I needed some new things and *everything* is on sale. My mother gave me her card and we're buying the stores out. There are *so many* cute things here, I just can't resist."

I was acutely aware of my old jeans, plain cotton sweater, and running shoes. Knowing Mara, I knew she wouldn't miss any of those details.

"I haven't seen you in *ages,*" she continued. "What are you doing these days? Everyone is always saying, 'Where's Ashley? What's up with Ashley?' "

"I've been busy. How about you? How's school?"

"I'm at UC Berkeley," she said. "I wanted to go to UCLA, but my mother talked me into staying in the Bay Area. But I'm *loving* it. Hey, guys, this is a friend from high school, Ashley, *the one* I told you about."

I could just imagine what she'd told them. They didn't look like they remembered anyway. They just looked bored.

"Ashley, this is Morgan and Lauren. They're Tri Delts like me. The sorority is *so much fun.*"

"Great," I said.

In a tone oozing with sincerity, she added, "Do you live around here or are you just shopping? I heard you had a job at Starbucks or something. How *is* that?"

On hearing that I worked at a coffeehouse, her friends completely lost interest in both me and the conversation. They moved toward the store window I'd been staring at moments before.

"Wow. Isn't that darling? Look at that teal dress with the black lace skirt. I have to try that on," one of them screeched, and they went inside the store.

I wanted to follow that girl and choke the life out of her, but I managed not to show it.

"We just *love* Union Street," Mara babbled on. "The shops are so cool and at night the bars are *really fun.*"

"Yeah, it's *fabulous,*" I mimicked her, but she didn't get it.

"So, tell me, what's it like working at Starbucks?"

"I don't work at Starbucks. I did work at a coffeehouse for a while, but not anymore." No way was I going to tell her about the Madhouse, the fire, or anything else about my life.

"How was it?" Mara rambled on, oblivious to my curtness. "Did you meet lots of hot guys, or"—she dropped her voice—"were all the customers weird and psycho? I don't think I could be around those *types.*"

She shuddered dramatically, but I didn't respond. She spoke again in the pseudo-whisper and asked, "Did you ever hear from your mother? Do you know where she is?"

The bitch! I gave her a cold look. "I have to go. I'm late for an appointment."

She wasn't done yet. "With a guy? Is he cute? Have you heard about Scott? He's dating some chick from Beverly Hills. Her father is a movie producer or something. Isn't that *wild*?" She gave me a sly, sideways look.

"Wild! Great seeing you, Mara," I lied, edging away and moving down the street at a trot. It was all I could do not to run. I didn't have to turn around to know that she had gone into the boutique, eager to fill in her sorority sisters.

I found my car, crawled into the driver's seat, and sat motionless at the steering wheel, trying to gather my wits and catch my breath. I waited for the tears to start. But they didn't.

Instead, I laughed. Amazing! I laughed at the whole ridiculous scene. I laughed to think I had ever been friends with

Mara or had ever worried about what she said or did. I wouldn't trade places with her for anything. I'd rather live in a camper than be like her. I'd rather hang out with Earl and the Madhouse gang than listen to her malicious gossip. She and her snooty sorority sisters could have all the *hot guys* and *fabulous* clothes and *really fun* bars. I didn't want any of that anymore.

I was still laughing as I drove away.

chapter thirty

In late April, nearly a year after my mother disappeared, my life finally seemed to be under control. Stella and I were living in a three-bedroom house in Twin Peaks. I shared it with Amy and Shannon, a couple of small-town girls from up north who were full-time students at the Art Institute. They were silly and prone to prying, but I could tolerate them.

The Madhouse had not yet reopened because of some hassle with the insurance company. But thanks to a glowing recommendation from Mal, I landed a job waitressing at the Beach Chalet, a trendy restaurant overlooking the Pacific. Chalet customers had more money than the coffeehouse crowd and I pulled in decent tips.

In January I had enrolled in two classes, Written Composition and Introduction to Cinema Studies, at City College. I had even gone to the movies a couple of times with a boy in my Cinema Studies class. Life was okay, maybe better than okay. At times it was even good.

. . .

I was in the bathroom getting ready for my ten o'clock class when Shannon pounded on the door to make herself heard over the roar of my hair dryer. The sound startled me and I knocked a perfume bottle into the sink. It shattered, flooding the room with the scent of gardenias.

"Hey, Ashley!" Shannon shouted. Cursing under my breath, I turned off the dryer and opened the door.

She stood there in her yellow bathrobe and white socks, her face lit up. "There's a cop here asking for you!" she said, eyes wide with curiosity. "What's going on? Are you a secret drug dealer or something?"

I gave her a cold look. "Why? Are you looking to make a buy?"

As I walked into the front room, I saw Ted Strobel. He was staring at Amy's Eminem poster on the wall.

"Don't blame me for that," I said. "My roommate is the one who loves bad-boy rappers."

He turned away from the poster to look at me, and I saw he was wearing his serious cop face. I felt a sharp jerk in my chest. He could have been there for any number of reasons. He could be bringing me a message from Earl. But somehow I *knew.* I knew he had come about my mother.

"What is it?" I said warily.

"Sorry to stop by so early, but I have some news that I didn't want to give you over the phone." He nodded toward Shannon, who was still hovering, not even pretending to do anything except eavesdrop. "Can we talk privately?"

"Sure," I said, throwing Shannon a fierce look. She immediately ducked into the kitchen, no doubt to continue listening with her ear pressed against the door.

My legs suddenly felt wobbly, so I sat down on the edge of the sofa. Stella darted into the room and leaped onto the sofa, digging her claws into the upholstery. I pulled her down into my lap and began mechanically stroking her silky fur. Ted sat down in the armchair across from me.

"You've found my mother," I said flatly, sounding calmer than I felt.

"Yes," he said. "I'm sorry. It isn't good news. . . ." He stopped, reluctant to go on.

"Just tell me. I can't deal with the kind, gentle buildup. Is she under arrest?"

Ted cleared his throat. "I'm sorry, Ashley. The County Sheriff 's office found your mother's Mercedes, and there's a body inside. We haven't officially identified it as your mother, but we're fairly sure it's her."

All I could do was shake my head from side to side. My chest hurt, as if something had broken loose, and I felt disoriented. I stared at the wall as his voice went relentlessly on.

"Her car was discovered halfway down a deep ravine in that forested area between the coast and the watershed lakes. Apparently, she went off Skyline Boulevard on a sharp turn when no one was around. Then last night a motorist lost his hubcap on that turn. He drives one of those vintage sports cars and apparently the hubcaps are hard to replace. So, early this morning, he climbed down into the ravine to find it and spotted your mother's car in the brush about a hundred feet down.

He went farther down to look inside, saw a body, and called nine one one."

My heart pounded so hard that the noise of it filled my head. Yet it still didn't drown out his voice.

"Pending the outcome of the investigation, we'll be able to tell exactly what happened. Right now, though, we're guessing that she's been down there a long time, probably since the day she disappeared. Her laptop was found and her purse—"

Suddenly, I found my voice. "That doesn't mean anything," I interjected angrily. "It could be anyone. Maybe someone stole the car. It's not her. I want to see the body. I want to make sure for myself that it's really her."

His voice was soft, but his words were hard. "No, Ashley, you don't want to see her. The body's been there for almost a year and there's not much left."

I grimaced in horror as he went on.

"It's not something anyone should see. There's probably some jewelry or personal apparel you will be asked to identify. If not, we'll use dental records to provide conclusive identification. It's the best way, believe me."

Ted walked over and sat down on the sofa next to me, putting his hand on my arm. Annoyed, Stella jumped up and ran out of the room. But I sat motionless.

"I'm very sorry, Ashley," he repeated awkwardly. "I came to tell you as soon as we heard. I didn't want you to hear it on the news."

"I've been waiting for her to come back. I've been waiting all this time."

"I know," he said.

"She's dead?" I whispered, and the tears began to stream down my cheeks. "She's been dead this whole time?"

"How can I help you? Let me call someone for you."

I stood up, but my mind was a jumble. "I need my coat and purse. I need to see Gloria. I need Gloria."

"I'll take you there," he said.

I nodded and put my hand up to cover my mouth. A sick, sour taste had risen up the back of my throat. I swallowed hard to force it back down. Biting my lip, I walked back into the bathroom and stared at myself in the mirror. For a moment, my mother's haunted face stared back at me.

I went into the bedroom to grab a jacket and my purse. Shannon came out of the kitchen and started to say something, but I dashed past her to the curb and climbed into Ted's patrol car.

During the long, silent ride to Gloria's house, I stared out the car window without seeing anything. The cool and overcast weather was classic San Francisco, although the fog would probably burn off. As we neared Burlingame, the sun pierced through the fading mist, raising the temperature outside. But I felt cold and empty, like my old Raggedy Ann doll after the neighbor's dog had pulled out all of her stuffing.

When Gloria opened her door, I didn't have to say a word. She took one look and then folded me in her arms. I unleashed a new flood of tears accompanied by hiccupping, choking sobs. I would never be able to tell my mother I loved her. I would never have the chance to tell her I was sorry.

While I struggled to get myself under control, Ted repeated the same information he had given me. Gloria was composed enough to ask him all the questions that I hadn't yet put into words. We all sat down in the living room, as if it were some kind of social gathering. It seemed so wrong that we could sit there talking normally when nothing was normal. I was grateful Gloria's sons were at nursery school because I couldn't have dealt with the two of them at that moment.

"What was the cause of the accident?" asked Gloria.

"At this point, it's impossible to tell because any skid marks have long since disappeared. We'll check the car to see if there was a mechanical problem. A number of drivers go off roads in those mountains every year, and it's usually someone who's going too fast. Most vehicles hit a tree or another vehicle. Do you know the area?"

"Sure. We've gone for picnics up there and we get our Christmas tree from a farm off Skyline every year," Gloria said impatiently. "The road is curvy, but it doesn't seem all that dangerous."

"Not if you're careful. But if it's dark or you get distracted or you're going too fast . . ." His voice trailed off. "She might have had a blowout or a problem with her brakes. She could have swerved to avoid a deer or a squirrel. She could have been under the influence."

Both Gloria and I said, "No!" at the same time.

Then I added, "My mother didn't drink. Alcohol made her sick. She didn't take drugs or pills, either, except aspirin."

Gloria spoke up again. "I don't understand why no one would notice a car down there. There are so many cabins, and hikers use those trails all the time."

Ted shrugged. "It's unusual for a car to go down a ravine and stay hidden for an entire year. But it's not the first time this kind of thing has happened. The road can be treacherous and the drop is very steep where her car left the road. Plus that spot isn't near any of the popular hiking trails. The poison oak and brush are really thick in that ravine, and you'd have to have a good reason for climbing down there."

"But what was she doing? Skyline's an odd place for Diane to be driving, especially on a workday." Gloria's voice was thoughtful.

"Curtis," I said.

"Curtis?" asked Ted.

"Curtis Davidson," I said. "My mother worked for him. He has a cabin off Skyline Boulevard. I drove up there once because I thought my mother might be staying there."

My voice trailed off for a moment as the awful truth finally sunk in. "I must have driven right past the spot where my mother went off the road. Her car was there . . . she was there all the time."

Gloria reached over and put her arm around me. I had to ask the question that had been haunting me since Ted first told me about the body in the car.

"Do you think . . . I mean, will you be able to tell if . . ." A tear slid down my cheek and I wiped at it with my hand. "If she was killed instantly? What if she was trapped there for days, injured and in pain, waiting for someone to save her?"

"I don't know," Ted said, gazing at some spot on the wall over my head instead of meeting my eyes. Gloria sat motionless, staring down at her hands. I realized that they must have been wondering the same thing.

. . .

For the next few days I stayed at Gloria's. Mostly, I slept to keep the pain at bay. When I wasn't sleeping, I sat quietly, staring at nothing. I went through the motions of everyday life, but I wasn't really there. Gloria provided Ted with the name of our dentist. She went to the coroner's office and brought back my mother's wristwatch and the gold wedding band she had continued to wear even after Jimmy's death. Now we couldn't deny it anymore.

It took the police lab a week to confirm the bitter truth. The report said that she had died from injuries sustained in the accident. Because they found no mechanical problems with the car's brakes or engine, they decided she had lost control of the car for reasons unknown.

Ted told us that he was fairly sure she had been killed instantaneously, but I was fairly sure he didn't *know* and just said that to make me feel better.

Gloria helped me to make burial arrangements and organize a small funeral mass. Only a few people came: Gloria and Richard, Ted Strobel, Earl, Malcolm, two of our former neighbors. Phil showed up, alone, but no one came from Warren Simmons, and there was no sign of Curtis Davidson. Over and over the priest repeated, "Holy Mary, mother of God, pray for us sinners now and at the hour of our death" until it echoed through my head. I closed my eyes and prayed as hard as I could that my mother was at peace.

Afterward, I tried to talk to Gloria about how I was going

to pay for all this. She kept brushing me off and saying, "We'll talk about it later."

. . .

After that, I didn't hear any more from the police. I badgered Strobel for more information, but he claimed the criminal investigation was closed. If any incriminating evidence was found on my mother's laptop, no one told me. The laptop belonged to the Simmons Company, so I couldn't even ask for it. Two suitcases were found in the trunk of her car, one of them filled with a jumble of clothes and the other empty. None of us knew what to make of that, but I hoped it meant she had planned to come home for me.

Then Gloria heard a rumor that Curtis Davidson had left the Warren Simmons Company, so at my prompting she tried calling Arthur Warren. He coldly referred her to his attorney. His attorney refused to discuss the case with her, claiming it was confidential. All my questions were left unanswered, and I was very frustrated.

I could think of only one other place where I might be able to get the answers I needed.

chapter thirty-one

The door in front of me was painted a bright, glossy red. Mounted on it nearly level with my eyes was one of those ornate door knockers shaped like a lion's head. I assumed the lion was merely decorative and rang the doorbell.

As I stood there waiting for the door to open, I smelled the sweet fragrance of the star jasmine crawling up the trellis alongside the entry. I turned around to admire the lush green lawn and the daylilies blooming in carefully laid-out borders. The house and its garden were breathtaking. It looked like the kind of place where nothing bad ever happened—or so I used to think. I knew better now.

A slim, well-groomed woman in her forties opened the door. We both stood there a moment, appraising each other. She was tanned and fit, as if she played a lot of tennis or golf. Her makeup was so subtle and flattering that most people would think she wasn't wearing any, and her silvery hair had been shaped into a chic bob. Her cream-colored sweater and skirt were beautifully cut.

"Hello. You must be Ashley," she said in a steady, carefully modulated tone that would project well when addressing a meeting of the Symphony Guild or Garden Club. "I'm Claire Davidson."

"Thank you for seeing me," I said as she stood back to let me inside.

The foyer was as impressive as the front lawn. It was large and bright with cathedral ceilings and a curved staircase leading to the second story. A gleaming tiled floor extended all the way to the back of the house.

"It's such a beautiful day. Let's sit out on the patio," she said.

I followed her through French doors onto a flagstone terrace. I saw trees and flowers off to the left and the blue glint of a swimming pool to the right.

We sat down across from each other at a round table shaded by a huge white umbrella.

"Can I get you some lemonade or a soft drink?"

"No, thank you. I'm fine."

I had pushed Gloria to use her contacts to arrange this meeting for me, but now I wasn't so sure it was a good idea.

Claire looked as if she never felt awkward anywhere. She leaned back in her chair and crossed her legs. Nice shoes. Expensive like everything else here.

"So, I understand you have some questions for me."

I hesitated, twisting my ring nervously.

She broke the silence. "I'm sorry about your mother, Ashley. I didn't know her well, but she seemed like a nice person."

I twisted my lips into an uncomfortable smile, as much in appreciation for her good manners as the sentiment. She misunderstood my smile and added, "I didn't blame Diane for what happened, or at least I understand. Curt is very persuasive."

I stopped fidgeting and looked straight into her eyes.

"That's what I want to understand—how it happened. So much of what went on is still a mystery to me, and I hoped that you might know more than I do."

"I don't know how much I can help." Her voice was cool.

"Please," I said. "Whatever you say, it will be between the two of us. I won't tell anyone. I just need to know."

She paused and studied me for a few seconds. "All right. I'll tell you what I can."

"Well . . ." I hesitated, and then plunged in. "I need to know how my mother ended up at the bottom of that ravine. She must have been going to see your husband at your country house, or maybe she was leaving? It could have been either. I assume they were, uh, involved." I faltered. "I mean, outside of work."

"Clearly they were," she said, shifting slightly in her chair.

"I don't mean to offend you, so please excuse me if I'm blunt. Did the two of them steal the money together? How did my mother die?"

She sighed and answered my last question first. "As I understand it, your mother was in an automobile accident. Are you thinking she might have been distraught enough to commit suicide?"

"Never. My mother was Catholic. She would never have killed herself. I guess I've seen too many movies and have a lurid imagination, but . . . could your husband have killed her?"

She laughed with real amusement. "No, never. Curt isn't

action oriented. He doesn't make things happen so much as take advantage of situations that present themselves. He couldn't kill your mother or even make a plan to kill her, but he is capable of taking advantage of fortuitous circumstances. Her disappearance allowed him to pretend ignorance about the missing money and blame your mother."

"So they were in this together?"

"Not initially. He claimed it began out of pity when Diane came to him in tears and confessed she had 'borrowed' from company accounts to help your father. Curt promised to help her. She probably thought he was a white knight coming to her rescue. Instead, of course, he exploited the situation for his own ends."

"He told you all this?"

"I persuaded Curt to tell me the truth," Claire said, smiling to herself with satisfaction. "Or at least his version of it. I doubt he even recognizes the truth. He claims the company never appreciated his contributions or gave him the money he deserved. I took that to mean he convinced your mother—and himself—that he was entitled to help himself to the company's profits. Curt can be very convincing, especially with women."

"I can see that happening. All he would have had to do is make Diane feel sorry for him. She would go overboard to help someone who was being treated unfairly."

"At any rate, when Arthur arranged the merger and the auditors were brought in, your mother panicked and wanted to confess. Curt said he didn't want to discuss the situation in public because your mother was emotional. He told her to meet him at our cabin. She drove up there and they argued.

Curt said she became hysterical. I assume that means she was crying—he always describes any outward display of female emotion as hysterics."

Her lip curled as she continued. "Anyway, he said she drove away, visibly upset, and he never saw her again. He waited, expecting to hear from her or to hear that she had gone to Arthur."

"So you believe him?"

"Yes," Claire said, smoothing an invisible wrinkle in her skirt. "I believe she was distraught and that's probably what caused the accident. That's the most reasonable explanation."

"How much of this do the police know?"

"When the police questioned Curt, he admitted she came to see him at the cabin and she was worried. He said nothing about their personal involvement or anything at all about the missing funds because there's no proof now that your mother's . . ." She stopped, and then continued, "Gone."

"I'm surprised he admitted this to you."

"I've had a lot of practice getting the truth from my husband. Arthur is an old friend of my father's. When he called me about his suspicions, I confronted Curt and forced it out of him. This was more than I was willing to overlook. I'd been aware of his infidelities for years and chose to ignore them because he's a good father and the children love him. But criminal activity is another matter."

Her voice had become angry. "I couldn't let our children be humiliated and embarrassed by his financial improprieties. That kind of scandal could destroy their futures. Even my own social standing in this community would be in jeopardy. I couldn't ignore all that."

"So, what's going to happen? Will he go to jail for the missing money?"

Claire gave me a steely look. "Certainly not. That's what I'm trying to avoid. I've negotiated a private financial settlement with Arthur and the board has approved it. In return, Curt is leaving the company. The whole matter won't be pursued any further—legally or otherwise."

"In other words, he's getting off scot-free while my mother's reputation is ruined, and she's dead."

She raised her eyebrows. "She's not an innocent party in all this, after all. Even if she was only foolish and gullible, she set the whole thing in motion. There's nothing any of us can do to bring her back. However, Curt isn't getting off without consequences. He's lost his position and he's lost me."

"You're divorcing him?" I asked.

"My lawyer will be filing the papers next week."

"Good!" I snapped.

Claire stood up. "Forgive me, but I'm due at a luncheon soon. I hope what I've told you has helped. You understand, of course, this conversation can't be repeated. As far as I am concerned, the matter is now closed and I will not discuss it again."

"I understand." I also stood up.

"You seem like a very determined young woman. I'm sure your mother was very proud of you."

"Maybe she could have been," I answered. "But now she never will be."

epilogue

In a few hours I will don a cap and gown and stride across a makeshift stage in the noonday sun to receive my college diploma. Gloria and her husband, Richard, will be watching from among the gathered throng. Earl and Malcolm too. Even Tattie will be here. These people, this rather odd group with nothing in common except me, are my family now. Still, I'm glad to have every one of them in my life.

Nicole is still back east, working on her master's degree. I tease her that she may end up with a doctorate just to avoid going home. But she's already planned her final escape. She recently became engaged to a New Yorker named Andrew, and an August wedding is planned. Cindy must be delirious that her daughter has beaten me to the altar and is probably planning a wedding lollapalooza where Nicole will, at long last, occupy center stage.

Tattie came back from Mexico and began tending bar at a place on Market Street. She changes jobs and addresses about as frequently as she changes boyfriends. Periodically she takes off for a month or two to Costa Rica or Belize or some other tropical paradise. While she hasn't made it to Amsterdam yet, she swears she's still going.

Malcolm remodeled and reopened the Madhouse with great fanfare. Even with new floors, new paint, and new furniture, the coffeehouse remains much the same as ever. The Scrabble games rage on.

Earl still works the night shift at the gas station. Sometimes when it's late and I'm restless, I give him a call. Recently he announced with great pride that his granddaughter had won a scholarship to Mills College in Oakland. From Earl I know that Ted Strobel continues to protect and serve the citizens of Burlingame.

After my mother's funeral, my life took another sharp turn. I was finally ready to go away to college and Gloria became my champion. Like a pit bull, she sank her teeth into the firm of Warren Simmons & Co. and wouldn't let go. Since Diane died in an accident and her guilt couldn't be proven, Gloria made sure I received all of my mother's company-funded life insurance. She threatened to sue if the company tried to claim any part of the insurance proceeds, and they backed off. No doubt their decision was influenced by Claire Davidson's payback of her husband's off-the-books "bonuses." In the end, the company hushed it up and the whole ugly mess went away.

Instead of shelling out big bucks for Boston University, I enrolled in the University of Santa Barbara, where I could pay in-state tuition. I lived in a tiny but cute apartment with Stella and majored in Comparative Literature. My second year I took a lot of elective theater classes, slowly edging myself into their cliquey crowd. I had good parts in *The Waiting Room* and *The House of Bernarda Alba,* and managed to get the lead role of May in *Fool for Love.*

What's next for Ashley Mitchell? At first, I thought about trying my luck in Hollywood, but instead I applied to the Yale School of Drama. If I don't get in, I'll try the Neighborhood Playhouse in New York. Nic says I'll love the East Coast.

Traveling is also on my agenda. I'm thinking of going to Europe this summer, including a side trip to Ireland and look up a certain someone there.

Whatever happens in the future, I'm pretty confident of my ability to handle it. I'm no longer Ashley the stuck-up homecoming queen or the girl Phil described as pouty, sulky, and sullen. I hardly even remember that girl. Even though my life didn't turn out the way I planned, I'm happy with the person I've become and the new life I've found.

Yet, sometimes at night, just before I fall asleep, in that twilight between waking and oblivion, I see my mother's face floating before me. I want to reach up and hold her thin arms in mine and say over and over, *Forgive me, forgive me.* I whisper it into the darkness, but I never get an answer.

If only she had left a note behind. If only I could be sure that she knew I loved her. If only I had been with her to hold her hand. I would give anything—anything—to know that my mother forgives me. Earl keeps telling me I have to get over it. He says I have to forgive myself the way he had to forgive himself for his own mistakes. I know he's right and I'm working on it.

My mother made herself responsible for everyone else's happiness, and in the process she crossed the line between right and wrong. But I can't hate her for it. Whatever she did, she always loved me. I am still, and always, her daughter.

Acknowledgments

I am deeply grateful to the friends and family members who read this book at various stages in its creation and encouraged me to keep going, especially Lynn Lasner, Suzanna Musick, Lorraine Flett, Nancy Staltman, Rochelle Worthing, Mia Cingolani, Patti Roth, Rebecca Johnson, Betsy Brill, Liz Watson, and Sue Bostick.

The members of the San Francisco Writers Group deserve recognition for the support and feedback they've given me, particularly Scott James, Maria Strom, Arlene Heitner, David Gleeson, Shana Mahaffey, Erika Mailman, Joe Quirk, and Tamim Ansary.

A special thank you goes to agent Andrea Somberg for loving my book and the character of Ashley (even in the beginning of the novel when she's not easy to love). Thanks to Celeste Fine for picking up the torch.

I also am grateful for the kindness and enthusiasm of everyone at Bloomsbury, especially my editor, Julie Romeis, who demonstrated amazing forbearance.

I would also like to express my appreciation to Janet Fitch and Joyce Maynard, whose words and writing inspired me, and to Margo Perin, for helping me get started at her workshop in San Miguel Allende.

And thank you, Charles Michelson, for loving me and helping keep the wolf from my door as I wrote and rewrote this novel.